BLACK
ROCK
WHITE
CITY

BLACK ROCK WHITE CITY

A NOVEL

A. S. PATRIĆ

MELVILLE HOUSE
BROOKLYN · LONDON

Black Rock White City
Copyright © 2015 by A. S. Patrić
First published by Transit Lounge (Australia) 2015
First Melville House Printing: September 2017

Melville House Publishing
46 John Street
Brooklyn, NY 11201
and
8 Blackstock Mews
Islington
London N4 2BT

Book design by Richard Oriolo

mhpbooks.com
facebook.com/mhpbooks
@melvillehouse

Library of Congress Cataloging-in-Publication Data

Names: Patrić, A. S., author.
Title: Black rock white city / A. S. Patrić.
Description: First American edition. | Brooklyn : Melville House, 2017.
Identifiers: LCCN 2017019905 (print) | LCCN 2017029899 (ebook) | ISBN
    9781612196848 (reflow able) | ISBN 9781612196831 (hardcover)
Subjects: LCSH: Refugees--Australia--Fiction. | Political fiction. | BISAC:
    FICTION / Suspense. | FICTION / Political. | FICTION / Literary. | GSAFD:
    Suspense fiction.
Classification: LCC PR9619.4.P375 (ebook) | LCC PR9619.4.P375 B58 2017
    (print) | DDC 823/.92--dc23
LC record available at https://lccn.loc.gov/2017019905

ISBN: 978-1-61219-683-1

Printed in the United States of America
10 9 8 7 6 5 4 3 2 1

for Emily
my love

Wherever I look there are poems
—whatever I touch is pain.

IVO ANDRIĆ

BLACK
ROCK
WHITE
CITY

ONE

JOVAN PUSHES THE SWITCH. THE WINDOWLESS room shudders with white flashes. He holds the cleaning caddy tight and braces himself against the solid post of the door frame. The fluorescent tube in the ceiling flickers one last time, yet Jovan is still blinking. Long moments pass without movement. The fluorescent above emits a static hiss and the light strobes almost imperceptibly. He blinks once more and refocuses on the overhead light. He'll have to replace the tube soon.

A minute before, in the darkness of the hospital exam-room, there were glowing red letters leering through three shattered skulls—the crash victims of a triple fatality. The plastic of the X-ray photos has been glued to the interior of the X-ray light boxes and it's going to be very difficult to remove. He'll need to soak the glass panes in a solution. **The / Trojan / Flea.** These are the words on the inside of the bank of three X-ray screens. Jovan wonders why the fluorescent tube had not been removed from the ceiling. The graffiti would have been made more effective if there was no other illumination. Perhaps the vandal hadn't thought that far ahead.

Mr. X-Ray walks into the room as Jovan begins removing the glass from the light boxes. The hospital director is with him this morning, so X-Ray doesn't whistle or sing his usual song. The director talks to Jovan as if he's never seen him before.

"Please do not, under any circumstance, damage that glass while you're cleaning."

"No problem," says Jovan.

"Please, be careful not to chip the glass."

"No problem."

"Do not scratch the glass."

"No problem."

"Please," he says again, and leaves.

Mr. X-Ray mouths "please" when the director is gone and scrunches his features in a full-face wink. "Notice how 'please' can be used more offensively than any obscenity?" Mr. X-Ray has a name though he prefers the comic book hero sound of calling himself Mr. X-Ray. He comes up with these kinds of monikers for a lot of people in the hospital.

"Director is angry," Jovan says, pouring hot water and detergent into a wide bucket. "Not for glass. He wants graffiti to stop and there is always new problem. Maybe I angry too."

"You're not angry." Mr. X-Ray walks to his desk and its computer, leans over into a hunch, and clicks the mouse. "At least, you don't look angry," he says, over his shoulder.

"It waste my time," Jovan tells him.

"Mate, you look at the world a certain way, and all you'll see is waste." The printer begins to slide out paper. X-Ray walks over to the machine and picks up his pages—pictures he took of the light boxes yesterday when he found the vandalism. He puts them in a blue plastic envelope and walks to the door.

"Dovi gen ja, Joe," he says before leaving.

"*Dovidjenya*," Jovan says, and turns back to the white foam and the glass within. For a while he gets to think about nothing other than not scratching or chipping the panes.

IF I WAS *washed away, if I was faded by the sun until my text was as vague as the tracery of veins below your blushed skin, if I was breathed in and out and whisper gone, if I evaporated with the thought you have just forgotten, and weighed as much as the word love weighs on your tongue.*

Jovan had been a poet in Yugoslavia when that was still a country. Two collections of his poetry had made it to the shelves of libraries and bookstores. He imagines that most of the paper printed with his poetry has burned. He'd never had a particularly good memory and hadn't memorised any of those poems. In Australia he never commits a word to paper. He finds himself recalling phrases, some old, some new, playing them over and again in his mind.

Many of the hospital's employees speak to Jovan as though his slow, thick words are a result of brain damage. When attempting to pronounce his name they become retarded themselves— "Jo . . . Ja . . . Joh-von. Ja-Va. Ah, fuck it, we'll call you Joe."

"What is hard to speak Yo-vahn? Jovan. The sounds all in English," he says to the dentist he's been fucking since the boozy Christmas party a month ago.

She says, "Whatever, Joe. Does it matter?"

"It matters. I hate the fucking 'Joe.'"

"They call me Tammie. It's a cat's name for God's sake. What are you complaining about?"

"Then there is Mister . . . the X-ray man. He always sings the song when he see me. The Jimi Hendrix. *Hey Joe. Where are you go with the mop in you hand.*" He waits. "And now you laughing."

"Well, it's funny," she says.

"What's funny?"

"You singing for one thing. And the mess you make with English. *Where are you go . . .*" She breaks up laughing again.

"He sings all the time. Can be funny hundred times?"

"We'll see. Sing it once more for me."

When he is ready to leave her office she tells him it will have to be the last time she sees him. She has said that every single time since they started what she would never call an affair. A fling maybe. No, not even that. It's barely a thing. She's married to a lawyer who is always working, even when ostensibly home alone with her. The law is his religion, she has elaborated. And this faith keeps him chaste when he's home with Tammie.

It doesn't matter, because Jovan is married to Suzana. His wife can't have sex with him anymore. Suzana wants him to find this necessary release. That's what she calls it. Perhaps she thinks of it as a bit of biology, another basic procedure performed at his hospital. Her proviso is that a lover needs to be married. Less chance of losing her husband. Jovan, on the other hand, knows he's already lost his wife, though that has nothing to do with Tammie.

Jovan tells the Australian his tooth is still hurting, and maybe she can do him a favour, since she's a dentist? She laughs because she thinks he's joking. He's been feeling pain in his jaw since Serbian Christmas. He tells her every time he sees her and he doesn't know why he can't make her believe him.

THERE WAS A *startling white winter in your blood, and there was all our springs and autumns and children in long laughing summers that will never end, though now, when we close our eyes, we see a blank expanse and it gets harder to hear through the clatter, the din of our disused, unoiled, derelict hearts.*

Jovan cleans graffiti off a wall in the cold hospital stairwell. His thoughts never register on his face. Looking at him you would think there's nothing more to him than the effort to dislodge ink from a concrete wall. Maybe that's why Tammie doesn't believe him. She doesn't see the pain when he tells her it's in his teeth.

Jovan is six-foot-four and broad, thick boned with hands that can wrap halfway around a basketball. He still looks fit enough to play. Years ago he even had unrealistic yet delightful dreams of a professional career running up and down the glossy blond wood, propelling himself up and finding drift in the air.

The stairwell is lit by a fluorescent tube from the floor below, and some sunlight struggling down through a door held open with a mop bucket, three flights above. Jovan wears a mask because the cleaning chemicals are toxic. A mask is good for about an hour before it's useless, he's been told by a workplace safety officer, and even that hour has a question mark hanging over it.

The graffiti says:

I am so full of your death I can now only breathe your rot.

The cleaning chemicals don't work today. A different kind of paint. Oil-based and applied thickly in layers. After scrubbing for half an hour and hardly affecting it, he steps back and looks at it again. It's not worth cleaning off words written on a darkened concrete wall, within a stairwell that almost no one uses. It's not offensive or crude. Doesn't even make sense. The hospital administration, however, are adamant about graffiti. About *this* graffiti especially.

A few weeks ago, on the walls of an operating room, the words, **I am a god of small knives . . . I am a devil of deep cuts . . .** The punctuation points were a different colour to the black of the words. The dots were a brownish red, and were meant to imply blood. They'd been applied wet with a thick brush and had dripped down in streaks of red. It was discovered they were blood, in fact—the doctors weren't sure whose. They all assumed it was blood from their own surgery fridges. Every drop was recorded in precise measurements and none was missing when they checked.

Admin called in Jovan as if it was another vomit spill. But they were beginning to panic. Fear in doctors involved talking in low voices, standing wordlessly in silent examination, staring at the graffiti in the operating room as if it was a brain scan of newly discovered tumours in their own heads.

The graffiti kept coming, and after long discussions in hospital halls and offices the police were called in. Bored constables wrote down indecipherable jottings that would never go anywhere. Detectives arrived with no preparation to pursue this kind of vandal, doing their duty with a disinterest they didn't disguise. It was graffiti that, no matter the highfalutin language, was the petulance of a medical school brat. In another few days the wanker would certainly be caught in the act.

The hospital can't believe it is one of their own doctors. They need it to be someone like Jovan though his English is a square block for a round hole. Further afield they simply can't attribute this kind of articulate existential suffering to someone who wears overalls every day.

It hasn't been voiced once by anyone, yet what disturbs people in the hospital, Jovan thinks, is the idea that the ellipses were the graffitist's own blood. Enough of a bloodletting to have required opening a vein. The problem is that if it is a doctor writing the graffiti, then the same hand writes prescriptions, it orders procedures, and it presses a scalpel into the soft flesh of another human being.

IF I WAS *the dream of water, you'd insist on the desert in your mouth, only because you never remember the rolling blue kisses of waves come the cold light of day.*

The lines of poetry are tracks he can run his mind along, again and again. There's less chance of finding the kind of crash he'd seen in Mr. X-Ray's office—skulls caved in with garish red lettering.

Today he's thinking about Suzana. Her pale white skin, the colour of milk, or rather, as if she's full of milk beyond the pink partition of flesh. Some white substance that fills her soul like black does for the stars and the distances between them. He seeks ways to describe her skin, contrasted against his own darker body.

Jovan has inherited the genes of a Turk somewhere along the line. The colour of his skin mystifies Anglo-Australians. Prompts them to ask, is he Greek, Italian, Jewish, knowing that he isn't any of those before they ask. Tammie, loving his skin this Australian summer, telling him if he could bottle it, he'd be a billionaire by autumn. That, and his yellow eyes.

"Is that a Serbian feature?" Tammie asks, on the next time that she said was never going to happen.

"There is no Serbian feature," he answers, feeling a distaste for the question. "I have brown eyes."

"In the light through the window they're yellow. It's nice. And just an observation. You look as if someone asked to borrow a kidney."

"You think 'feature' of the Serbs?"

"Whatever Joe. Make sure that door is locked."

"What is—*The Trojan Fleas?*" He asks her as he moves towards her, unbuckling his belt. "Is that expression in English?"

"Why do you ask?"

"More graffiti. I had to clean this words other day."

"Ever think about what kind of a maniac needs to write on walls?" She opens her eyes a millimetre wider. "I wouldn't read too much into it." She props herself on the edge of her desk and opens her legs, bare feet beside her arse, already without underwear.

"It makes me think . . ."

"Don't think too much Joe. You're here to do something very easy; very clear and pleasurable."

Jovan isn't used to women who love fucking as much as Tammie does. He doesn't believe the elaborate moaning with her head thrown back or the whispering through clenched teeth.

He looks out the window while he delays his own gratification, watching people wait to park their cars when others vacate spots. Hot enough outside for a heat shimmer off the concrete and wilting people to hurry from cars to shade. Thinks about the pain in his tooth. Her nails begin to dig into his back. He tells Tammie no scratches, and then speaks in Serbian, calling her a fucken stray cat in heat. She places her ankles on his shoulders and lifts her arse off the table, holding herself up. Loud enough to be heard from behind the locked door, in the dental surgery, and maybe beyond to the waiting room. He still finds it hard to believe her when she shudders to climax, and allows himself—lets himself fall into the rushed air of their breathing. Blood on his lip from a bite she gives him, makes him think about Suzana. The excuse she'll never ask him for.

Tammie puts on her white coat, the name Samantha Ashford sewn into the pocket. He points to it, "How is this Tammie?"

"Samantha. Sam. Sammy. Tammie. Like Teddy from Edward."

"I have a friend, Slavoljub. Slavko, we call him. Australian call him Sam."

She looks at him for a second, apologising with an expression on her face, giving him a pat on the shoulder. "I've got a root canal in a few minutes."

"What do you call this?" He leans over her face, breathing across it as though to blow away a frosting.

"Freckles," she says as she opens her eyes. They don't speak for a moment. They are close enough to kiss.

"Is this feature for the Aussie?" he asks.

She looks at the door and then back to his face. "You have to go."

WORDS ARE SPRAY-PAINTED over the wall of an empty hospital room for children. In thick black over the pictures of fluffy dogs, cats, and ponies, and across crayon drawings some of the children had made of themselves and their families. Jovan has to throw all those away and decides to give the whole wall a fresh coat of paint. A vivid colour he thinks, which he could bring from home tomorrow. A bright warm orange. The hospital only pays for drab colours.

The message this time reads:

The dead will not bother you. The dead have left you a world. The dead will welcome you. The dead have slept here. The dead have been born here. The dead look like you. The dead have the same names. The dead already own your father. The dead have already fucked your mother.

All of these statements are jumbled. There is no order to them. Some are repeated many times and some written once. The final line is written over the top of everything as though the doctor found the courage to use the word *fucked*, and then became braver and more insistent in its use. The words that might have been carefully placed initially, turned into a wild crescendo that reached a climax in this children's room last night.

JOVAN STEPS OUT into the afternoon light. Or is it evening light? Strange, living so close to the South Pole. It's past eight and there's still sunlight in the sky. A fingernail moon is pushing through the indigo curtain rising from the suburban Sandringham houses. He walks out into the warm air, exhaled now from the ground, heavy on the skin, light in the lungs.

He leans over the top of his first Australian car, feeling the heat of the roof radiating through his arms, and drifts into poetry.

The air that breathes me, the air that moves my life, that evaporates my soul, the air that kisses me and kisses me, the air breathing in the bliss of my longest exhalation . . .

He doesn't own this tranquillity. Moments like these are rare gifts that come his way accidentally, wrapped and intended for others. He can hold them, briefly as he does now, pausing beside his rust-spotted white Ford panel van. Soon he'll have to surrender them.

He opens his chest and takes a few more lungfuls of air and thinks of Suzana again. She will be at home, somewhere in that empty Frankston house. A rental that still feels like a rental after three years. He unlocks his car door. He pulls it open and doesn't wait for the heat to leave the cabin before he gets in.

There's a long drive home to Frankston. The brakes are spongy. He will have to fix them this weekend. And it has to be this weekend. He bought the brake pads a month ago. He doesn't leave important things—at least, he never used to. His brakes have been bad since winter. As he waits for a space in an endless stream of traffic on Bluff Road he remembers he's signed himself up to help Slavko paint a house in Toorak, both Saturday and Sunday.

THE HOSPITAL DISCOVERS a body on a trolley in the lobby on the weekend. Cut into the flesh with a scalpel, from throat to navel, is the word

I
N
S
P
I
R
A
T
I
O
N

The body belonged to a woman who died in the hospital from a heart attack the day before. It has been prepared for the undertakers. An optometrist finds the body on the trolley in the morning with that strangely inappropriate word cut into its chest. The victim of the heart attack was a mother of four children and a grandmother of two. She owned a milk bar in East Bentleigh and there is no reason in the world why someone would have wanted to cut a word into her chest.

It is determined that the letters were made post-mortem and that these cuts were not tentative. They struck bone on every letter.

THERE ARE A few quiet days with no new instances of graffiti. Mr. X-Ray and Tammie complain that the hospital has become boring again.

Jovan is called to the Doctor's Cafeteria. One of the other janitors had joked that Jovan was a specialist in graffiti removal and it soon became an accepted fact. So Jovan is now the only one who is called for any instance of graffiti.

In the Doctor's Cafeteria, the blackboards that inform everyone what they might eat today have all been washed clean. Across them is a new message, written in a mixture of melted sugar and chalk:

DOG

EAT

DOG

They are repeated over and again. That isn't the problem. Hot water and a bit of scrubbing from a kitchen sponge is all that is required. It's a repeated message on every available plate and bowl that causes distress. These letters are burned into the ceramic surfaces by a blowtorch through a metal stencil.

The police shake their heads and give the hospital the same message—it is going to need to get more cameras. Surveillance everywhere. More security guards. New locks. They've conducted interviews and done background on everyone after the Inspiration cadaver. These police interviews either went nowhere or into areas of people's lives that were destructive and disturbing but non-pertinent. Nothing moved nearer to the origin of the graffiti. Everything got drowned in a toxic whirlpool of unrelated questions and answers, speculation and accusation, crying and shouting, murmuring and mumbling, finally dissolving into confused silence.

Blanket surveillance isn't a popular idea with most of the doctors and nurses who have gone through police interviews for the first time in their lives. They don't want so permanent and invasive a security feature for what they still hope is a nuisance, soon to pass. They agree to new locks and another bleary-eyed security guard.

Every few years, rumours circulate that the Sandringham Hospital will be closed down. It occurs to Jovan that this graffiti debacle is not merely an annoyance or embarrassment, it's a threat to every doctor working here that the government will take this as an opportunity to close down a small, outdated hospital.

The message burned into the plates reads:

Masters of Destiny
Victims of Fate

Jovan suggests that if the plates are washed thoroughly they are still perfectly usable.

The managers order new plates (that will take months to arrive because they'll have to be tabled and approved in the next budget) and decide on paper plates while they wait.

After a week, the cafeteria is filled with a motley array of plates and bowls, mugs and cutlery, brought in from fifty different homes.

Jovan puts all the ruined crockery into two big cardboard boxes and drives home. He doesn't know what to do with them so he slides them onto a shelf in his garage, looks at them for a while before he turns off the light.

They resemble artefacts. Not in the way of being ancient. It isn't what they might mean—that's been interpreted in different ways. Old plates with the vague traces of cutlery marks across their faces, chips and hairline cracks from contact with clumsy hands, and blemishes from thousands of trips through the dishwashers. Now they can't be used because of these new marks trapped in their surfaces. It seems nothing much more than the result of a burned meal, yet now they are unusable.

Whoever Doctor Graffito is, he would know that Jovan is the man obliterating all his words. That they would drip from his elbows in black foam when he washed the graffiti from the walls. That the message on the plates would be shattered into pieces, and it would be Jovan sweeping that desperate communication into a pile of rubble. They must walk by each other in the corridors of the hospital occasionally and maybe both men nod at each other in passing.

Jovan thinks about the plates as he washes his hands in the laundry and walks the hall to his kitchen. Why brand the plates and use chalk on the menu boards? Who are the victims and masters, and what is the difference between fate and destiny? What is the meal and who is to eat it? Dog eat dog is easy to rub away, easy to ignore. Masters and victims both just bones for those chalk dogs to gnaw and crack for marrow. All of it washed away easily from the mind as everyone continues to feed.

Suzana is talking to a friend on the phone. After listening to English all day, as well as the various languages patients speak, he enjoys hearing perfectly understandable Serbian, particularly with his wife's Belgrade accent and expressions.

She's speaking with Jelka, a Croatian woman from Dubrovnik, who calls herself Yugoslav when she's in Suzana's company. They almost never meet outside of work because her husband, Ante, is the kind of Australian Croat that grew up hating Serbs as if it was the central feature of his identity. Jelka avows that Croatians who are from Croatia, as she is, are pretty much over all this nonsense.

Suzana doesn't ever talk to Jelka about having lived in Bosnia for a few years, Jovan notices, maybe because that's where the loveliest illusions of Yugoslavia were most thoroughly destroyed. Other parts of that fractured world can blame politicians and governments for the catastrophe, and still evoke those sweet daydreams of fellowship, community, and a shared spirit of place. Jovan can hear Jelka's voice, but not the words. A tinkling of pleasing tones through the small speaker in the kitchen phone.

Jelka got Suzana a housecleaning job after they met on a Frankston bus one day. Realising they spoke the same language because one swore at the other, saying "fuck your bitch of a mother," the other responding, "watch your mouth, fat slut." The bus had swerved and braked, dumping Jelka into Suzana's lap. Or it was the other way around. Annoyance and embarrassment instantly turned into laughter and banter all the way home. They still call each other *fat sluts* in happy greeting.

Jelka is Suzana's first friend made in Australia. Her only friend here. They talk a few minutes on the phone every evening before Ante gets home for dinner.

Jovan sits down at the table. His wife pours him a glass of wine as she moves around the kitchen—attached to the wall phone by a long cord. He has forgotten the sore lip he got from the bite the dentist gave him when they fucked a few days ago, but the wine glass reminds him as he brings it to his mouth.

Jovan waits and listens to his wife's side of the conversation. Good to hear her sounding so everyday. Carefree.

When she puts down the phone, they say hello to each other and then find little to say. The day before, they almost talked. An actual conversation. She asked Jovan whether he remembered what he hated most about the university they both had taught at in Sarajevo.

He said, "I think the staff rooms filled to choking with tobacco smoke would be close. Winters were always unbearable. It made me think about how in Scandinavian mythology hell was a place of ice and cold and how we should have had that kind of idea for hell in our part of the world as well. The devil could be some sinister version of the Snow Man. Good old Frosty with horns."

She didn't smile. She told him she didn't remember the winters anymore. Not really. It was now white without the bite of cold. It was the ceaseless sounds of chaos she remembered, as students rumbled through the halls and rooms, that used to give her these dizzying headaches and nausea, because it would never stop the whole day long. As she was waking that morning she thought she was hearing it again, until she realised it was the sound of an almost-tuned station on her clock radio.

He knew she couldn't remember anything she hated about Sarajevo University or their lives as teachers there. That's the unvoiced in her asking. It was the students she remembered. Their vivid faces. The animation and energy. The rampant movement and hanging limbs at rest. The way it had exhausted her then. The way it now leaves her numb and dead.

He can't speak to any of it because it isn't about words anymore. It's about another existence. Neither of them is sure about the present but this is some kind of afterlife.

They eat their meals and they wash the dishes. Discuss what needs to be bought next time she goes shopping. Sit on the couch. Watch a movie. Fall asleep halfway through, her head on his chest, both of them with their closed eyes, flashed with what could have been afternoon light from above, passing through the branches and limbs of trees they're moving through, lying back on a creaking hayrick wagon, on some long journey back home.

In the morning they wake in bed. He has a vague somnambulist's recollection of Suzana towing him down the hall from the couch and into the bedroom. He turns his mind from conversations of the university, and other thoughts of Sarajevo, and directs them towards the day ahead. Feels her hit the clock radio a few seconds before it sounds, as she always does. Hears her heavy sigh.

Half out of bed, sitting on its edge rubbing her eyes with the heels of her hands. Bent over and breathing through her nose. Every vertebra visible. Each rib defined. *Skeletal weariness my dear. Skeletal cherishing in my love. All of it clinging to the bones. All of me cutting down to bones.* The ribs and vertebrae disappear as she stands and wobble-walks to the bathroom. Calls out his name and tells him he better get up. After her shower she comes in smelling of soap and shampoo and pushes him awake. He hadn't noticed himself drifting off.

"Come on, I need a lift today. Some place called Black Rock. Do you know where that is?" She's sitting on the edge of the bed again, his side this time.

"Not far from the hospital," he mumbles into the pillow.

"What kind of name is that for a place?"

"I don't know," he slurs into a deeper, whiter oblivion. "Give me another minute."

"Sounds as though you could find another thousand in that pillow."

He drifts away from her soap and shampoo, thinking about the irony of her coming from a place called White-City, which was the literal translation of Belgrade. He could almost hear Dr. Graffito whispering some absurdity in his ear about burying a Black Rock in White City.

THERE'S A JOURNALIST asking questions today. When he comes around to Jovan he doesn't accept the janitor's only answer, which is, "pain in fxxxing arse."

Dog eat dog eat dog
Every man for himself
Winner rapes all
The last man standing
Dog eat dog eat dog

This is printed on the back of the hospital newsletter. Patients get the newsletter and read the message before anyone realises. The red slashed words are overlayed onto a full-page Rorschach image. Most people think it's a bit of enigmatic poetry not worth reading or perhaps a bizarre ad for something to do with mental illness.

"Who do you think is responsible for this?" The journalist has a recorder which he has switched on and off a few times.

"You reporter—you job to make the theories."

"I'm asking *you* whether *you* have any suspicions. *Any* intuitions? *Any* guesses?"

"I am hundred per cent not sure," Jovan says. The journo stands nonplussed, going cross-eyed over what sounds like a Zen koan.

He shakes his head to uncross his eyes. "One possibility is all I'm asking for. Any kind of theory. Something I can use." The line would be, *inside sources say . . .*

"Ask police," Jovan tells him.

"I'm asking *you.*"

"How could I know?" Jovan is mopping the floor and sloshes hot, dirty, soapy water on the journalist's shoes to get rid of him. He continues down the hospital hallway talking over his shoulder. "Why you ask me?"

"Have a wild guess. Say anyone you can think of, for God's sake."

"No one here can do this thing. Maybe anyone, everyone, as well, does this things."

"And you haven't seen anyone suspicious? In *particular.*"

"Yes suspicious. Very suspicious."

"Who have you seen looking suspicious?"

"Everyone. This is hospital. Everyone has secret. Not much of the secret. So suspicious is nothing different from must be obvious."

"Do you even know what the word 'suspicious' means?"

"Maybe you explain me one day."

The journalist walks away shaking his head and swearing

under his breath. He returns a few minutes later with his card and the promise of money for a photo of the body with the engraved message, or perhaps another incident if it is equally bizarre.

THE NEXT EVENT is discreet. In fact, it takes days to become clear that it is an incident. The watercooler in a hallway near radiology looks almost normal. It is rarely used. When a nurse tries to get a cup of water it oozes out of the blue plastic tap. It trickles out oily but doesn't smell as oil would. It raises the hackles of everyone who comes near enough for a sniff. They don't need to press the blue lever. The look of the yellow viscous stuff alone is enough to force a person to step back with an alarmed expression forming on his or her confused face.

Management asks Jovan to put a tape around the area and they call the police again. Detectives arrive and ask questions. The journalist takes photos. They seem dull pictures of an ordinary watercooler. It's difficult to catch the difference in the liquid, on film.

It starts being whispered that it's human fat in the watercooler, taken from the plastic surgeon's liposuction waste storage. Jovan isn't asked to take the cooler away. A quarantine waste worker wearing yellow and black hazmat gear does that.

The journo gets a headline from Dr. Graffito himself. Or so he says . . . after his own run-in with the reporter, Jovan thinks he's liable to make the news as much as report it. A man speaking in an undisguised voice, well-educated, middle-aged, phones the journalist to tell him that above the ordinary looking newspaper photo of a watercooler, the words should read:

Origin of the Species

JOVAN IS PARKED near a railway line. Four trains have passed. Two heading towards Frankston and two going to the city. There were mathematical problems that he'd been given in school when he was a boy, using trains to figure out various sums. He might be able to work out how long he's been sitting in his panel van on this street. First he'll need to start thinking again.

Jovan doesn't know how long that will be. Sometimes it has taken an hour to get going again after he's been derailed. At this moment he's not sure about anything. He might never be able to think again. He has seen that happen in Bosnia and knows it might happen to him. A ruin beside the tracks. He runs his own name through his head and he's not even sure about that. He repeats it: Jovan Brakochevich, Jovan Brakochevich . . . It's like a sum that needs trains to be calculated and he doesn't know which stations are where and hasn't been given the appropriate timetables and the people at the stations are family, strangers, everyone in between, looking at him, waiting for him to disappear so that they can get on with their days, and then there is nothing but a crashing of glass and metal in his endless calculations.

Please, he says. Murmuring the word into the silent, dead space of the cabin. Please, his lips barely moving.

About ten metres away is a house he's been invited to. He will be welcomed. He is an expected guest. A name will not be necessary. He might not be required to say anything. Perhaps they'd let him sit. If there was no demand on him to speak he'd be delighted to nod at people as they talked and toasted his friend's *slava*, raising glass after glass to each other, celebrating the world they were living in. He wants to be able to do that—nod at them as they enjoy Slavko's feast day.

There are cars on both sides all the way up and down Raymond Avenue and some are parked on the nature strip. Kids are playing in the street and some have already noticed Jovan in his vehicle. Sitting motionless. Wondering what he's doing. Trains passing and the man in the panel van not moving. Maybe they'll call their parents out soon to investigate the strange behaviour.

He knows his body will still work even without being able to think properly so he removes the keys from the ignition. He opens the door. He moves his legs out to the asphalt. He puts one foot in front of the other trusting that by the time he gets to the door he'll be able to respond sensibly if someone says hello. The children greet him in English and he knows he doesn't need to say anything to them. Concentrates on getting through their play area. All these Serbian children playing cricket and speaking English. They don't expect a man like Jovan, a refugee from the wars of their parents, to smile and speak.

They allow him to pass without comment, as if the giant lumbering through their field of play is barely visible. A ball is lofted from a cricket bat and another kid runs to catch it and crashes into the huge Bosnian. The kid falls to the ground. He might have thought he'd run into a parked car. The child is stunned, begins crying even though he has caught the ball.

Jovan doesn't need to think. It's OK if his mind is derailed for this. He picks the kid up and sets him on his feet. Kneels down with one hand on his shoulder, the other hand behind the boy's head, lightly assuring him that everything is as it was before the crash. "Dear heart," he calls the child—words he hasn't used since his own boy died. The kid still has the tennis ball in his hand and realises it means it's his turn to bat, so off he runs, as if nothing at all happened.

I

GO

COG

ERGO

COGITO

ERGOSUMNON

OGREERGO

ERGOOGRE

GOREGOREGORE

OGREOGREOGRE

COGITOERGOSUMNON

TWO

THE OPTOMETRIST DOESN'T MAKE A FUSS about the replacement charts. She asks Jovan to get rid of them. Specifically, she asks for the pile of them to be incinerated. He nods, says "no problem."

The optometrist is a woman getting old quietly as much as gracefully. She doesn't colour the silver streaks through her black, shoulder-length hair. There is a drift to the way she moves around her self-contained office. A delicate and precise focus about how she puts her hands to the equipment within it. Her patients come and go without disturbing anything. Without the usual troubles that they carry with them into the rest of the hospital.

It isn't the kind of work a dentist does, which is all gums and pain, clamps and drills, blood and spit. The only thing that ever needs to touch a person is the bridge piece of the Optical Refractor, the immense apparatus she swings around her calmly seated patients. She asks a gentle question with the slightest click of her gears and dials. "Worse or better?" are words she uses hundreds of times every week, and she enjoys their simplicity. The basic, clear improvement of someone's vision. "Sharper or fuzzier?"

The Cogito eye charts have no place in her world.

They are almost identical to the actual eye charts and striking from a technical point of view. The numbers along the sides the optometrist uses to gauge visual acuity, the card that it is printed on, rather than thin paper. Even the *made in USA* at the bottom. It doesn't matter because she knows they are wrong instantly. Every single random letter on each eye chart she can recite by heart. Has been doing so for thirty years already.

Her name is Miss Richards. She is known as such by everyone from Jovan to the Chief of Medicine. Miss Richards smiles at most of the hospital staff when she passes them in the halls, and mostly they smile back. She doesn't think about who it might have been, of these people passing her daily—one of them going to such an effort to create fake eye charts. Miss Richards knows it isn't a message for her. She thinks it's more or less random.

There's a large bin outside her office and it's emptied every day. Jovan wonders why Miss Richards didn't dispose of the charts herself, as he takes them away. Instead, she uses the word "incinerate" twice, as though it's not enough that they be thrown away. They had to be incinerated.

JOVAN PUTS UP one of the modified eye charts on the inside of his locker door and stares at it as he changes into his overalls. He understands the Latin, it takes him a while longer to work out the anagrams in plain English. For one thing he'd never heard of an ogre (the *OED* tells him it is a man-eating giant) and didn't know what *gore* meant initially, though he'd seen enough to know the difference between it and a bloody wound.

Another janitor, called Bill, tells him he's the only man he's ever seen study for an eye test and then laughs as if that's about the best joke he's heard all year. He repeats it every time he comes into the change rooms and guffaws. Elaborates by asking Jovan if he also studies for breath tests when he's driving home. And he must be studied up by now for a blood test. Or has he prepared sufficiently to go into the staff cafeteria today and see if the new lunch menu passes the taste test? Does he think that if he goes to watch Australia play South Africa in the cricket that he'll pass that test? Jovan isn't sure what he's talking about. It's getting more and more absurd. Jovan doesn't take the eye chart down from his locker door.

The rest of the eye charts are at the bottom of his locker, beneath his sneakers. Almost all the eye charts are the same. There is one that wasn't the Cogito. It repeated itself a number of different ways, reading in disorientating upside-down letters with this message:

Do You know Me

Do You know

Do You

Do

I

Jovan closes his locker. There's a space in his life these messages fill. It isn't that he thinks they're profound. He finds them interesting.

It's a shame they have been made by a madman, because that worries Jovan—having these insane messages floating around in his head.

The right thing to do is what the optometrist has done. Ignore these messages as though they are the million and one words leaping out at everyone, from every angle, countless times every day. The advertising, graffiti, brand names of clothes, newspaper headlines, all the bare-knuckled words that keep hitting with as much force as can be mustered by the cunning of their multitudinous authors.

Jovan isn't doing that. He's wondering why a man would say that he thinks and therefore he knows he's not alive. When the graffitist wrote *I Go Cog*, was he saying that any kind of thought made him a gear in the greater machinery of language, that he himself didn't own? Within the apparatus of the Optical Refractor itself, unable to simply be, because he can't see without the words that had been flooding through his mind from numberless sources, since before he'd even conceived of a self who might express being as idea.

Jovan knows he's overthinking it. Who knows what goes through a madman's head? Who'd *want* to? Jovan knows about Gore and about the Ogre. He also understands that when it comes to being alive, to *feeling* it, thinking doesn't mean shit.

He yearns to be the same as Miss Richards, with her headphones plugged into her ears, her book before her eyes, ignoring as much of the clamouring world as she possibly can. He contemplates the image of her doing that, swaying in the rapidly moving train, as it shudders through graffiti-ridden tunnels and overpasses, splashed-out images from billboards and signs, swaying her head ever so slightly as the bodies in motion and voices in chattering profusion pass over the clear reflective surfaces of her indifference.

He sees her doing that in the cafeteria often enough, sitting over her meal, placidly munching away on the wholesome home-cooked food she always brings along with her, plugged into her music, and her own chosen words screening her face, and she seems so self-contained and unstained. Until he realises that he himself has been that way long enough. That he's his own version of a sealed jar, and that maybe this is the first time in years he has felt himself being twisted open.

Jovan knows that the optometrist might be nothing as he imagines. She rarely speaks, so he finds himself looking for clues. Dr. Graffito is nothing but clues and yet Jovan can't imagine him walking around the hospital, caring for patients.

As he lifts a mop off its hook on the wall and rinses out a filthy bucket, he wonders if people might be little more than products of their professions. Mr. X-Ray drives home and feels the crush in the screech of brakes a hundred metres away and lives with the intimacy of loved ones being smashed and broken. The optometrist's world gets dimmer and darker, filled with more and more of the indecipherable all around her. For Jovan, now and until death, a janitor (a "cleaner" as they say in this country) there will be nothing other than deepening waste and grime. Perhaps that's the reason he never puts his thoughts down on paper anymore. And yet what kind of person burns words into plates, cuts letters into cadavers, paints messages in stairwells almost no one uses, carefully creates eye charts? Dr. Graffito passes people in the corridors, smiling and saying hello.

Jovan walks down to the delivery room. Pushes his mop and bucket along, leaving the sharp smell of cleaning product along the halls of the hospital. The grid pattern on the plastic floors is three tones of a comforting grey. He's already been warned what's awaiting him in the birthing room. It seems a kind of medieval event, yet some women still die in childbirth, bleeding out through a birthing wound. He dwells on the grid pattern of broad, grey rectangular shapes. Squares also cut into the ceiling. Pictures along the walls. Photographs of the many happy mothers who have come through these same corridors. Their offspring as well, not even babies yet. They could hardly be called infants. Exorcised embryos. New, trembling, half-blown balloons of life.

A gory entry to the world for someone, whatever you wanted to call it, in the birthing room. Blood and faecal matter on the floor below the table. A silver bucket kicked over in the desperate panic of a dying mother. This is what Dr. Graffito means by *gore*. Many of the clean soft white towels and sheets not now clean or white. Bundles of paper towelling scattered across the ground in wet, brown-red splotches.

A devastated nurse bustles past Jovan, leaving the room with an air of evacuation and disaster. It's odd to see a professional nurse so affected that she's scrambling to get somewhere quick, some place to release her sobs into weeping. It reminds him of the time he saw a policeman crying. A world-weary cop, with perhaps twenty years of investigating theft, murder, and rape—in uniform and standing on a busy street—crying. Tears and an open mouth. Outside a newsstand in Sarajevo with the headline in his hands declaring war.

Two clocks on the wall. One the time in the outside world beyond this windowless room and the other the time in this room. Stopped at sixteen hours and twenty minutes. A long fight, particularly if you weighed each of those minutes for what they were. Not at all the same kinds of minutes as those that passed when waiting for a train at a station. Not those passing through the night as you slept.

There's an armchair beside the birthing bed and its pillows. The space about the distance of two hands reaching out to grip and grapple. There's blood on that chair too. It would need to be cleaned after the floor was done. It has the kind of heavy-wearing material made to deal with human blood and other stains.

Jovan raises and releases the mop, watching for the right amount of steam and foam. He places his foot on the pedal to squeeze out the water he doesn't need. Brings out the mop and pushes it through the mess of this birth.

There is an entry. There is an exit. There is the escape of cold pierced skin. There is the seal of flushed flesh. Never to remember that first crown-

ing coming into light. Never to know that last drawing away. There is the long loving sigh of the in-between . . .

"What are you thinking?" the dentist asks him, closing the door behind her. Locking it. The blood on the floor has gone a bright red again, mixing with his foamy water. It is diffused and easily ignored.

"You'd have to call that a profound light in your eye," Tammie Ashford says with a mocking tone, that doesn't quite mock. As though she's willing to accept that he's capable of deep thought, if she was able to acknowledge that he had any thoughts at all. She often speaks to him as to her own imagination—a tool for her sexual fantasies. She leaves her heels at the door and walks to him barefooted across the wet floor.

"There's something about you with that mop in your hands, the way you wield it like a weapon, the blood at your feet." She stands before him. Close. Doesn't touch. "We've got to get you out of those overalls. These mundane overalls." She tugs at his shoulder strap. She perches on the birthing bed. Pulls back her skirt.

She's a pretty woman. It surprises Jovan that she acts this way. Beauty doesn't need to behave like this. And yet it was *because* of it. Her bare feet had been placed in the watery blood, and now her heels drip with it. Jovan gets a towel to clean her feet and wishes he could leave it at that. That he could close her legs and plant a chaste kiss on her misguided forehead.

He could imagine how all this mixed in the hungry imagination of Tammie Ashford and worked closer to the bone, tearing open her anaesthetised layers of mind to get to a core of pulsing life, where she could feel something primal and actual. Her lips pull away from her bright white teeth.

He asks, "This word. Ogre? Do you know what means?"

"What?" She really doesn't hear him, but the heavy words spoken with his crude accent struggle through. "A monster, I suppose," she says, watching his immense hands clean her small feet, the pulse at her throat beginning to visibly beat. She places both hands around his neck, his head, her fingers through his hair. Tries to pull his head down. He won't bend. Won't do that; not for her. She grits her teeth and feels an impulse to tear out his eyes, to reach into his mouth and pull his tongue out—some impossible act of destruction.

"Monster yes. What kind?" he asks.

Again the words are slow and heavy. Her blood is so loud. Her heart is so fucking desperate. She has to watch his lips move to hear him.

"I don't know. Some type of monster." Opens herself up to grind naked and raw against the hard fabric of his dark blue work clothes.

"He is the giant. Eating human meat. You did not know this?"

"All monsters eat people. Wouldn't be much of a monster if it didn't." Wanting more of his stupid words to fill her mouth, his brutal rock-crushing hands to reach inside her and ease her heart out for a bite from his crooked teeth, yellow in a slight diastema. She leans her head back, becoming breathless. "You should know, some of us taste good."

Jovan looks down, standing in the blood he's supposed to be cleaning, and feels revolted—impelled by his body. He allows her hands to pop open the front of his overalls, button by button. Her hungry mouth reaches up for his neck. Her teeth, perfect and white. Breath beginning to rush and moan. There's anger in the hand that takes hold of the back of her hair and pulls her head away, and hunger in the mouth that comes down on that clean smooth pale skin rushing through with moaning blood.

She pushes him away as he gets close, and drops her feet to the floor, turns around and has him enter her another way. A different kind of revulsion now, blistering with heat breaking through them both, rippling fevers of violent energy. Leaving them barely able to stand. Out of breath. Out of thoughts or words. Out of everything and now just dead for a few seconds.

One of the two clocks ticks out into the room. They begin to move in silence and then to the sound of their recovered breathing. Jovan doesn't know why but he tells her the word "vampire" originally came from the Serbs. It's true, yet she looks at him as if she should have been gone five minutes ago and this little bit of trivia is more than a waste of time.

"Why do you always feel compelled to talk after fucking?" He doesn't respond. "Isn't fucking enough for you?" He shrugs into his overalls. She refastens her bra. She fixes her hair. She straightens her shirt. Flattens her dress. She says, "He came from Transylvania, didn't he?"

Jovan has finished dressing. Moves towards his mop again. "Dracula is not same thing. This is one story by the Irish man." She gives him a shake of the head that should vaporise him and all his words as sudden sunlight for the damned in this windowless room. Leaves without saying another word. Light and ready to live again.

That revulsion grows stronger in Jovan after Tammie is gone. So much of what happens shouldn't happen. There is a kind of helplessness that we learn, he thinks. A helplessness that is bred into us from the very earliest moments of our lives and the world goes on happening in ways that it should or shouldn't. There is an illusion of a clean bright room where it is all laid out for us and we get to make our choices, say "yes, this will be good," or say "no, I do not want to do that." The room these choices present themselves in is windowless; airless and without light. With more than one clock on the wall the one for the outside world hardly matters. The other clicks on beyond twenty-four hours into calculations that can't be understood anymore. The tick, part of a cacophony of clicking, as though this room is full of watches and timepieces and grandfather clocks with swinging metal pendulums and cuckoo-clocks with opening doors and a helpless little yellow bird, popping out and announcing, "do this" and "do that."

He pushes his mop. He picks up his bucket. He lets the water run down a sink. Washes down the foam. Thinks about the pain in his jaw. Locates the fear somewhere in his stomach, almost nothing at all now. He knows that's not true. It wants to rise and fill his chest with black feathers, desperate to lift the top of his head off with screeching released in full-throated screams.

Clean virginal snow, a disguise for the Blue Sky, in love with its floating White Angels, draped over the everything below of Shambling Feet, burying all in the heavy Broken Beneath.

He has been overcome before. No matter how much time passes he knows it is there, that it will descend and lay a heavy blanket of suffocation over him again. He has tried to think his way out. He has tried to allow it to wash away; ease it through to nothing. It persists, perches on a cornice of his brain, glaring down on his mind like a gargoyle. A different kind of monster. Not a flesh-eater at least. This one, a devourer of peace and soul, memories, sleep, and dreams.

There was another time he saw blood on the floor. He saw it cleaned away with mops. Something else to be washed away. He'd watched the way it was done with a clear simple expression that looked at it all and understood it and cleaned it away, as if what needed to be done could be accepted and it could be carried without crushing the soul or mutilating the mind.

The same eyes that came to his low metal cot and the same hands that removed his pyjamas and cleaned the bloody diarrhoea from his helpless legs and trembling spine, and smiled at him afterwards as if there was nothing in the world to be ashamed of in any of this.

A nurse with a name: Dragana Mihailovich. A mother of three dead boys. One daughter, alive and safely in London, who sent her letters every day. Which Dragana couldn't get because they went to her address in Sarajevo. They were waiting for her, those messages. She knew that. A Muslim neighbour collected her mail, and when it was possible would send another parcel of messages on to Dragana, at the ever-moving camp. There were pictures in those letters, of her grandchildren, and there were those delightful, painful glimpses, resemblances to her brave, lost sons.

A human being is made. Made by the world. And made to go on, even after these kinds of losses. She must have been speaking more for herself than for Jovan, drifting as he was, closer to death by the hour. He can't remember her voice anymore. He remembers her form, the permanent hunch in her shoulders like she wanted to be closer to the ground. As though there was nothing in the world above the shoulders she could possibly be interested in. Huge breasts as if she could have breastfed grown men. The way she wore black instead of nurse-white, saying white was a luxury this part of the world couldn't afford. She always carried a whiff of bleach. She talked as she cleaned him. Basic words that were anything but simple. Saying that the course of human evolution was a blind walk, through a long, long cave, littered with human bones that we stumbled across; that we kept walking over, thinking that we would reach the end of the long tunnel—eventually we will all sit. "Don't worry my darling," she said. We will rest and let ourselves part at the ribs, unfold our vertebrae, and let our skulls roll along at the feet of those continuing to move along to the end of the tunnel. He can't remember what she said and he knows these weren't her words. Only that refrain, "don't worry my darling" remained distinct. Something she must have said to her sons countless times as she raised them from their cradles, and went on saying until all meaning had been exhausted and the words barely meant anything and she could say them to the sick and wounded she cared for without payment or thanks—to Jovan and the rest of the patients she didn't need names for. "Don't worry my darling," she murmured, as she adjusted Jovan's limbs from contorted positions and lifted his blanket to his chin when he shivered. A hand on his forehead. Even the end of the world was a part of human evolution, "Don't worry my darling."

The water finished gurgling down the drain minutes ago. Whistling along the corridor outside pulls him out of his reverie. The footsteps come and go, the happy tune with them. Jovan washes his hands. Washes his face. Can still smell Tammie's perfume on himself as he walks out of the clean birthing room. Looks into his mind for some poetry. Finds none. Nothing but the fluttering feel of glossy black feathers rising ruthlessly through his intestines.

AN ELDERLY PATIENT comes in Tuesday morning to see Miss Richards. While she runs him through the usual lenses to cope with deteriorating vision, he complains about letters appearing before his eyes. She doesn't know what to make of it. It doesn't make sense. Maybe because Mr. Donaldson has difficulty explaining things at times. She tells him anxiety, or various emotional states, can affect how well the eyes worked. So they can reschedule and he won't be charged for this appointment. He leaves mumbling about that damned contraption of hers doing diabolical things to his head.

Miss Richards sits in the chair and swings the Optical Refractor around to look through his last lens. There's a letter scratched into the lens itself. A very small, very precise letter T in the middle of the glass. She swings the machine around. Finds the next lens in the series has a letter also scratched into the lens—a capital R. *Scratched* isn't the right word. *Engraved* is better. They are exact. It is the same blockish font as the Snellen eye charts she used. When she lines up all the lenses on her small desk she finds the message reads:

TEST TO DESTRUCTION

It is a term used in medicine. Manufacturers use it more commonly. If they develop a new design for something, perhaps a brake pad, they need to work out what its response to the stress of its function is. The way to test full tolerance is a test to destruction. So she knows what it means though she has no idea what this vandal wanted to say by it. She throws those lenses away. Checks all her other lenses. Finds nothing else. Miss Richards orders replacements and arranges for new locks to be put on her doors.

The first thing she does the next few mornings, when she comes in, is check her charts. Goes through all her lenses carefully. Sometimes more than once a day. She calls Jovan to make sure the eye charts were incinerated.

JOVAN ENJOYS READING the local rags more than the proper newspapers. He is amazed that someone has caught a massive barracouta off Frankston Pier. Every time he's walked up and down it, the fishermen, with their three or four rods each, seem so hopelessly fishless—sitting forlornly against the wooden railing with lines slack in the shiftless waters.

Last week on the front page there was a picture of a tall, lanky youth, with a stretched out, crooked smile—his two-metre-long barracouta beneath it. Jovan examines his smile in this newspaper image and wonders what it was about the big fish that made William Hay feel so joyous. He'd merely cast a hook in the water. A fish had sniffed out the little bit of bait and thought it could eat it. Fell for the deception. Was William Hay a man happy because his little trick had paid off so handsomely, or was there a larger feeling of cosmic blessing he felt on Frankston Pier?

This week the local rag had a picture of the watercooler near radiology with the tape Jovan had put around it and the senseless words above the image: **Origin of the Species.**

Jovan reads the article. An interview with a local psychologist and Frankston-based writer who is good for a few quotes as well as the appearance of some solid research done.

David Dickens opined that from what he'd been shown of the graffitist currently pestering the Sandringham Hospital there was a frustrated artist at work in all of it. He also stated that this should not be underestimated as a cause of the mental illness widespread in our society.

Jovan folds the paper up again. His break is almost over. He spends the last few minutes thinking about the young man who caught a big fish. A barracouta resembles a small dinosaur. It's strangely long and thin and its jaws have miniature alligator teeth. Jovan had never been fishing but he would enjoy catching an Australian barracouta from Frankston Pier—when it dangled from a line held in his outstretched arm, still alive and flapping.

An odd bit of data floats into his mind about how the early Christians didn't use the crucifix as the central symbol of their faith. It had been the fish, a representation of the soul in the ocean of the Holy Spirit. Everyone has scraps of mythology in their minds, and it's probably foolish to spend more than a few seconds considering them, yet he does enjoy the idea of a barracouta soul.

IN THE AFTERNOON Jovan carries leaking green bags of refuse from the kitchen to the skip a few metres from the back door. One breaks open and spills out onto the hot asphalt. He's swearing at it, and at the thought that he'll have to clean this mess up now, when he finds that a bald man has materialised behind him.

He's watching Jovan quietly, listening to Serbian profanities. He smells of incense and wears the kind of Indian apparel you can buy in the stores that sell that incense. It's a strange fashion some people wear in Australia. Back in Bosnia the poorest wouldn't have worn it. Even Gypsies would have ridiculed it.

Jovan picks up the pile of bones and rice and carrot, all soaked in gravy and a variety of unknowable juices. Strides away from the man to the mini skip. He walks to the kitchen with the man following him. He washes the putrid stink off his hands, applying the pink liquid soap three times before he is satisfied. Cleans beneath his fingernails with a dishwashing brush. It's not only the odour. It smells noxiously of the rotting chicken flesh he'd found in the mess and Jovan has been paranoid in the extreme ever since he'd suffered through food poisoning back in Bosnia. The word alone, *Salmonella*, feels toxic in his mouth and ears.

He shakes the water from his hands in one big wave from elbows through wrists to fingertips and looks at the man patiently waiting for Jovan to finish. The bald fellow is wearing small round glasses. He lifts his right hand as if to clear his mouth before speaking, then doesn't get the chance to talk because Prasad, the kitchen's chef, has stepped between them to tell Jovan to go help the delivery man bring in a large shipment of frozen meats hanging in his truck.

"Not my job," Jovan tells him.

Prasad is dumbfounded, blinks it away, and says in a rising voice practised at throwing around orders, "Your job is what I tell you. You go and help him. Now."

"Not my job proscription. Kitchen not my job. Hospital is my job."

"What do you mean? The kitchen is part of the hospital." He speaks in an accent that makes Jovan think it's an attempt at posh English, that gets carried away with some Indian flowery vowel sounds.

"Part of this job. Not part of you," Jovan says flatly as he shakes his hands one more time over the sink and uses a towel he keeps in his back pocket.

"What the bleeding hell are you talking about? Part of this? Part of that? Do you understand basic directions?" Prasad leans forward without moving his feet. Jovan starts towards the door and the small, pot-bellied chef is quick to dance out of his way. Jovan walks out the door with the silent man still following him.

"My name is David Dickens," he says, as they walk towards the next cleanup request that came through on Jovan's pager fifteen minutes ago. A woman's waters have broken in the lobby. When Jovan hears the name he stops and turns towards him. "I'm told you're the man to speak to regarding the graffiti. Because you're the man that cleans it all away. And I found myself interested in the watercooler that was in the *Bayside Bugle*."

"Yes, and you this psychologist they ask to understand him." The man nods without really hearing. Intent on following a set of sentences he's already prepared. "It seems interesting what he's doing. I've been told he used his own blood to write a message on the walls of the operating room. I was interested in what the message was."

"The dots in his blood. *Maybe* his blood. Maybe from somewhere else."

"What dots?"

"After the sentence there is the dots, to say there is something more, but it is not . . ." Jovan taps his finger in his palm three times to indicate the trail of ellipses.

"Oh, the dots were in blood. What was the message?"

"I cannot tell you right this time. I have my job I have to do."

"I understand," he says, reaching out a hand to touch Jovan's shoulder. Realising instantly it's a mistake and dropping his outstretched arm. "I'm wondering if they tested the blood. They could still match it to a hospital employee."

Jovan lifted his fingers to his nose and sniffed to make sure they were clean as he thought about the question. "Can hospital afford this?"

"Well, yes, of course. They do blood tests all the time. Matching

DNA wouldn't be exorbitant. It'd be an expedient response to the ongoing cost of this vandalism."

"No. This is not my question. Can hospital afford if vandal is doctor. If this doctor works here—in *this* hospital." For the first time Jovan feels as though Dickens is listening to him. "Not story for small paper, asking *you* for answers. This for real newspapers, for radio and the television, and the patients and lawyers and judges talking for years about big money."

"Yes, but what are they going to do? Just let it go on?"

"They ask me to clean. Maybe his blood. Maybe no."

"He seems smart." Dickens walks with Jovan, moving to the service entrance together, as though they were friends. "Probably too smart for that anyway," Dickens says, as he stops at the door. "I just think it's interesting. Anyway, thanks for your time." Dickens offers his hand and they shake. Dickens gives him a nod and a smile before he starts to walk away.

"I want to talk to you about something you say in the article," Jovan tells the hippy psychologist. "We talk again later."

THEY MEET AGAIN a few hours afterwards in a café on Bluff Road. Dickens had been drinking herbal tea while he waited. He is now satisfied with glasses of water. He watches Jovan devour three different kinds of muffin and drink two cappuccinos. Jovan's hair is wet from the shower he had after work. A feminine berry smell to the kind of shampoo he uses.

While he watches the big janitor feed, Dickens talks about what he's mentioned in the article—how the frustrated artistic impulse lay at the root of many forms of schizophrenia, also contributing to the ever-rising instances of anxiety and depression, even in people that did not consider themselves artistic in any way.

It was due to the artistic impulse in itself being a function of imagination, and imagination being unavoidable in the human animal. Imagination wasn't simply a reflex action of higher cognitive processing, it was the reservoir of all experiences and passions, positing within itself such speculative notions as God and Soul, even Ego, Superego, Id, and whatever other names we chose to use for its contents, including Life, Humanity, and World.

This went to say that Imagination was not a discrete function of the brain, but a fundamental explosion of everything we knew, everywhere we looked. The repression of this artistic impulse led many people into lives that continued to diminish until they collapsed in on themselves. The simple equation he put forward was that everything that cannot find expression will melt into a molten subterranean river of repression.

Expression rising from repression equals liberation. It wasn't a way out of emotional pain. It was a way out of neurosis because it contextualised the pain. It let the imagination develop an image of psychic contents. Anything could be tolerated if it was understood. A person could develop, and imagination has always been a tool of evolution, so this was critical. The idea of the *path*, or course of life, was crucial if the individual was to allow the power of evolution to push him forward. There was destruction expressed as disease in anything counter-evolutionary.

Jovan presses the last bit of muffin down into the plate so it will stick to his finger, raises his hand, and eats the crumb. "Hipip-hooray," he mutters to himself.

David Dickens continues without pause, "With a man like the graffitist that you have running amok in your hospital, we find an interesting mixture of desperation and philosophy, the waking mind and the unconscious, a desire to destroy as it seeks to be understood, a hallmark of this whole current generation—"

"A question for you," Jovan says loudly, placing a full stop into the doctor's mouth, because clearly Dickens could go on pleasantly theorising for the rest of the afternoon and evening.

"What if the man has this monster in the imagination?" Jovan asks. "And monster wants to come out? Into this world? He wants to live here. Making a story for him does not make him something else. He is still the monster. He still want to eat people. Monster want to be real."

David Dickens drinks his glass of water and clears his throat as though he's ready to launch into another psychological sermon, which might or might not answer Jovan's question. Jovan tells David he must go home now.

"Well, I was just starting to enjoy our conversation."

"If we fish in Frankston we catch no barracouta. Noise is good for catching nothing."

Bewilderment passes across the psychologist's face, as he seeks to appear understanding and to bid farewell, all at the same time. It's an expression Jovan enjoys remembering on the drive home.

IN THE KITCHEN sits Jovan's birthday cake. Something Slavko's wife, who loves to bake, thought would be nice. Thirty-nine candles stuck in the top. It will sit there for a few days and get thrown away without comment, into the green wheelie bin outside, not the kitchen bin in the cupboard beside the stove. Those unlit candles and the unsung cake—quietly covered by household refuse.

Jovan goes to bed. He doesn't sleep. He gets up and takes a sleeping pill. When he still doesn't drift away, he gets up and takes another pill. He does this in half hour instalments until he is unconscious. Despite this, the night feels long and broken, hard and relentless—Suzana is waiting for him at the other end of it, saying happy birthday and kissing him for every year of his life.

And perfume, in heavy drops of redolence, filling nose and mouth. Drowning in the wake of passing love.

In the morning, Jovan buries his face in a clean face-towel in the shower, then rubs it across the back of his neck. Lets the water run across his face for long minutes as he wakes up slowly. The dream drifted in and out of his recollection, ready to disappear completely and forever. He coaxes the dream back and tries to remember some of its features. It came from something Dr. Graffito wrote.

Jovan had been asleep when Suzana started kissing him this Friday morning. She had the earlier start today. She'd pulled him from the dream—he'd fallen back into it as soon as she left him to his sleep.

A man, already half-dead, can drown in a few centimetres of love.

In the dream, he walked from house to house, through unknown suburbs looking for his wife, because he knew she was cleaning one of the homes. He walked into twenty or thirty, maybe forty different houses, knowing she had to be close from the wafts of her perfume. Every house had been cleaned yet was also empty of everything. No furniture, pictures, plates. The wardrobes without clothes. He was mystified, wondering where everyone and their belongings were. It felt epic, a search that could go on for the rest of his life, looking for his wife through the many empty houses of the suburbs. That it would go on, forever and ever, as in fairytales. He walked into an empty, antiseptically clean kitchen, and saw a spotless glass on the bench. The only bit of anything indicating domestic life he'd seen in all the houses. It still had a cardboard smell to it and it sat on a flyer—serving as a paperweight. He lifted the piece of paper. It was a welcome to his new home on this new planet. Soon to be populated and called Crumbs.

The water runs off his face. He lets the strange dream wash away as well. He wonders what Dickens would make of it. He might tell him about it when they see each other on the weekend. The doctor is coming over to see the plates in Jovan's garage. The ones that read **Masters of Destiny / Victims of Fate**. Why is the planet called Crumbs, Dickens might ask, and Jovan would say that he'd heard somewhere that's what the planets were. The crumbs of exploding stars. And the doctor might be able to infer something from that regarding how empty or abandoned Jovan felt, or how it was only people like Barracouta William Hay that had God's good light shining down on them. Not for people like Jovan, who dwelled in some unpopulated underworld of . . . No, in general Jovan doesn't have much of an appetite for psychology anymore. He has done more than his share of reading in regards to Freud, Lacan, Miller, Jung, etc, etc.

He turns the shower taps off, remembers not to turn them so tightly that Suzana will have trouble the next time she uses the shower. One of those things he forgets sometimes—turning them too tight. Creating that instant of despair for Suzana as she stands naked in the cubicle unable to budge the handles without calling him out of bed.

The dog next door is barking his head off about something. Quiet usually, thank God. Not much of a guard dog for Mister Silvers. Charlemagne saw every human being as a potential friend instead of a possible enemy. A devastating hunter of possums however, and appreciated as such by the neighbours in the vicinity, who couldn't legally kill the protected animals—despite the fact that cute little possums got into the walls of houses and screeched at any hour of the night with the spine-chilling effect of horror-movie creatures.

The barking goes on for a while, as Jovan pushes his thoughts away from the hopelessness of the entire field of psychology for him, and the fear that all he feels on a daily basis will go on being felt in the same way for the rest of his life. He often thinks he has just enough strength to cope with a few more hours (sometimes it's minutes or seconds) and yet the days keep coming relentlessly like those trains the other week at Slavko's place. When he was young he might have played happily near the tracks like the cricket children. These days he feels as though he uses a rail for a pillow—always listening to the vague rumblings of oncoming annihilation.

He leans out of the cubicle and picks the towel off the open door of the vanity unit. Dries his thick black hair which silver has begun to glint through in the last year. Wipes down his torso, then his limbs, and steps out clean. Strange how little his body shows the evidence of his life. How rarely the flesh has been nicked by catastrophe. Almost no evidence in scarring outside a few abstract burn marks on his back. His stubble has gone white. It seems odd. When he shaves he becomes just another man living a quiet life in the suburbs.

He brushes his teeth, gingerly around the painful area in his jaw. Feels the fear building somewhere in the open space of his ribcage. Doesn't have a thought or a reason attached to it. It comes and tears at his heart and lungs. He continues to brush. Spits out a little blood with his foam. Stands up and wipes his mouth with a hand towel. Can't see it in his own face. When it fills his chest with a hundred crows, scrambling with their claws and beaks through black feathers for immediate release, even then, he can't see it. It's as though the past never writes itself into his features and expressions. Only that which ghosts behind the face can summon white-terror spectres and black-dread phantoms; the dead and living writhing in the muddy grave of his mind.

He puts his hand towel back on the rack. Breathes through it. Shrugs as he moves his head from the steel rail to let another train hurtle past. There is nothing those men who still have faith in the rational, as does David Dickens, could tell him about any of it. So he pushes his mind along to thoughts of Dr. Graffito and what he might do next.

Jovan looks at his reflection in the mirror. He'll stay that way, paused before his reflection for a few moments. Jovan will not reflect on the war. Those who have suffered a breakdown, such as Jovan has, often remember events during the crisis in chaotic clouds that roil through their minds. Flashes of lightning reveal electrified horror amidst the details. The narrative sequence of Jovan's life is not something he can lay out for himself.

The Serbs fought for Sarajevo from the hills and mountains of the surrounding Dinaric Alps. They were vilified for firing mortars into the city. For snipers taking shots at mourners at funerals. At musicians playing music for peace. At children skipping along the footpath or kicking a ball from one side of the street to the other. All of this happened. Yet this is also true: for the first time in tens of generations there are now almost no Serbs left alive in Sarajevo.

Jovan and Suzana were forced out of their homes during this civil war and then out of the university. Into a camp. Given food they thought was from the UN. It had been passed through different hands and it wasn't clear who poisoned the food. It could have been Croats, Muslims, or Serbs.

The result was the same. Suzana didn't eat dinner, so no poison for her. For Jovan, the worst agony of his life as he struggled to go on breathing every minute of two weeks, eventually coming through some fifteen kilos lighter. His boy and his girl, his two children, were gone before nightfall of the first day, while he was burning in hell. No one told Jovan until he stumbled out of the camp's hospital a week after he was deemed recovered, which meant he was well enough to travel and it wouldn't kill him.

They slowly made their way out of Bosnia and Herzegovina to Serbia on a trailer pulled along by a farm tractor, new maybe when Tito was still a young man. They didn't speak about their boy or their girl on the journey. They never spoke about them when they got to Belgrade. Not with each other. Suzana's family talked and cried with them. When they left the busted, burnt remains of Yugoslavia and came to Australia as refugees, the Brakocheviches went back to the trailer behind the old diesel tractor which never moved faster than five kilometres an hour. A funeral procession of two. Never to reach its destination. Or it was two small bodies thrown into a group hole and eventually the trailer would tip two more bodies into it. What was there to talk about along the way?

Jovan is an articulate man and he wants to speak to his wife. What stops him time and again isn't the pain, it's a feeling that talking makes it trivial. Not that it makes it real—it makes it small. The reality is clear from when they open their eyes to when they close them, perforating even that boundary almost every night. The death of their two children isn't the erasure of two beings. It is the loss of God and the skies, it is the loss of the past and the future, of all their small-voiced words and their hearts. The only possible response is suicide. To survive they have found a way to live without response.

Jovan opened a suitcase a few weeks ago. It was the day he came home from having attempted to clean the graffiti that said The / Trojan / Flea. He'd done the best he could but the glass couldn't be made pristine again. The outlines of the words were still faintly visible when the light boxes were illuminated. The director chose to update to more modern X-ray viewing screens.

Jovan brought out their photos. He put them in frames. He set them on the chest of drawers in the bedroom. On the fridge in the kitchen. On the mantel in the lounge. He put them into more frames and hung them on walls in rooms and halls. They didn't talk about the pictures. Suzana kept the glass clean in all of those frames Jovan placed around their home. The two dead children within them smiling.

He was four. She was six. They died within the same hour, eight years ago. Both born in Sarajevo. Their names were Dejan and

Ana. And there's nothing more that can be said about the dead that doesn't make them small, lost, and forgotten.

Jovan leans closer to the mirror. He runs a hand across the white stubble and remembers another birthday. A cake that Dejan and Ana made with the help of Grandma Radmila. Wincing on some bites because eggshell had made it into the mixture. Eating it anyway because they kept asking how he was enjoying the crunchy birthday cake they'd baked for him. Jovan takes a breath that wavers on the exhalation and tells the reflection that he won't shave today. Leaves the wet towel on the bathroom floor.

IN THE LOUNGE, stuck to the front of a book he was reading last night, a note from Suzana. He lifts the book and reads: *I've made an appointment for you with a dentist next Monday. You're going to call in sick at the hospital that Monday. Or you can inform them now. This is not optional. I won't listen to any more moaning. I won't hear any more excuses. Consider yourself locked in. Consider yourself half-done with it.* On another Post-it, which he won't find until he's reading his book at lunch, a quote from Cervantes stuck within the pages a little further along from where he'd stopped the night before: *Every tooth in a man's head is more valuable than a diamond.*

He puts the book down, the note still stuck to it. He doesn't screw it up and throw it away because she hadn't written a note in all the time they'd been in Australia. Because he'd screwed up a million of them already. Because there was no calculating how many times she had left these kinds of notes around their flat on Pehlivanusha Street.

Post-it notes on the paper halfway through his typewriter on his desk, or on the centre of a television screen, at times a few of them, and some hanging from the screen from the day before, on the inside of the front door if it concerned something he should do before he left home, sometimes on the other side if it was the rubbish that had to be taken down, on the kettle, on the seat of the bike he'd use to ride to Uni. On the seat of the toilet or its water tank. The mirror in the bathroom if she wanted to share a quote with him: . . . *Dame Dafina, otherworldly and radiant in a flurry of snowflakes and flames, in a mingling of Slavonian woods and heavenly constellations, saw the face of Vuk Isakovich.* A quote from *Migrations*, by Milosh Tsernianski, a book she was reading for the fifth time. Or it was a quote from her favourite author, Ivo Andrich: *You should not be afraid of human beings. I am not, only of what is inhuman in them.* That one had been stuck to the book review section of the weekend newspaper, *Liberation*, that she knew he'd be reading as soon as he had the chance.

Anywhere she knew he would see it. Where it was unavoidable. He picks it up. The note about a dentist Monday. Folds it. Puts it into his wallet. Nods, and mumbles, "Monday. OK." He walks into the kitchen and prepares a quick breakfast, and does not think about the birthday cake, sitting inside the fridge as though it's a bomb. The note on the fridge says: *Dinner tonight. Restaurant by the sea.*

ON THAT SAME Friday morning, the optometrist, whom everyone calls Miss Richards, is standing at her usual train station. She hasn't brought her customary music or book. She has a ticket still worth over a thousand dollars because it's a yearly pass. Hallam is a small, unmanned station on the Pakenham line. The V-Rail trains never stop there. She's seen them speed through countless times. There has been a notion on many such occasions. It has always been a small idea barely the size of a full stop in whatever she was reading. She's read that famous novel by Tolstoy and remembers the images of a flame being blown out and a book being closed. But it's not as easy as that. Or poetic. It is more like a pig hung from its rear legs and getting its throat cut. It is a mutilation the splintering bones of her skeleton had never prepared for. It is a demolition of her soul her imagination could never have conceived. There is no book to close. There is no candle. Such absurdly poetic images for the pages of a story.

When Miss Richards leaps off the platform at Hallam, she hits the shiny, clean steel rails and breaks bones in her wrists and knees, and then the impact of the train shatters everything else, and tears her meat into bits, and spatters her blood across the hot dry rocks of Hallam station. She is in all of those cells for an instant too long. For the briefest moment she knows what it is to come apart in millions of different directions, none of them a release or relief.

THREE

A SOFT PATTERING SOUND AGAINST AN upturned plastic bucket beyond the bedroom window peters out. Jovan notices the drizzle of rain only when it begins to ease off. He's been dozing. Acid trickles through his veins as he wakes. It's the reason Jovan rarely takes afternoon naps. The five- or ten-minute spells of unconsciousness he gets when fatigue overwhelms him are never restful. He keeps his body still. His limbs ordered. Palms folded atop his chest. Eyes closed and teeth unclenched. Breathing in slow, measured intervals. His heels balanced on the crease at the end of the mattress.

The house is empty. It sounds abandoned and feels hollow in a way only Sundays can. He swings his legs over the edge of the bed and blinks, waiting for the acid to leave his blood, hoping it'll be sooner rather than later. Checks the clock for the time. Twenty-after-seven. Ten minutes before Suzana comes home from Black Rock. There's a house out there she's regularly attending to now. Not just cleaning—some cooking is required. A dinner tonight for the Coultas family of Prospect Grove that has her coming home so late. *Seven-thirty*, she said. Often, it's later than promised. "Promised" was too strong a word for it. He wasn't sure what word he should use.

While he waits for his nervous system to ease up, he watches Charlemagne stroll around his yard, roaming through the lemon trees and across the dry grass. The dog sniffs at a turd some eight centimetres long. One of many that Charlemagne has already left out there on Jovan's lawn over the last few weeks. When they're dry, they're easy to scoop up with a shovel, but the days get away from Jovan. The grass doesn't need much cutting at least. It's an Australian type that creeps across the soil in a lattice rather than growing from individual blades. Perhaps it's a weed that merely looks grass-like. Or maybe the grass evolved in this country to survive the regular droughts. Charlemagne stretches in the middle of the yard and opens his massive jaws for a huge yawn.

"Just look at that thing," Jovan murmurs, feeling a burble of laughter dissolve in his chest without surfacing. "That's a big fucking dog."

Charlemagne is a shaggy behemoth, almost as tall as Jovan when he leaps up to put his paws on his shoulders. Children stop mid-stride when they see the dog. Heads stop talking in their cars and slowly turn as they drive by. Over a metre high at the shoulder, Charlemagne is about as tall as a good-sized pony. Obviously he eats about as much as one as well.

An Irish wolfhound, his neighbour told him, when he came

searching for his dog the first few times. A man of inverse proportions to his dog. Silvers would never have been big and, as he ages, seems smaller every year. More frail and withered, though he isn't out of his fifties yet. There's a slight depression above his right eye and it extends across his forehead and over the top of his skull. The circular shape marks an impact, the same way as the surface of the moon reveals an asteroid strike. A car crash years ago means Silvers trembles almost constantly and speaking more than a few sentences can often be difficult. Many words are impossible to say.

Silvers can still read, he assures Jovan. In the local paper there's usually something Silvers can share with his neighbours. Most of his neighbours don't want to speak with him for any length of time; some of them even swear at Silvers. Jovan talked with him for a while yesterday about the boy who caught a barracouta off the pier. Silvers told Jovan he has fishing rods that he hasn't used for years, just sitting in his garage. Jovan explains he's never been fishing and wouldn't know the first thing about it. Silvers can't work out where the pier is. He knows it's not far away; within walking distance. He can't remember which road leads to the ocean, so he wanders around the few streets he does know, and talks about barracouta with neighbours he catches when they're getting out of their cars.

They shake hands every time they meet in Jovan's drive. The small man puts out his jittery arm, giving him that one word to go along with it every time. "Silvers." For a while Jovan thought it was a greeting rather than the man's surname. His first name was only discovered by Jovan when Silvers's wife came looking for him, and apologising for Charlemagne's human-sized shits on the Brakochevich front yard. Looking for Bob again. And aren't their names also in inverse proportions? "Funny," murmurs Jovan again. "Look at that monster."

A few minutes later Silvers stutter-walks into the yard across the road, and picks up the garden hose. Turns the tap on and starts watering the grass going blond in the Australian summer. No one around here seems to care about dry grass and mostly they let their lawns get what water they can from the skies, so Silvers goes from house to house in his neighbourhood watering the dying lawns.

Jovan sits on the edge of his bed feeling the acid run out of his blood. He can take deeper breaths now.

Memory of comfort, how easy, how quick, I forget myself.

When he comes out into his front yard it's with his shovel and Charlemagne is happy to see him. He follows Jovan around as the shovel moves in swift slashes across the dry grass. Before he's half-way though cleaning his lawn a car pulls up into the drive. A beat-up navy-blue Datsun 260c, as much of a bomb as Jovan's panel van. The psychologist gets out of it. He's told to get back in and park it in the street.

"Sorry. My wife come home soon and I want her to park on driveway," Jovan explains as Dickens hobbles over. "What's wrong with you legs?" Jovan asks.

"Ah." Dickens waves his hand. "I fell down some stairs. Other-wise I would have walked here. I walk everywhere usually. Anyway, Friday morning I'm coming down stairs I've walked down three or four times every day for the last ten years without incident, and I missed the top step. Tumbled all the way down. Hurt my neck and coccyx, bruised some ribs, and sprained an ankle. My GP told me that I should consider myself lucky I didn't break my neck. I felt I was unlucky to have tumbled down my stairs in the first place. You would have laughed if you saw it. It's pretty disturbing to fall though. My first thought as I started to groan was an accusation, and a feeling of anger. I don't know at who since I don't believe in God. Certainly not a prankster god sticking out a foot when I wasn't watching. I sometimes suspect that there is an atavistic blueprint for the mind that no matter what we do, we can't really alter. Which is to say, two thousand years of social evolution and generations of civilisation is a layer as thin across the psyche as the skin on boiled milk."

Jovan steps back with fingers passing across his forehead.

Dickens leans forward slightly, saying, "I'm sorry to go on. I had a second cup of coffee today, and I really don't think I should drink any coffee at all. I saw this experiment once, when they gave wood spiders various drugs like cocaine, heroin, THC, LSD, nicotine, etcetera, etcetera, to see the effect on this phenomenal web builder of a spider. Interesting results, though I don't know how controlled the experiment actually was. In any case, the fascinating thing was that the wood spider given caffeine built exactly the kind of web he would have built without the caffeine, except very quickly. The actual effect on him was the most dramatic of all. I mean, more than cocaine or heroin. The other wood spiders continued to function after building their bizarre, drug-induced webs, but the caffeine spider went into a rocking, semi-catatonic state after completing his web. In human terms you could call it a complete psychotic breakdown. Oh my God! That thing's coming at me! And I'm sore already. Don't let it jump on me!"

Dickens is stumbling back as the Irish wolfhound emerges from a possum hunt in Jovan's backyard. The psychologist falls onto his bruised coccyx with a yelp.

Charlemagne stops and looks up at Jovan as if to ask, *What's the deal with this guy?*

"This is friendly Carlo. He won't make you any pain," Jovan tells David.

"Jittery, I suppose, after what happened. And I won't sleep tonight," Dickens says getting back to his feet. "I keep forgetting how addictive coffee really is. It's the commonplace nature . . ."

"You did not come for this," Jovan says. The Irish wolfhound stands beside Jovan, leaning on him. A hand unconsciously reaches down and plays with the folds of skin at the dog's throat.

Dickens looks at the two of them, rubbing his lips with the back of his hand, and then says, "I take it you've heard about the optometrist."

"Yes. Very sorry for her." Jovan felt little about the incident. Having spoken now though, feels the words thump into his heart, the ghost of a train suddenly rattling through with all its carriages and then vanishing and leaving him feeling the same kind of nothingness again. That feeling was the lie. The truth was the train, loaded not only with Miss Richards and her small sad decision on the Hallam platform, but with others seen through the glass, blurred with reflections of Jovan and Suzana, and so many others still waiting at the station. The numbness of a long wait.

Purgatory is a nothing, fear is a nothing, love is a nothing.

Dickens leans forward, reaching out a tentative hand to Charlemagne. "We can't attribute the action entirely to her exposure to the graffiti. Clearly a tipping point was reached." A drizzle begins to descend in a mist, evaporating before it gets to the ground, warm from the day.

"Was it killing herself? Maybe she fall over. Or something else. Pushed by accident." They move beneath the foliage of a silver dollar eucalyptus growing in Jovan's front yard.

"Did you see the eye charts?" Dickens asks.

"Yes."

Dickens blinks. "Do you *have* the eye charts?"

Jovan nods.

"Is it possible from what you saw? Intentional, not accidental." Jovan shakes his head. "I am very surprised."

"Is it as simple as reading the message? Perhaps it was a part of it. What about the invasive nature of the act—the particularity of it. Everything else so far has been broad range. For anyone that came across it. Here we have a specific target for a message. And that target is dead a few days later. It certainly seems a related sequence. What do you think?"

"He knows her very well." Jovan shrugs, feeling tired and dazed. "Maybe. But he does not push. He has an instinct for how to find pain. This doctor with needles."

"Acupuncturist."

"He finds the nerve that hurts most and uses needle for ice."

"Ice pick."

"He is not planning the place like Hallam. He is not a mastermind from a bad grade film."

"B Grade. There's A Grade and there's . . . whatever. It's not Bad Grade."

"Enough with help. If you understand, nod your head. Or keep your mouth close for more than a minute. You don't catch flies in your mouth."

"Sure. Sorry." Dickens rubs the hand that touched the dog on his pant leg. "I would very much like to see the eye charts, if that's convenient for you at all."

A few moments ago Jovan had been in his bedroom. Dealing with a chattering psychologist sky-high on caffeine wasn't a pleasant way to wake up.

"As well as the eye charts, she find the body with the message cut in chest. Maybe this have effects," Jovan says.

"You didn't see the Inspiration cadaver yourself?"

"No."

"Did they take pictures?"

"What you think?"

"Of course." Dickens squints in embarrassment. "I didn't know the optometrist found the cadaver. Do you think that's what made her Graffito's next target?"

"Yes. Maybe." Jovan tilts his head back to stretch his neck and take a breath of air. He wobbles his head left and right, blinking as though he's just woken. "Trying to understand crazy can make the crazy." He plucks a eucalyptus leaf and brings it to his nose. A lovely smell.

Dickens doesn't blink or move his head. He keeps himself very still and focused. "How did she respond to finding that woman's body?"

Jovan exhales loudly, exasperated.

"I know it sounds like an interrogation. I'm not just asking questions. I'm very interested in your thoughts. There's a part of me that can't believe a woman killed herself over some graffiti. A bit of vandalism. But there's the cadaver, and you have to call that carved word a desecration. So that makes more sense. Did you see Richards after discovering that body?"

"Miss Richards always quiet. Everything was in tight jar. I think she acts like doctor, but she not surgeon and a dead body for the optometrist is dead body for the suburban person. I never see a word made into a human body this way. How do we respond? Maybe there is no respond to this." Jovan rubs the back of his neck as he speaks, pauses as he asks his question, and then lets his arm drop.

David Dickens pats the giant dog's head very lightly, pretending to touch him as much as anything. "I might write a book about these events. I've even made a start. It's early days and there's many a project I begin . . . but you can never tell which will carry you all the way through to the end. I thought the best way to tackle this story would be from his perspective. Dr. Graffito's eyes. Of course, I have nowhere near enough information, but we'll see how we go. The event is in progress and it's going to be interesting to see who this man is. One thing's for certain: he will not stop. The evidence of his behaviour indicates a deeply compulsive personality that is only becoming more obsessive with time. Sedation and restraint is all that might be recommended. So, he will be caught. Eventually. I might get a chance to talk to him. Maybe Graffito is a way for me to investigate a range of ideas I'm already exploring, but he might also end up being the way to crystallise what I've been working towards for years. I can show you the intro and you can give me your opinion."

"My opinion?"

"I mean your professional opinion." David leans forward, arms slightly raised, suggesting an actor might emerge from the wings onto a stage. "As a professor of literature in Yugoslavia you must have assessed many a manuscript."

"Not now. No more professional anything. I understand talking much more better than reading, especially with technical word. This way he looks . . ."

"Perspective," David fills in, then raises a hand in apology.

"It is impossible for you maybe. Where does he look from? How does he look? And what you could speak for him, comes from easy explanation you have already prepared. This is . . . just *you* again. Not a new perspective."

"I think I can find a different perspective. I don't want to shrink him into some easy categorisation. I want to try to understand him. See if I can . . ."

"The rain is falling from a full moon," Silvers says. "The water wets my face but I haven't been crying."

Silvers has returned to the yard after having watched the rain sifting across the lawns of his neighbourhood. Watering the grass wasn't necessary after all and he hasn't been called a "fucking mental," "stupid fuck," or "dumb shit" and hasn't been pushed away by any of the more territorial neighbours who don't want him touching their hoses or water to save their grass.

The full moon is clear even though the sky is still more blue than black. Silvers stands among the men as though to join the conversation, not paying attention to what they're saying. He's pleased to hear their voices engaged on some subject of apparent substance.

"Round moon in the blue sky," he says into a brief pause in the two men's voices. "I hammer it in with my eye. The head of a big nail."

A car coasts up the drive. Jovan's wife. The pretty lady that gives Silvers food she cooks herself—who has a cutting voice and hard sharp eyes as though she found them in broken beer bottles. Even when she smiles at him, or at his Charlemagne, or at her husband, the big man with hands twice the size of his own. The woman who never looks afraid of anything, even when he had to bring her over to the house because his Janey was so sick she couldn't get out of bed, and couldn't make him anything to eat, or even call on the phone for people to bring around food and Silvers had already eaten all the bread and cereal in the house. This woman with the broken-glass eyes came and made everything alright again. As though she was changing the bed. She called the ambulance and Janey came back because it had been a mild heart attack. Now Janey was always resting and she promised she would live to be a hundred and one. Silvers worries that she might not be telling him the truth and he doesn't want to ask Mister Jovan's wife for help every day, even though she was very nice, because he doesn't want to look at those eyes.

Charlemagne barks and Jovan sees Mrs. Silvers making her way over. To collect her "two strays." At the same time Jovan sees a sleek new Saab roll up behind the Datsun that Dickens owns. Tammie sits behind her steering wheel, smiling at the sample of the local community here in Frankston. She gets out of the car and walks towards them.

"Hello there. I think I'm a little lost. Not used to driving around the boondocks I suppose. I was wondering if anyone can help me. I'm looking to get to the Church of Christ. Do any of you know where it is?"

She's looking at Jovan when she asks. He lifts the shovel that he's been leaning on, but remains silent, watching her and the smile snaking around her mouth. Jovan smiles despite himself. It's a good joke: *the Church of Christ.*

Silvers is pointing up at the moon by way of comment. He says, "It would hurt more. This kind of bright round moon. No sleep on the cross. A dark night would be better. The iron nails cannot disappear when there's no darkness."

Charlemagne trots over to Tammie. She gives the dog a whack on the snout with the back of her hand. A hard hit showing experience with animals and discipline.

Suzana lifts the bags of shopping she'd put on the ground and Dickens takes it upon himself to help the woman. He moves out to the kerb and begins pointing out directions and estimates of travel time.

"I'm surprised you need the address at this time of night," Dickens says. "They're closed right now, aren't they? Though I don't suppose it's like a hairdresser or haberdashery. Actually, you must have passed it coming here, down Cranbourne Road. It's the one with a needle on the roof. Don't ask me why it's a needle. Perhaps it's a directional needle. A symbolic gesture reminding us of the Assumption or the struggling soul's aspiration in general—"

"Thanks." She slaps Dickens on the shoulder. Hard enough that it barely qualifies as a friendly pat. "I appreciate the directions."

"Still, what could you possibly want at the church at eight in the evening?" asks Dickens with a polite smile.

Tammie tilts her face forward, closing her eyes. "That's between me and Jesus." She waves at the group of people gathered in Jovan's front yard without looking at them again. "Shame you're holding a shovel. If it was a pitchfork we could call this lovely little tableau Australian Gothic," she tells Jovan, before she gets back into her silver bullet of a car.

Suzana whispers something into the cup of Jovan's ear, and walks into the house with the shopping.

Silvers is dragged away by his wife, announcing before he leaves, "It's a shame we don't all live to a hundred and one years."

Dickens returns to the motionless Jovan and continues talking about the ideas he has for his new book. *The Graffiti Artist of the Caves* might be a good title, Dickens says and goes on for half an hour without noticing that Jovan isn't listening to a word he's saying.

MONDAY MORNING JOVAN drives from the dentist to the hospital, pain in his jaw, knowing now that he'll need seven fillings. Rescheduled to go in for some drilling Friday. Lucky, they tell him, to get in so quickly. A cancellation, and it could have been a month's wait instead, and who knows, maybe another cavity. As it was, lucky number seven. Every time he got fillings they took six months to settle in, and there was no feeling lucky about any of it, anywhere in the process. Well, at least he hadn't taken a fall down the stairs as had the Caffeine Wood Spider.

He is forced to manhandle the van, leaning into the column shift, and swinging the metal crate of a vehicle this way and that, through the alternating gliding/grinding traffic. The brakes are still spongy. Gearing down to stops whenever he can.

David Dickens hadn't fallen down the stairs. Jovan hadn't believed that when Dickens told the story, though he'd accepted it in the wild flow of the man's words yesterday. The over-elaborate lie that students had tried on Jovan in the past so many times, going to ridiculous lengths to explain a late assignment. He pulls his van in and out of the combative lines of traffic.

Because another thing Dickens had talked about last night was the kind of graffiti he'd seen on trains, under bridges, on brick walls along the tracks and at train stations, and what it meant to desperately need to scrawl your name across concrete, rhapsodising about the liquid vision passing across those words and images, as though witnessing a river drowning all in a rushing anonymity. Generating questions: Why did oblivion of this kind hurt? Why did it force these boys out to the desolate concrete near the gleaming steel rails of a rapidly passing world?

Jovan considers Frankston station and what it's like late at night. When Dickens did his research for *The Graffiti Artist of the Caves*. A book that was (metaphorically speaking) also graffiti scrawled beside the tracks, "and as much a response to the hurt as it is for those lost boys buying their cans of paint," Dickens said after dinner as they walked to Jovan's garage to see Graffito's plates and charts.

The man with careful glasses set on his nose; those inquisitive eyes; those hippy clothes; crawled up into a ball as the youths of oblivion kicked into his legs and arms and back. Booting into the sag of an aging body. Kicking into his bald head to see it bounce. Had anyone ever really fallen down the stairs or collided with a door handle when explaining their bruises?

These thoughts shove away from Dickens and those boots crashing into his body and push instead into the traffic Jovan's trying to get through.

Written across the chalkboard-black streets is the mathematics of chaos. Everyone going off in a million directions, scrawling their intentions in Morse code flashes and dashes, behind glass hissing at each other in the lost languages of silence, sometimes colliding and crashing into each other, mostly passing untouched across the unalterable long black mark of a destiny road through an anonymous fate.

Thinking about chaos again, and the difference between fate and destiny. Jovan wonders if he is affected by Dr. Graffito in the same way Miss Richards was. Not so simple an act of destruction. Something at least; not knowing where this will eventually lead him.

Jovan gets out of his white Ford panel van and walks through the hospital car park. He rarely spots anyone he knows from Bosnia. It seems an impossibility that someone from the life over there might pop up all the way over here in Melbourne, though it's happened a few times. His hand is raised to the side of his sore jaw to dampen the jolts of every step. He doesn't pay much attention to the woman pulling along a reluctant five-year-old across the shimmering concrete. He remembers how difficult it had been to go to a supermarket or get on public transport with children. Any kind of movement became a matter of logistics. A child isn't a sack of potatoes you can throw over your shoulder, dumping it here or there. They need to be coaxed every step of the way. Their opinions of the heat taken into account. Their distress negotiated. So he smiles at the woman yet doesn't recognise her from Sarajevo.

Silvana Pejich passes Professor Brakochevich. His smile reaches her with the force of a full-blooded slap as they pass. Manages to keep walking. Doesn't turn around. It hasn't been a good day for her. The bleeding over the last two weeks was the initial stages of a miscarriage, though the doctor hadn't put it that way exactly. The obstetrician was very clear in other ways. A strict recommendation for bed rest. In effect, saying that she should stay in bed for the next six months. Impossible of course. Two wages kept them all barely afloat as it was. She feels damp. Not sure if it's urine, regular fluid, or blood. She pulls her daughter along, promising ice cream on the way home if she'll be a good girl for a few more minutes. *Chocolate* ice cream, she asks. *Strawberry?* she asks—so that her daughter can almost taste the reward. So she'll keep walking and not break down and cry in the middle of the furnace out here. Six months bed rest!

Silvana doesn't look as she did when Jovan knew her. Was it only six years ago? She has gained weight and doesn't dress as daringly these days. Her hair was much longer then and there was that surprising beauty she used to own. Not quite ugly, yet close enough for those pressurised years of school to be an endless, slow-growing agony. Then flowering into something extraordinary in university, the bony, gangly girlhood smoothing out into graceful curves and gentle sways of loveliness. Or so the boys seemed to say with every glance her way. Their mouths were often far more crude. She preferred to keep in mind the lingering gaze of adoration when she passed. Hair down to her hips. All her movement keeping to the rhythm of a dance she had finally discovered. A radio station she never knew was there, playing in the background of her mind all the time. Making her feel plugged in. That she could move along with any kind of bustle, not getting knocked around anymore at all. Grades beginning to slide towards failure because of all the things she wanted to be doing. The ways she preferred to spend her time, waltzing along from one lovely moment to another. Student life in that university would have challenged the most ascetic temperament. She'd had enough years of boredom and silence in Mostar. Feeling the hectic, brutal old movements in the background. Not too far away. So near at times. Kept her moving very quickly. For the first time discovering that there was power in the world that didn't belong exclusively to politicians and soldiers, that she could find and use some of it herself. That she enjoyed the new power she had, simply because she'd grown up into a woman that people thought was beautiful. Yet there would always be an awkward girl within, looking on with mouth agape.

"Have you even fucking read the damn book Silvana?" Brakochevich asked.

She blinked. The lie. It didn't matter what she said, she realised, so she didn't bother with the excuses. "I've always liked you Professor. It would really be my pleasure, you know. It wouldn't be an effort making you happy." She got up, moving around his desk, and let her body find its new rhythm, showing him all the things it might do for him. That it could bring him such joys. Bliss would last longer in the next few minutes than it had ever done before. It would resonate long after she left his office. Unbuttoning her shirt and lifting her skirt, already within her groove when the silence came through a ringing slap. For an instant, she was totally awake. Nothing had changed. It was just Silvana—alone in the world. Her professor standing before her, his huge hand returning to his side. No indication that he had struck her. He might have waved away a fly from his face. Sitting down at his desk. Arranging paper. Picking up his green-ink grading pen. Silvana knew that he'd been careful. Only the fingers had connected. Not the full weight of his massive hand. She wouldn't have been left standing otherwise. Thankful for his restraint.

"Read the book. Get me that assignment by the weekend. I don't want to hear, or see, anything else from you. Now get the fuck out of here you silly little girl."

Silvana reaches her car and opens all the doors to let the heat out. Her daughter says she wants butterscotch ice cream, the same as you get at the movies. Six years later and she can still feel that Sarajevo slap.

"**WHAT ARE YOU** doing here Joe? I thought you were at the dentist this morning?" Mr. Sewell, Jovan's supervisor, stands at the staff entrance, dropping his smoke, crushing it with an old black shoe. The sole looks paper thin.

"This was a plan. They check today. Scrape my tooth clean . . . teeth. So nothing, until Friday. Arvo Friday," Jovan says.

Mr. Sewell nods and lights another cigarette. He smokes, watching the cars circle in the car park, slotting into a space as soon as it opens up. A grimace every time he draws in his tobacco. Smoking as part of some grim duty.

"It's a fucking nightmare out there." Robert Sewell raises a chin at the cars, all in some kind of commerce with illness or death. Depositing their wounded and maimed, picking up their leg- or arm-plastered kin, the all-too-glad-to-be-escaping visitors. A woman in her nineties, trying to exit her spot without turning her head; her handbrake on.

"Maybe you should have gone to the beach," Sewell tells Jovan. "Why do I find that hard to imagine? You ever go to the beach with your wife, Joe?"

"We should go more times," Jovan says, not sure what Mr. Sewell is thinking, standing in his worn-out black shoes. What he sees out there, and why it makes him draw on his cigarette with that ugliness around his mouth.

"Me too. I don't have a wife though. It's good to have one when you're contemplating a jaunt. That's a word you might not be familiar with. It means to get out there on the spur of the moment. For the hell of it, you know. Have a picnic by the Yarra or the Melbourne Botanical Gardens. My parents used to get into that. They never did the traditional Christmas or birthday bullshit. A BBQ by the river was always a brilliant idea. Not only on the twenty-fifth of December. You and your wife should check out The Botanical, Joe," he says blowing smoke at the cars. "Me and Gillian moved all the way out here and never got out anywhere when we were married. We forgot lots of great places and things we used to do, like the jaunt. Used to seem too far away every time we considered it but it's really not a long drive to the Botanical Gardens."

"OK. I'll get address from you." Jovan takes off his sunglasses and moves towards the door.

"But that *fucken* van of yours, *mate*. You can't take a woman *anywhere* in that. A woman doesn't want to feel as if she's a part of the equipment." Jovan lets out the first breath of a chuckle—knows from previous experience that his supervisor is quick to begin talking from his loneliness. "You can borrow my car, mate. I'm not saying it's a luxury vehicle but it's got air con and a great stereo system. I listen to most of my music on the road."

"Thank you. Maybe we have some time soon." Jovan makes a move for the door.

"No new graffiti."

Jovan stops, his card held above the swipe-scanner that will unlock the door for him.

"Maybe he'll stop now. After Hallam," Mr. Sewell says.

Jovan turns around. Waves off the proffered cigarette. It was as if Mr. Sewell didn't believe him when he told him he used to smoke—that he no longer did. Every time they saw each other the pack of smokes came out and he would urge Jovan to take one as though there needed to be a reason for the two of them to be standing together, having a conversation.

"Not a generosity to welcome a friend to poison," he says in Serbian. In English, "No thank you very much."

"Life could go back to the way it was."

"Maybe, yes," Jovan says.

"You don't think that's likely?"

"This going in one direction. Worse. And more worse."

Sewell remembers to blow the smoke away from Jovan as they stand at the staff entrance. He's about to raise the cigarette again when he says, "Look at that old woman, struggling to get out of that spot for the last ten minutes. Her windows up on a day like this. I hope she's got air con. What do you reckon? Is it nice and cool in that piece of shit Mitsubishi Colt?"

They watch the old woman, shrunken white head on stiff shoulders, swivelling in confusion. Two hands that have seized the steering wheel, unable to let go. Not being able to negotiate the tight spaces and narrow angles that will allow her to get out. Jovan swipes his card to release the lock.

"I've already given you the day off, mate. It'd take you five minutes to walk down to the beach. Why don't you go down and have a swim?"

"Maybe you should go water, Boss."

"Me? What would I fucken do in the water?" He smiles. "And I hate smoking on the hot sand. You can't get any satisfaction from a ciggie at the beach."

"I go work now." Jovan smiles at him with his hand to his jaw. "I have this pain. Not so easy to relax in sun."

"OK mate. I want you to go straight up to maternity. Nurses up there complaining as usual. Can't ever be clean enough for them."

"Life go back to way it was," Jovan says with a smile. Sewell blows more smoke at the carousel of cars out in the car park. The old woman has released herself from her purgatory. Jovan swipes his card again and enters the hospital. He hears Sewell behind him say, "Who knows what the fuck that looked like anyway?"

Jovan descends the stairwell and opens a door that will lead him past the laundry rooms and then on into the change rooms. He stops by a sign above the largest of the immense industrial washing machines. Made to look like a regular sign that might have been up on the wall for decades, except it wasn't. It couldn't be. For one thing it's in German, *Arbeit macht frei*. Dr. Graffito's work. Perhaps it was new yet Jovan is certain it isn't. It hadn't grabbed anyone's attention. It is a failure for Graffito. Maybe his first piece. Surreptitiously placed on a wall. No one noticing it for months. Derivative. Uninspired. Before he started getting creative. Before the mania really took hold.

A middle-aged Hungarian lady in her white cleaning uniform unbends from a washing trolley and gives him a malevolent look. He points up at the sign, to indicate he wasn't watching her bend over. She doesn't look. She walks away mumbling something in her language.

Another woman in the white cleaning uniform, a dinky-di Aussie, with that broad type of English he can barely understand, is returning from a break, and stops beside him. She's gazing over to where he's pointing.

"How long has that been there?" she asks. He shrugs. "What's it mean?" Her voice rises from the gut. Always comes with a heavy swing to it, as if she's using her fists as much as her lips.

"Work is . . . work make you free," he says.

"Huh! That's bullshit if eva I heard it," she says. "And why's it in Croatian?"

"You mean Serbian?" he asks.

"Same difference." She looks at him as though he'd climbed down a ladder after having hung the sign. "Why's it up there?"

"It is German." He takes a step away from her. "And I don't know."

"You don't know. Of course you don't know. But you'll stand here looking at it like it's the *Mona Lisa*." That last, *MownahLeesuh*, comes out as nothing Jovan can identify.

"This is Dr. Graffito. You know, the graffiti we have been having."

"What, he's a Kraut, is he?" she asks as she walks back to her work station. "Huh! Should'a known it'd be a foreigner." She turns on her iron, and starts bringing out the white coats of doctors she'll be ironing for the next few hours.

SUZANA IS STILL in the house when he wakes. Jovan stumbles out, eyes refusing to operate properly. She's got the coffee on. A pile of French toast. Cinnamon on the table. Broke-open eggs in a bowl, ready to be poured into the pan. The smell of coffee squeezing his stomach tight and then releasing, opening a vast space of hunger.

"Not working today?" Jovan mumbles through a thick mouth, slumping at the table; hands scratching through his hair and then rubbing at his face.

"Is that disappointment in your voice?" She puts down her book. An Ivo Andrich collection of short stories in English he bought her on her first birthday in Australia. To practise her English with something familiar. Turned out an annoying hurdle for something too well known. Unused until now.

"That's fatigue. And my eyes—not being able to open them— that's age. The stumbling around for half an hour before the coffee kicks in, that's death."

"Hey. That's not funny. Not fucking funny." She rises, waving her hand at him to dispel fate-tempting words. She switches the gas flame on and strikes a match. Waits a second for the pan to melt some butter.

"No, I save the funny for the dilemma of the toilet on this kind of morning, an erection and a full bladder."

"And now disgusting. The scratching of your arse, that's just gross." She uses the English word, *gross*, like a cliché teenager from an American film. She pours a dash of milk into the bowl of eggs. Swishes them around a few times (Jovan's preference).

"I might want to do that, scratch my arse, yet I resist that temptation in your presence, because that's love."

"Love in refrain. Sing me a silent song darling," she says. Presses her mouth closed afterwards. And he doesn't speak because it strikes him as unusual, these days, that she'd even speak of love in jest. Fear struggles up out of his intestines and freezes his lungs into a gasp that she doesn't see, and he's able to swallow it with some French toast. Maybe because this is the first time they've talked this way in years. As though nothing had happened and they were allowed to be themselves again.

The familiar silence goes on now.

They eat. She reads her book and Jovan looks out the window.

They're surrounded by trees. Down Reservoir Road, the street they lived on, was Jubilee Park. In their elms and the park's pines and gums, vermillion birds were leaping around from branch to branch. Brilliantly coloured ones they call rosellas. Australian birds, he thinks. About the most beautiful birds when they're seen altogether. A neighbour, Mister Karistianos, breeds them. Cages and sells them sometimes. He prefers to sit on his front porch these days throwing them seeds as he listens to classical music on the radio. It seems a shame that the music comes through a small speaker, from a cheap stereo the size of a hardback book, that he's owned for a decade or two. Orchestras had produced the music in concert halls.

"I had this dream last night," Suzana says, bringing over the plate. He's putting the piece of French toast he's taken from her plate into his mouth.

"What are you doing? There's plenty of toast in front of you. Why you taking it from my plate?"

"I don't know. I thought you were finished."

"In the first place, that's revolting. And in the second, damn strange behaviour. Why would you do that?"

"There was something appealing about your bite marks in the bread. I don't know. Move on. Tell me about the dream." She sits there looking at him, shakes her head.

"I was back in Belgrade. Walking along Kalimegdan. I used to do that in my angsty student days. Anyway, it starts snowing, and I'm bothered by that because I'll be wet by the time I get to my car. I'm dressed for summer. A dress I got for my birthday; from you. The one I had to wait six months to wear because you bought a summer dress in winter." She gives him a look with the pause. "Then it really starts to snow, and I'm trying to make my way through half a metre of it blanketing the ground. It gets worse, and I'm panicking because I know I'm going to get covered. Suffocated. And I do. The snow falls in blankets. The suffocation is slow. When I woke, I was desperate for another breath. Snapped my eyes open, and saw nothing but white. Woke up from that and for a second still felt an oblivion of white airlessness."

"Good dream," Jovan comments around his last mouthful of wolfed-down eggs. He picks up his coffee cup.

"Good? It was terrible."

"Yet interesting. I never remember my dreams because they're too boring. I had a good one about moving to a new planet called Crumbs."

"What happened in that one?"

"That's all I remember. Planet Crumbs."

Looking at the clock on the kitchen wall, she stands up.

"Eleven o'clock start for me today, in Chelsea. Jelka is picking me up. And then I'm in Black Rock again until dinner. You've got ham or pastrami for lunch today. I baked some bread yesterday as well."

"Alright," Jovan says, drinking his coffee and shaking some cinnamon onto his toast. Cinnamon was never something they used for French toast back in Yugoslavia. It's an idea she has picked up in the Black Rock house.

Suzana stands in the doorway, watching him as he moves with sleep-clumsy movements. She looks out the window, at the garish birds that drive her crazy with their ceaseless squawking and twittering.

"I want to have another child," she says.

He looks over at her, his face immobilised. He turns his body towards her, a slight swivel in the wooden kitchen chair. "Is this something you want to discuss?"

"You want another child, don't you?" she asks with a very small question mark. It's a statement really.

"Yes." He swallows the piece of bread in his mouth. "I do."

"So do I. What's to discuss?"

"Alright," Jovan says.

"And I want you to clean up the yard today, OK? I'm walking through a minefield every morning. Not to mention the impression it creates of our house. I mean, we live here, right?" She leaves the kitchen, saying, "Someone should put that monster dog on a chain."

"I started to clean the lawn the other day but then the Australian came over. He wouldn't stop talking and I suppose I got distracted."

"You can finish it today."

"No problem," he says in English and doesn't move from the kitchen table for a long time.

FOUR

THE STREETLIGHTS BUZZ AND SEEM TO be smouldering in the wet air. Glowing like fireflies left in a jar too long. A mist of rain falls as if there's all the time in the world to come to a final rest on the ground. Summer warmth exhales through concrete. Thick black blanket clouds have brought the evening early to these Melbourne suburbs. The branches in the trees sprinkle heavier drops of water as they sway above. The damp wind blows strands of Suzana's long hair across her face, making her seem like the young woman she had been only a few years ago.

She slots her key into the door of Jovan's Ford panel van. She hears

Mr. Coultas calling out to her. He's jogging up the long driveway and to the street. To the ugly vehicle that neighbours have complained about in over-the-fence conversations. Rust stains along its bottom like unwashed underwear on display. About the roar of the stuttering engine, a crass brute belches at their pristine Mercedes and BMWs. She has heard snatches of conversations on the phone and between Coultas and his wife. They have both agreed, the panel van is a problem. Suzana has been waiting for them to mention it to her for the last two weeks.

Glen Coultas has followed Suzana out into the night even though it is drizzling. He's out of breath. Isn't it pathetic when a man can't run up his driveway without having to gasp for air?

"Missus Brakochevich," in that carefully over-pronounced way of his. "Hang on a tick."

"Yes Mister Coultas." A hard edge to her voice. Knowing it should be a soft tone of voice when speaking to an employer. Unable to help herself. "I need to go home now." She pulls the key out of the lock and opens the door. She continues to face him over her shoulder.

"Well . . . we forgot to pay you, is all," Coultas explains.

What does he want looking at her that way? Desperation in his hands, flapping uselessly at his sides. Why doesn't he fold them or put them away in his pockets? One hand is now palm up before her as if he's presenting some kind of fortune in its lines.

She opens her mouth for a moment and then speaks. "Okay. We should arrange payment every week if you want me to come here so regularly." It's only on that final word that her accent stumbles. It's such a sing-song word, and she might have put one too many *la*'s into it. "Paying me every day is stupid. Also not easy for you." It feels as though she's getting paid pocket money.

A quick nod of his head. He looks afraid that the next thing Suzana says to him will be an insult. A skittish smile fails to take hold on his face. "We can do that. What day should we make pay day? What day is good for you?"

"Whatever day is good for you," she says. Gets into the cabin of the van. Coultas goes on standing there, gathering glimmering beads of rainwater in his black beard. "It doesn't matter for me. You pick the day."

He says, "Sure, well, we'll make it Wednesdays. From now on. Oh-kay." He has about ten ways of saying *OK*. "So OK. I'll see you tomorrow at about three."

"It can't be before four. That will have to be enough time for everything." She stumbles slightly on *be be four four*.

"Four? Oscar gets home at quarter past four. Yet you'll be here at four. That's barely enough time. But OK. Sure. O'Kay." She doesn't know what is Coultas-with-her, and what is Coultas-himself. Is it possible that he has this desperate edginess to his eyes when he talks with people in general? As though he wants to tell them something that might make all the difference in their lives, his life, to life in general? And if only he can articulate the thought, he can share the news, and somehow a fresh accord will be brought about in the world. Why does he continue to stand there, a fool collecting rain-drops in his beard?

"So I'll see you then." The indigo shirt he is wearing, an evening sky gathering black stars. His glasses spattered with droplets. She reaches to pull the door closed. To hell with the idiot. Coultas is now leaning forward, a nervous waiter with a question for a seated patron.

Amazing that this man is a lecturer at the University of Mel-bourne. How does he survive amongst the brash students plucking the feathers of his knowledge to stuff their toys with, leaving only mockery for the naked, trembling man beneath? There has to be a costume he puts on when he goes to his university and walks into a lecture theatre. He cannot lean forward there with this weak uncertain smile on his face. Or, it's possible things are different in this country. Maybe the students go to university in sedate lines and quietly absorb his lessons with patient questions and feel no need to test his mettle. That had never been her experience as a student or teacher.

He says, "I also wanted to thank you. For doing . . . what you're doing . . . for Rae."

"Don't be stupid." A kick in that word rather than a caress. "Go inside now." He walks away, raising an arm in farewell and then letting it drop. She puts the key into the ignition. She doesn't turn it. She watches the water on the windshield gather and run in rivulets.

Coultas makes her think of Belgrade, and of course, the Demon. It's the contrast between the two lecturers, yet she knows how many things got her around to thinking about that son of a bitch, Vladimir Mitrovich. How is it that a man can become a devil even before he's dead? Entering a woman's ear and living in the grey whorls of her brain—a gleaming red imp with a sharp little cheese fork. The two long thin prongs perfect for skewering a precise memory and forcing it down her throat.

Moving into that Belgrade lecture theatre as if he was the man a whole generation had been waiting for. To the board, and chalk, writing across two metres of it in slashing letters the words:

Vladimir
Mitrović

And then standing there—glaring at his students. A long (maybe it was only twenty seconds but it felt like twenty minutes) staring contest with every one of the first-year history students new to the University of Belgrade.

"If there is any doubt in your minds that excellence is possible, here in this room right now, I want you to leave. If you bring me a conquered mind and a cowed soul, I want you to take them back out with you. Spill your drivelling words of defeat out in the halls. Do not bring me this fucking cooler-than-thou attitude packaged as the sneer of a hipper generation above the bullshit of the past. I want you to pack up your fucking books and get the fuck out of here." Speaking with an incomprehensible rage. "I do not want your masquerades of glamorised ignorance and parades of chic stupidity. Here we have the possibility of greatness. You will approach knowing you know fuck all, and that you may be pathetic and pitiful, but that all you need to do is see a fire. All you need to do is see it. And if you can see it, you will be able to take a light from it back with you into the dim cold cavern of your brain and illuminate the walls of a cultural and genetic memory that is your birthright as a member of the most powerful, awe-inspiring species to have emerged in the millions of years this planet has been churning out life—from the pterodactyl to the AIDS virus. I will show you the fire at the centre of history. Not only our history as Serbs, simmering in the cauldron of Europe above the burning coals of the Middle East, but also, our story as human beings, the history of a Godless planet in the galactic void of brainless stars and lifeless dust, creating God from our own molten blood."

And then he stands there again, motionless except for his eyes, and looks at his students blinking back at him. Standing within a philosophical battlefield, surrounded by the glorious, fluttering battle flags and pennants of his words. A mad general looking to enlist an army of insanity on the possibility of true vision.

The history lecturer had then wiped away his name and had written in its place:

The Engine of Evolution
The Drive of Divinity

He asked the class to begin writing as he continued to watch, moving amongst them. He stood over those that dawdled, until they began scribbling. One that sat there, a rabbit in his headlights, had a finger placed in her collar, and was yanked out of the class. Readmitted later when she was able to respond to the anomalous eight words written without explanation on the blackboard.

Suzana didn't know then that those who most closely resemble angels are those who are the most powerful demons. All she could see of Vladimir Mitrovich was the halo of an explosion from his fusion-powered mind.

Her own response in that essay, on that first day, was a black stream of words that could have flowed as an ink vein through the rest of the year and still broader and longer, flowing on through the rest of her life. Because she did indeed *see* the fire in the cave in that instant. Understood the miracle within the curse the history lecturer was referring to. Knew it intimately even though she'd discovered it for the first time, cleanly and clearly, and was ready to flow through, on into the ancient black inkwell heart of the planet itself.

"You alright?" Coultas stands by her window again. His shirt dark with rainwater. "Are you okay?" He talks from beyond the closed window.

She winds the window down a few centimetres. "Yes. Fine. I was thinking." He goes on standing there. She starts the van and it roars into life, then stutters, so that she has to feed it big gulps of petrol. Jovan tells her that she should run it for a minute to give the engine a chance to warm up. Usually she forces it to grumble and grind along, warming up on its own time. She wants the fucking thing to die, though she couldn't kill it if she tried. Whatever happens to the Ford, Jovan repairs it. He took the whole engine apart and rebuilt it when he bought it. She'd have to burn it by the light of a full moon and hammer a solid-silver stake through its carburettor to destroy it.

She asks Glen Coultas if he is ever overcome by memories, above the dying engine of the Ford, which falls silent after she's asked her question.

For a moment he seems to understand. Perhaps he hasn't heard clearly because he shakes his head and says, "You can park in the garage from now on. OK." He passes her a clicker for the automatic door through the open part of the window. "Oh-kay! So I'll see you tomorrow." Glen Coultas waits for her to drive away. Waves at her in her rear-view mirror. Standing in the drizzle. The old Ford roars on through the nice suburban streets of Black Rock, the anti-Christ of ice cream vans.

FIVE MINUTES DOWN the road her mobile starts ringing. Jelka again. There is a record of five missed messages during the day, and she's already talked to her twice in the morning. Jelka wanting Suzana to come over to her place in Seaford on her way home. It's a left and a right off Nepean Highway yet it isn't as easy as that to make the turns for Suzana. It isn't easy to drive on towards Reservoir Road, Frankston, either. Sometimes it's easier to just drive anywhere else rather than where she is expected. She almost laughs at the thought of making a getaway in the Ford panel van.

As she nears Station Street she makes the left without deciding to. Makes the right onto Chapman Street and stops in front of Jelka's house. The engine threatens to stall but doesn't. Idles with hiccups that have something to do with timing. Jovan has explained it to her; never clearly enough for her to understand why it can never be fixed. It's something he seems to need to adjust every few weeks. So it runs to rumbles and she switches it off and listens to it die out with a shudder. Sits and listens to the car make ticking noises.

Hands on the wheel. Looking at the streetlights on Chapman Street that shine out for no good reason. No one around here goes out for walks. Dogs barking from every barricaded backyard. Children ensconced before their glowing screens behind the walls. Family cars left out on the streets make her think of discarded bits of clothing, forgotten shoes to be picked up when needed the next day for school or work. All of it done tiredly, against the will, with an obligation that works on them like a disease. People around here collapse into bed at the end of the day. They rise every morning with their cheap suburban alarms forcing them out again.

No, she knows this isn't objective. This isn't the life around her as much as the poisoned life within her. She's seeing reflections. There are the streetlights beyond the rain-spattered windshield, with their useless illumination over patched asphalt streets and cracked footpaths. Behind one window, a child with a blue zombie face stares at the screen of a computer as though he'd been there hours already and would spend hours more, lost in a comfortable oblivion. Wasn't it possible it was just a child having fun, playing a computer game, and what was wrong with that? And if it is indeed subjective, she wants to know how she can look at things around here and find a more satisfying, objective picture to dwell on. All she can see is this suburban wasteland. Feel herself within it trying to find a way to live. Perhaps it's in the way each bead of water on the windshield spins the lights in "its microscopic heart"—a line from one of Jovan's poems.

She knows that Jovan used to be able to turn almost anything over to a new perspective, see something deeper, redeeming, more beautiful even if pitiful. It was what made him such a superb poet back in Yugoslavia. And it still takes her breath away, an actual gasp of air at the top of her lungs, when she thinks how crucial poetry used to be to him. How Jovan used to wake in the mornings with poetry emerging in rhapsodies. How it used to drive him, his body slumping over a bedside table and writing with eyes that couldn't open from sleep, and with a drowsy hand, poetry that cut through all the usual bullshit poetry was, the usual mediocrity, and opened up new ways of feeling, seeing, understanding, and being. And now nothing. He doesn't write anymore and it's as though he never did.

She gets out and walks up the drive to the door. The streetlights don't buzz in Seaford, though she remembers now that it was Jovan that came up with the line about streetlights that resembled the glow of fireflies left in a jar too long. Perhaps he'd seen fireflies when he was a child in Banja Luka. They certainly weren't around Zemun, her corner of Belgrade. The door opens before she gets a chance to knock. Her friend is already stepping outside to give her a hug. Not an embrace as such. Jelka places both hands on Suzana's shoulders to halt her. Making as if to kiss Suzana's ears.

"Come inside," Jelka says.

"No. I can't. I'm on my way home." Suzana lifts her wrist, looks at her watch without seeing it. "Dinnertime. I've told you how useless he is in the kitchen."

Jelka is dressed in white designer jeans, in a lovely chartreuse boutique shirt. Her hair is done up anew after work. Her makeup is an intricate detailed artwork she might have spent half an hour before a mirror labouring over. Not going anywhere. She's decided to dress up for the occasion, though the occasion is simply Suzana coming over.

She makes Suzana think of the flush and thrill of a girl emerging into a woman, of the rush of barely understood allure even in plastic jewellery from the local chemist bought with the pocket money of a few dinars. The whiff of unimagined possibilities in a mother's abandoned jewellery box, and medicine cabinet perfumes, and ghostly gowns from forgotten balls and dances hanging in wardrobes. All of these things full of the mystery of womanhood that was rich to a growing girl and usually sucked dry within a few years after being offered up to the ceaseless, limitless hunger of men.

Not for Jelka apparently. The myth took firmer hold in Jelka, until she was a shrunken Cinderella dreaming in eternal sleep on a glass slipper. A confusion of fairytales. Lost at the roots.

No, it isn't that simple. Suzana knows that the world of work clothes growing paler every wash, and flat, cheap runners bought from the Frankston Target isn't a preferable existence. This is a life looking after the seven dwarves as they would have been outside of cartoons. A world of diminished men labouring without end, for no good reason, and a woman's job thrown in there after them, some-how, somewhere, however she might fit the shoes provided, broken crystal slipper or otherwise. Suzana doesn't want the face bleached of everything she saw in Jelka's eyes and yet the Witch's apple seemed to have different effects on different people. If anything, she wishes she could find some of that eternal sleep.

"But I want to talk to you," Jelka says.

"OK, talk. I'm sorry, but I shouldn't have stopped. My stomach is starting to eat itself."

"I'll give you something to eat." Jelka steps back, waving her inside.

"Please Jelka . . . Don't insist. Tell me what's going on."

"Am I on a meter?"

"I just finished work and came straight over. I thought it was an emergency."

"Sit down for *five* minutes. What's the problem?"

The problem is that it is a house that also belongs to her husband, Ante. And Suzana doesn't want to step into Ante's home. He doesn't want her in his house, though of course he's never even seen Suzana.

"Come inside," says Jelka. The first time, in the year she's known her, that Jelka has invited Suzana to her house.

"If you're not going to start talking, I'm leaving." Suzana takes a step backwards and begins to turn.

"What are you doing? I thought we were friends." Jelka steps out and grabs hold of Suzana's arm.

"We are friends. Not schoolgirls." Suzana shakes the woman's hand off her arm. Notices a tremble in Jelka's eyelids. "I've got a life that demands my presence," speaking every word softly, and eventu-ally, it's an apology.

"That's what I want to talk to you about," says Jelka.

Suzana can imagine Ante coming home and parking his car in the driveway, stepping out and walking up the cracked concrete path, blocking her exit. Asking her to explain herself. Who she is. Why she's there. Through the doorway there's the red and white chequerboard of the Croatian coat of arms. This is the first thing Ante wants you to know when you come to his front door.

"What do you mean?" Suzana asks.

"I mean life demanding a presence. Can I demand anyone's presence? You won't come in, even for a few minutes. Ante comes home any time he wants, and thinks nothing of practically never seeing me at all. I mean, do you know I haven't seen my husband for a week?"

Suzana moves back towards her only friend. "Has he left you?"

"I don't know. Maybe. Maybe he left me six months ago. Maybe it was a year ago. I don't know when."

"What do you mean?"

"Won't you please come in?" The trembling eyelids shut.

Suzana shakes her head yet moves closer to her, lifts a hand to cup Jelka's elbow. "What's happening?"

Jelka doesn't open her eyes. Nods and then says, "Alright, I understand. You need to get home. To your husband." She opens her eyes and nods. "And this is nothing new. This has been happening for a while. It gets on top of you all of a sudden sometimes. I don't know how it happened. It just happened. Day by day."

She'd begun assuming that there was another woman. Of course she had. The truth disturbs her somehow more than this divorceable offense, and now has her bewildered. What should she do with what she knows? She feels too embarrassed to bring it to their shared family; the people that know them both intimately. Because they would laugh at Jelka. They wouldn't understand what was disturbing about it at all. What is Ante doing after he finishes a day's work as an electrician? He travels all the way out to Prahran, where you have

85

to climb three flights of stairs to enter a room filled with quiet men. Silently they walk around green-felt-covered tables and push around polished sticks, propelling red balls into leather pockets. And this is all it is and no one would understand why it has begun to disturb Jelka as much as it does. She didn't tell him she'd come to see what he was doing when he said he was going to play snooker. She quietly watched him from a distance playing for hours on end. Day after day, surrounded by other men who talked in murmurs. When Suzana tells her it sounds peaceful, Jelka says, yes, it's nice. It doesn't end, though. He goes out after eating his dinner and doesn't come back until two or three, sometimes later, in the morning. He goes to work and doesn't call her between jobs. For a year now, and longer still that it had really been going on.

When Jelka and Ante got married, they'd known each other for a few years. It was as friends of friends, as acquaintances seen at other people's weddings and parties, and they knew each other a bit better going into marriage, with the promise that they would be going on in that direction. That the general intimacy they'd established would become deeper and more lasting. Perhaps she'd believed in the fairytale of marriage, without knowing it. It seems to her now that they are still friends of friends, and that he is still someone she doesn't know personally. When she'd met Ante, she knew he was quiet. She'd made the assumption that familiarity would breed an ease in him that would open his muted heart to her, and unfold his bound-up soul. It was as romantic as that. Was she wrong to have made that assumption, she asks Suzana, not expecting an answer. She's starting to think that the brief glimpses of something more to him than a kind of brooding, brute silence, have been massive efforts on Ante's part to reveal areas of himself, submerged since childhood, and in future will be as accessible to her as Atlantis. His soul a myth long lost to vague belief, even in himself. And she has tried everything, from attacking him day in, day out, and long silences that numbed her mouth and paralysed her brain, going on for weeks on end, with no success.

She has a neighbour who is dying of bowel cancer. She owns a Chihuahua. The neighbour has been dying for months now. They are going to scatter her ashes in a park where she walked her pet dog every day. This little rat-dog that Jelka loathes. Does Suzana know that Chihuahuas are the only creature in the world that can cry, outside of human beings. Not dog moans. Actual tears. Because this little rat-dog has been crying for its dying owner. Jelka starts laughing and crying at the same time as she says that a little rat-dog has more feeling in its little trembling body than the man she married. Because what it comes down to is this: if she was to die tomorrow she can only imagine how meagre a cluster of mourners will come, and how few, maybe one or two, might shed real tears of grief for her. For her, not their own mortality. For her, not because they lost someone once. And Ante will be sitting in the front row, listening to the priest. And afterwards, he will climb those stairs, and lean over the green felt of his tables, and hit those shiny red balls into those worn, brown-leather pockets.

Would Suzana cry? Jelka doesn't ask, but maybe that was the point of calling her over today. Feeling lost and unloved. That colossal sense of disregard from the world at large. Both of them perhaps like those fireflies left in a jar too long. The rain starts to fall in earnest, and as it does, the two women huddle closer, beneath the bit of roof overhanging the three concrete steps at the doorway of Ante and Jelka's home.

SUZANA STOPS AT a service station for petrol. After paying she takes out her notebook and scribbles a thought into it. And keeps scribbling for a few minutes until she reminds herself that she has to get home, and before that to the supermarket. So she turns on the van and gets it to move without a stutter.

She recently bought a Moleskine. She hasn't seen one since her Belgrade student days. She's been opening it and writing in it. The notebook begins with a quote by Milosh Tsernianski, which she knows from memory and has translated into English.

In the eyes of these bedecked and bedizened Imperial officers, the Serbian nation, privileged as it was by the Empress, was a target for mockery—but otherwise a blank, an obscure thing, in whose existence they did not feel the need to believe.

She's read his book six times. A novel called *Migrations* that doesn't feel like a novel. The characters don't feel like characters. It isn't history or myth, and yet it's all those things. That quote had been all she wrote for weeks. There is a lot more scribbled in the notebook now. Pages and pages have been filled in the last week. Ideas flowing from that inkwell she had first discovered in Belgrade—the one the Demon had helped her find.

There's a local newspaper sitting on the passenger seat. Jovan takes it with him to work. He's already read it and has left it open on an article with a picture of a sad little train station called Hallam.

Suzana has been reading newspapers every day now, as well as novels and non-fiction books, with an idea of improving her written English. She watches English films with English subtitles whenever she can, for the spelling. Suzana's spoken English has always been good. Even before everyone started learning it in high school. Her father loved languages and thought he knew a lot more English than he actually did. He tuned a powerful Soviet radio he owned to one of twenty different languages nightly and translated what he could. An American military base in Naples played blues music and jazz and they spent hours listening to Yankee DJs tell stories about obscure American lives and loves. Suzana's English still carries some of those American accents and music.

She enjoys speaking English though she continues to feel the bewilderment a native of a phonetic language experiences every time she encounters the chaos of English spelling. *Four*, but *forty*, not *fourty*. *Nine*, but not *nife*, it is *knife*. Where does the k come from? Why is it there? The w in *sword*. Where is it in the word *sort*? Why doesn't a person swort out the mail if they've just used a sword to kill the mailman? Why are there two l's in *Hallam* and r's in *barracouta*?

She wants to take a knife and sword to those that uphold this medieval language as supreme in the world today, then lets the notion go, and spells her words as best she can. The truth is that she's falling deeper in love with the English language. Her native Serbian is tied into everything she was and everything she had already thought and done. In English she notices things, as when Glen Coultas asked her to hang on a tick—she knows it refers to the ticking of a clock. Yet in English, she sees the words. The parasite that lives on blood, and hanging on to that insect with its full pouch is holding on to a moment with thumb and forefinger, in a pincer grip. Hold on to a tick. You can't get it back but perhaps you can smear it black and red between the pages of a book.

When she goes out to her houses, she cleans quickly and then sits in a lounge chair and reads for half an hour, noting down eye-catching expressions or strange spellings in her Moleskine. At the Coultas house she sometimes has as much as three hours of reading time in an eight-hour shift. They aren't the kind of family that want their light bulbs polished. They're happy when she deigns to cook them all dinner, instead of letting them order takeaway again, and each of them thanks her when she cooks for them, very politely. For Suzana this kind of appreciation seems a weakness, yet she knows she's not right in this.

If Rae is napping, she is glad that when she wakes, Suzana will be there, reading her book quietly. That when she rouses from deep groggy disorientation, she can ask for a glass of water and there is no need for conversation. Suzana simply goes and gets the glass of water. Has a very steady hand as she helps Rae drink. If Rae needs the television turned on, it is turned on. If she needs the wash-ing done, it is done, and her urine-soaked sheets aren't a problem. Suzana doesn't seem to notice. There isn't an issue in anything they ask her to do. And they find some kind of strength in simply seeing her move around, doing the things they need to have done for them. They're not the kind of family that needs a nurse or maid. They have found that they need Suzana.

SHE WALKS INTO the supermarket. She could go to every shelf blind-folded she's traced the same route so many times. Suzana brings the local newspaper with her to read if she gets stuck in a line. There's an article about a woman who has recently leapt from a Hallam plat-form to her death. The article is by a journalist who has tried to talk to Jovan once or twice about graffiti at the hospital. She remembers the journalist because of the name, which looks backwards. Appar-ently he is indeed Wilson Lawrence. The article isn't reporting the suicide itself, but the fact that suicide isn't being reported. It happens every week. People throw themselves in front of trains. Six or seven people go off the West Gate Bridge weekly. It becomes notable if a father throws his daughter off the West Gate Bridge. There are alarming figures in youth suicide. Australia has one of the highest rates in the world yet you couldn't talk about it in an article without raising the figures—writing about suicide encourages suicide. Triv-ial as they might seem to the general reader, they can't be tallied up like road accidents, because they represent a deeper social illness of disconnection. Our own ambivalence being . . .

The checkout boy calls "next" a second time as she's reading.

Someone behind says "next." From calm to berserk in less than five seconds in this supermarket line. An African boy with the name badge *Capon* on his chest. He doesn't say hello or goodbye. She wants to ask him if he knows that *Capon* is also a word in English meaning a castrated chicken.

Suzana pushes her cart out to the van. Opens its back doors and puts her bags in. Takes the cart back to the supermarket. Gets into the cabin of the van and thinks about a commercial she's seen on television about people wasting power by leaving electrical appliances on. Black balloons rise from the appliances, squeezing out of an air conditioner left on or an electric kettle on standby. It's a effective way of illustrating waste because the commercial ends with people's homes being filled with jostling black plastic, and afterwards, there's a sky full of those nasty balloons.

The quiet suicides of Lawrence's article might also have black balloons. People who have thought about killing themselves, with black balloons hovering above their heads, the strings reaching down, tied around their necks. Eventually it gets to a point where the string is tight enough, and breathing too difficult, and there are enough black balloons to carry a person off. It isn't an effort, as "suicide attempt" implies. It's just breathing out a final breath and letting the balloons lift away.

SHE DRIVES INTO Frankston and down Reservoir Road. Parks in her driveway, wishing they could organise a fence to go around their rental property. The giant dog from next door is nothing but a monstrous pest. He's in her yard again, ready to leap on Suzana as soon as she opens her door.

It seems the entire neighbourhood has gathered on her lawn tonight. The excitable bald man, who uses his arms too much when he speaks. Silvers and his wife, Jane. And a beautiful woman, asking for directions, and getting them from the bald man, looking at Jovan as though he's the one giving them to her.

Suzana whispers to Jovan when she doesn't need to whisper. Maybe to move that much closer to him and to have him bend his face down to her. Words for the cup of his ear. Telling him that he has an interesting collection of people here and she's going inside to make dinner, so he shouldn't be long.

By the time she is through her front door the woman is already gone. Call her a figment of the imagination. All that long black hair, the blue eyes amidst it all—a shock of contrast. The Chanel perfume the only thing clear, and all else a blur of unnecessary, unwanted details.

Suzana walks to the kitchen. She's going to make Jovan one of his favourite meals even if it's going to be late. An hour and a half from now would mean dinner at about nine in the evening. She's already made a bean soup called *pasulje*. Which would have to do if he was hungry sooner. For *lovachke schnitzels* she takes out the veal she just bought and beats it with a tenderising hammer. She cooks it slightly on both sides, throwing it into flour afterwards. She cooks up red onion, diced tomatoes, and pours in a good amount of white wine and a cup of water. Puts the flour-caked schnitzels back into the bubbling liquid and leaves it to cook an hour. The meat will absorb the wine and flavours of Vegeta and pepper.

It's a peasant's dinner she had never dreamed of making before she met Jovan. She'd learned the recipe from his Bosnian mother, one of her many rustic recipes. They argued a lot when they talked, especially if the conversation was in the kitchen, but she learned a great deal about Banja Luka and that region from the old woman. Even though she was dead, Suzana felt a combative impulse at the thought of Darinka, a matriarch who dominated everyone in her world effortlessly despite cooking like a slave for most of her life. The total concoction of smell and memory are almost able to obliterate the scent of Chanel perfume.

There is a part of Suzana that always stands aside, aghast at this kind of domestic performance. She learned no culinary skills from her own mother and never bothered with real cooking all the way through high school and university. In the first years of marriage, if they ate at home at all, it was Jovan who cooked. So she'd never made proper meals before she had children, and for Ana and Dejan she learned a whole array of recipes. She'd stopped afterwards.

Over the last year she'd become sick of the round of five meals Jovan is content to cook over and again ad infinitum, and finds the time in the kitchen to be a good place to gather thoughts for her notebook. Doesn't she look right now, to all intents and purposes, a drab housewife pottering around meekly in the kitchen for the man of the house? That woman outside, with her glossy black hair and silver Saab and those vivid blue eyes, must see only this diminished life Suzana is living.

Suzana sits down at her small kitchen table and writes in her Moleskine, surrounded by the aromas of the cooking meal. Previously it has all been notes and snippets of things that could be bundled together into a history. Today she has an image of a man riding the long road from Istanbul to Belgrade, during the height of the Ottoman Empire.

They warned children not to fall asleep near the poppy bush. The name of the flower in his native tongue sounded like a pagan god of the underworld. In that language of his mother and father, though no longer his. "Mahk" they told their children while they still had them in their possession. They told them that if they fell asleep near this flower they would never wake up again.

When he heard this story he was so young that he listened with mystified awe, because what he understood wasn't—"be careful here or you will die"—he understood it as, there's a place you can fall asleep and dream, never wake up, and never stop dreaming. He could close his eyes and imagine a rising ribbon of smoke, twirling up into the air, and through the dark clouds in the storming sky, and out to the stars themselves, rising on a stream of smoke on the still whisper of dreams.

He must have heard the story when he was five. He hadn't thought about it for maybe the whole of the forty years since then. Yet here he was riding through the hostile land of the Bulgars and Vlachs because of it. Already he had slaughtered two brigands that should have known better than to try to hold up a soldier, clearly carrying the weapons of a Janissary.

He would usually ride by a tavern without question. He didn't do that tonight.

The sun had dropped out of the sky, leaving him a few seconds of twilight. It wouldn't be a problem to continue down the road a half hour, or hour, find another place to stable his horse and a warm meal and bed for himself. The right kind of house for a man such as himself. Or he could find a spot in a field anywhere around here. It was the voices he heard coming out of the door that drew him in. His mother tongue spoken this way, at ease, boisterously, tumbling out with friendship.

All of their voices faded away when he walked in, and petered out when he sat at a table. He was going to order a drink, something alcoholic, yet when he saw the frightened face of the Serbian proprietor, he decided to ask for a meal, and water, in the language she expected from him. Turkish from the Turk.

IT'S A LITTLE after nine when she's finished. Jovan is still outside talking. She calls out from the front door, to tell him dinner is ready. He brings David Dickens in with him—a schoolboy with a friend. Laughing like children when she offers David a coffee before he goes home and Jovan answers "no" for him. Saying something about his friend the Wood Spider that doesn't make sense to her.

They continue, Jovan guiding the conversation with a word here or there. Letting the failed psychologist/aspiring author unspool his mind—now talking about how long it's been that human beings have used walls to communicate with each other, that it was indeed far longer, by centuries in fact, before paper came along, whether it was cave paintings, hieroglyphics, or billboards. And that the phrase "the end is nigh," is an acknowledgment of a certain culture and historical stream of public outburst . . .

They go on and on about the graffiti and she feels the embarrassment she's felt often about Jovan's English. She is beginning to think that with him it's some strange point of pride. That he doesn't want to rid himself of the heavy accent that makes sales assistants or doctors or the landlord talk to him as if he's a cretin. That he knows how to form perfectly constructed grammatical sentences and feels more comfortable at a distance to English—a language to dabble in, and play with, only. Everything that he has been serious about, all his work, left behind with his native tongue.

Suzana thinks of nights when a group of students would migrate to their apartment after their classes at the university, charged with the ideas of Jovan's lectures, and he would sit in the fray being fought around him, guiding and prodding them all along, enjoying more than anything circulating and sharing the enthusiasm for ideas.

It also reminds her of something Ivo Andrich wrote. "Not only every word, but every sound used to be accompanied for me by a whole procession of emotional and intellectual associations. Now that no longer happens. Sounds are isolated, and words weak, so that you have to repeat them: and that does not help at all. And this would be bearable if I were not tormented by the idea, clear and exact in itself, that all these associations still exist and live around me, only I do not feel or hear them. And that all this beauty, inaudible to me, is heard by others, gathered and carried home like armfuls of flowers."

When Jovan opened that page for her and asked her to share the beauty of those sentences, back in Sarajevo, she'd thought that Andrich had written them because he was getting old, and the beauty was a sentimental one she wanted to store in her soul—now she knew better, and wished she'd never seen those words; that Jovan hadn't shown them to her.

Jovan had pulled out a chair for David and they had all started eating without an invitation to dinner being offered or accepted. Halfway through the meal, David takes a breather from their conversation to address the silent Suzana.

He says, "So Jovan tells me you enjoy reading."

"It's Yo-Vahn. Not Joe-Van," Suzana says.

"I'm sorry?" he says, smiling good-naturedly at Jovan, and half-apologetically at Suzana.

"Don't be sorry. I'm not asking you to learn a new language. Learn how to say our names. That is if you want to talk to me. Go your own way if you don't."

The smile murdered on his face, he leans forward. "Sorry. Did I say something to offend you?"

She chews before answering. Places her fork into another piece of meat. Suzana says, "Take a moment. Think about what I said."

"Alright. And how should I pronounce your name?"

"Does it matter? I ask you, because I suspect that as soon as I tell you, it will slip away from your memory, with about as much importance as the name of that dog outside. You do remember his name don't you?"

"Yes." He's been holding his cutlery, halfway through his meal. He glances at Jovan, who looks back at him as if he's simply interested in this new direction in their conversation.

"And what is the dog's name?" she asks, chewing slowly. He puts down his cutlery and it's clear he wants to simply rise and leave.

"Isn't it Charlemagne?" He tries a smile. Suzana with the fork in her hand. She doesn't move it to her mouth.

"And since you remember how to correctly pronounce that dog's name, tell me, what is my husband's name?"

He pronounces it carefully, "Jovan."

"OK." She smiles at him. David Dickens looks relieved.

She picks up his question. "Yes I read. I have read in the past and I will continue to read in the future. Who do you enjoy reading, David?" He picks up his cutlery and they continue to talk. He doesn't return to his exclusive conversation with Jovan again. David Dickens is also careful to compliment the food and the wine.

When they finish their late dinner, Suzana asks them, "Both of you talk about that graffiti as if it was something more than scribbles on the wall. I mean, it's just more *graffiti*. What do you think it is, that it deserves this kind of continued examination?"

"If it's just the graffiti then it's how he does it. It's pretty amazing that he's getting away with it for as long as he has. If it's a message, we're interested in what he's trying to say. Because if we look at his Dog Eat Dog statement, there is the text, which isn't all that remarkable, telling us little more than a certain disenchantment with the world. The shortcomings of Consumerist-Capitalism are fairly cliché. Then there's an overlaying of this text on a Rorschach test image, which is also contextualised within the framework of a hospital newsletter. The meta-narrative of all such messages already presented and various methods of presentation in all of them. There's also the aesthetic success of the particular message, which might strike some as somewhat superficial, yet there's a feeling of artistry in all we've seen him do. His "installation," we might call it, Origin of the Species, gets a front page of the local newspaper because there's something about the seemingly innocuous watercooler that fascinates the eye. And the mind, of course. A watercooler full of human fat. The juxtaposition astounds the imagination. We must then ask what do we think of when we think of the watercooler? It's the pseudo-mythical place for gossip, and if not secret talk, then privileged conversations among the general people of a workplace. We're very far from the origin of the species and yet we have gone on with this kind of monkey chatter from the beginning. Is the substance itself the origin of the species? What's compelling is how all of these works do seem to connect and change meanings and interpretation. His Rorschach image was displayed in the paper and has been circulating on the Internet. They're becoming immensely popular. People want to see these images. So they are things in themselves. There's also the effect of these displays, which is an interesting phenomenon. I am one, I mean, me being here at all, to discuss it. More significantly there's the suicide of a respected woman to consider. Certainly this could not be attributed solely to the graffiti, though clearly it was significant. There's what he might choose to say next, if it is a "he." Because what interests me in particular is that we have yet to glimpse the person behind these outbursts. I simply see no psychological profile. There's no thumbprint in any of the paint, so to speak." Dickens stops, blinks, and asks, "I mean, who is this person?" He blinks again. "Jovan probably talks with Dr. Graffito every day."

JOVAN BRUSHES HIS teeth in the bathroom. Charlemagne barks at a possum somewhere out beyond the fence. With the bedroom door open, Suzana can hear the fridge go silent. She hadn't heard the buzzing while it was going. Only the silent contrast. Now Jovan washes his mouth out with water, seven, eight, nine times. It seems excessive. She hears him switch off the light, and she hadn't noticed how much light had reached down the hall and through their bedroom door until it was off. The heavy sound of his footfalls. As though he's twice the size he is, and he's already such an oaf of a man.

She's lying in bed. Too warm for sheets. Boxers for Jovan, and Suzana in knickers. The silent k in that word. He looms above the bed. Perhaps he pauses above her body. Perhaps not. Always the feeling of abeyance with him now. How much of it comes from him and how much from her? If he were to decide he wanted her, desperately came to her, maybe she'd feel his passion come and sweep her away as it did in the past. It wouldn't be the heavy flesh impact of skin-covered bones. It wouldn't feel like a collision.

"What's that woman's name?" she asks Jovan, after having not wanted to ask that very question for hours. After driving it from her mind. Almost fooling herself into believing she'd succeeded. The familiarity of the perfume (the Chanel—Marilyn Monroe's No. 5) has also been caught in Jovan's overalls. Makes it unavoidable now; something she can't help but see even if the agreement is for closed eyes.

"I thought you were sleeping," he says, head falling onto his pillow. The whole bed moves, the word "elephant" warbling in her head, settling after a moment. She spells the word in English to calm herself. She remembers ph instead of f.

"You should know better," she says.

"Maybe I don't. Who am I to question the rules of the game?"

"What game?"

"The game you play when you're not playing a game."

"What does that mean?" She hears the fridge click back on, and thinks about whether it's better to be bothered by that noise and have the air circulating through the open door.

"I'm not keeping secrets. I'm just surprised by the question."

"I don't know what you're keeping. Do you?"

Jovan says, "Her name is Tammie Ashford. She's a dentist at the hospital. She's married to a lawyer. I've heard they've got some political future together."

"You might want to draw a boundary for Tammie Ashford," she suggests.

"Some people drive right into walls for the fun of it." He shifts onto his side to face Suzana.

"Do they?" She turns her head on the pillow towards him and opens her eyes. "They drive into walls?"

"Maybe because their heads are full of those monkeys, blind, deaf, and dumb, not sure what they're hearing or seeing in the commotion of the cage." Tapping his skull. "Is there a point in putting a sign on the wall?"

"I'm *telling* you to put a sign on it. Hang a light up. Paint the road in yellow warning stripes. Put up a fucking barricade a hundred metres down the road." She turns her head back and closes her eyes again. Her hands neat, beside her hips. Breasts exposed. He rolls back. She listens to his heavy breathing. Knows he's lying there, his eyelids blinking. Outside that damned dog starts up barking again.

"Do you hear me?" Suzana asks.

"I don't need to hear you. Wasn't I thinking the same thing myself?" They don't speak again. She listens as his breath gets deeper and slower. As he moves into sleep and leaves her behind on the warm bed to trickle sweat down her ribs. To listen to her own eyelids shutting and opening.

"I saw you smile at her Jovan." She says it quietly.

It isn't that uncommon, is it? Glen Coultas has underwear that often shows evidence of another woman. Even having hushed conversations, while Rae dozes in her medicated sleep. His own wife incapacitated by something called symphysis pubis dysfunction, and her depression making things worse. So he goes out to a prostitute called Isabelle. Whispering that name into the phone. Yet then he takes his son out to water the grass and talks about the world and the wisdom that can be found living in it with open eyes. Glen then comes back inside to wake his wife with kisses, and a love that seems sincere in every way that matters. Rae's grateful for it, because her depression is an affliction that has fallen on her as though from the sky. Not making her bitter, but apologetic and grateful for every sign of his enduring love for her, cripple that she is, with a womb that doesn't work properly. Keeping her in bed for six months of a pregnancy that should have been easy after going through it all once already, and happy that he doesn't chuck her in as a defective.

Suzana doesn't feel that way about Jovan. She is aware of how much she means to him, and she wonders if it's this that so often makes her feel sick around him. Or angry, and a kind of seething hatred when he comes close; when he's physically near. Twisting everything inside-out in her mind, because seeing his overalls hang on a hook in the garage, a half-deflated balloon (in the shape of his body), just seeing it, can make her cry. An empty glass he's drunk from, bearing the marks of his lips. Muddy boots sitting on the back step, laces hastily undone and the tongues lolling half out in the rush to get into the house without tracking in mud. A half-read book, laid down in a collapsed tent to keep his place, glasses perched atop. Any of these things have put needles through her chest. And the same now, when she can take deep breaths from his body, and fill herself with his smell.

Suzana gets out of bed. She walks to the fridge and opens the door. The weak illumination of the fridge light offers her some comfort. There's the mundane quality it has, the frosted pearl illumination, making its way past milk, bread, and cheese. Another instant in the immense dark of the evening. Another night in this house that she and Jovan are living in. They don't own the building though they own this fridge. That's nothing different. They hadn't owned a house back in Bosnia either. They'd been talking to their landlord about buying their rental in Sarajevo. It had gone from cordial discussions about the paperwork to coming home to the locks changed and what they owned in boxes and piles by the gate outside, much of it already stolen or damaged from being dropped. Their books heaped along with crockery and cutlery, summer dresses and underwear, and their children's toys. Possessions like their fridge, bed, couch, washing machine, these stayed in the house—the mundane spoils of war. She leans into the fridge to feel the cool air waft out. Imagines all those black balloons escaping. A rushing mob of them pushing past her and milling up on the ceiling of the kitchen. Bobbing up there and gathering, accumulating and coming down lower until she was down on the cold tiles, taking shallow breaths of refrigerated air. She shakes off the image and closes the fridge.

She gets a glass of water. She notices the water beading inside the glass after she finishes, she thinks about the glasses Glen Coultas was wearing in Black Rock. Standing in the mist of rain as he watched her drive away. Those glowing streetlights looking so lonely and abandoned amidst the swaying trees. The fear she'd had in her stomach that what he wanted was something else. That he'd make the same demands Vladimir Mitrovich made back at the university in Belgrade. Worried that she was as crass as to be a potential fuck for Coultas. She feels that ease away as she realises that the man is grateful. It's as simple as genuine gratitude. Almost a kind of divine favour that someone could come down and look after his desperate wife, crippled as she was by a body barely able to take their precious unborn child to a sustainable threshold; poisoned as she was by a depression that ate her—a cancer of the soul. Grateful to Suzana for holding her when she cried, for long rocking sections of time, and then simply opening her windows to a new day afterwards. All those suicide balloons allowed to escape into the clear blue skies outside. Glen Coultas was grateful even as he saw a prostitute with the warm-whispered name of Isabelle, wringing Suzana's heart when he bent down to kiss the emerging bump of life on his wife's belly. Despite Suzana being in the room (and everything else about this couple and their family existing under layers of reservation and polite do's and don'ts), putting his lips to that mound—a lustful penitent finding God's grace for the first time returned to him in a kiss.

Suzana washes out the glass with a swish of hot water and

then lets it drip from the dish rack. She returns to bed and Jovan.
Lies close to him. Her face very near his.

let me go
drifting
on the waters
above the stars
let me go
adrift

Poetry Jovan had beside a bed he slept in long ago. It had been
printed onto red paper. The antique strokes of a typewriter. Blu-
Tacked to the wall in the one-room boarding house near the university he'd begun teaching at. It was faded though, so it had been
with him longer than he'd been staying in that room. And she
hadn't thought about it much and had always assumed it was something he'd picked up from a book somewhere. Maybe a lyric from
a song. Something fairly anaemic and not worth considering. As
it emerges from her memory right now, she knows it's something
he'd come up with himself and put there, and that what it meant
for him then and means to her now are very different, and very
much the same.

She brings her face close to his massive, bearlike head, so that
their noses are almost touching. Love for those breaths. Love for
that life moving with such gentle, steady heaves, so intense in her,
that it makes her choke. Love for those closed eyes. Hatred still
so very close. Just below. For those eyes. For the man lost in sleep
somewhere. Maybe it comes from him forgiving her so easily for
murdering their children. His simple ability to see it as a blind act
of fate that has nothing to do with her deciding to give her dinner
to their hungry children. Believing in her act of sacrifice and that

it simply turned out bad. What he never takes into account is instinct, and the feeling that somehow she knew the food was poisoned, that as death's shadow came close, she was able to pass it across to her children, and give them the food that was meant for her.

He breathes on her face slowly and deeply as if she isn't the woman who put poison into the mouths of his children.

FIVE

JOVAN UNROLLS ONTO THE LONG CHAIR, almost horizontal, drifting towards sleep quickly in the minute-long wait. He's wearing the sunglasses they gave him and he opens his mouth when they say good morning. His jaw is forced to its limit. The needle that pierces his gums sends numbness up the side of his head and does nothing for the teeth themselves, now shooting bolts of pain straight to the centre of his brain. The second injection doesn't take either. It only makes his cheek feel warm and it's back to drilling and suction and his heart goes into palpitations, sweat popping out over his face. His body becomes rigid, as if it's being executed in an electric chair, cell by cell.

He apologises to the dentist. To the assistant. "I must be stress," he tries to explain around the fat white pellets in his mouth. He unravels words in his mind to calm himself as the other side of his jaw begins to scream white-hot shock. Maroochydore and Mooloolaba, Noosa and Coolum. He thinks about the Glass House Mountains, and the stars out there at night, between those compass points in paradise.

The sunglasses in this room are for the overhead lights above his face. Jovan keeps his eyes closed and thinks about the way the hills rise just beyond the beach, a clear Noosa green in the sparkling Australian light. Going below the buoyant blue, crystal clarity in every drop of water dripping from him when he rises again. Suzana on the sand, napping in the sun. For the first time in years sleeping naturally. Without the pills; letting the various prescriptions lapse in Queensland. Jovan walks through the waves, across the long stretch of damp sand and up onto the hot sand to her, the seawater from his body waking her before his body weight.

"What a strange dream that was," Suzana says after she's pushed him away.

They talk about other things and he never finds out what dreams she had that woke her up smiling like a girl. An inversion now, his dentist and the assistant looking down at Jovan, as though desperately worried he might fall asleep again. Using torture to keep him awake. "What a strange dream," he intones with tongue and throat, when they pause in their work for the suction hose to stop him from drowning in his own saliva. They understand as few of his words as before when he attempted to mumble around the cotton pellets.

The dentist told Jovan a story while they waited for the second needle to take effect. "I had a patient once who refused the anaesthetic. It was a root canal, and I told him I didn't think I could do it—cause that much pain without giving him at least *something*. The man must have been a believer in meditation. I've heard experts in that kind of thing can walk over hot coals and hang with hooks through their flesh."

Jovan has his own mantra yet now he's thinking about that man who refused anaesthetic for a root canal and he decides his dentist is probably wrong. It's not likely that the patient was a master of mind control. It was more believable that he was a recovering addict; that the fear of physical pain was secondary to the fear of succumbing again to addiction and disintegration.

Jovan finds those words again, silently chanting them: Maroochydore and Mooloolaba, Noosa and Coolum.

Afterwards Jovan is told to floss every day. He says, "No problem." He's never been one for flossing and, despite the dental torture, he's not sure he'll be able to commit to cleaning his teeth that thoroughly. They pencil him in for another appointment in six months and he nods again, feeling the pain still ringing through his mouth and his head, thinking about when and how he and Suzana might get back up to the Sunshine Coast, whether they'll have time, and how they can afford that kind of trip, especially with these dentistry bills.

It's got to be soon now, he's thinking as he walks down the stairs. He passes people sitting and waiting to see his dentist or the GPs that work in this centre. An old man with a walker, who brings along a small tank of oxygen the way some bring a bottle of drinking water. The two sixty-year-olds in matching tracksuits, assuring the five women of the reception that they are careful to look after themselves with diet and exercise. The child that drapes himself over a chair, moaning about how bored he is, coughing his head off in minute-long fits.

Jovan stumbles outside into the bright light, thinking *soon*, because a child will keep both of them near one of these purgatorial medical rooms for two or three years. Even if a new child turns out to be not as sickly as Jovan's other children had been, it will be difficult getting around. He wants to drive, and that would be crazy with a baby, yet without a car to explore that wondrous Queensland land-scape, he can't see the point of going. Neither he nor Suzana are the kind of people who can loaf on a beach for hours on end every day. So it would have to be soon if they want to get up to the Sunshine Coast again. Suzana had been all for it. In the last week or two she's been saying she wasn't so sure anymore. The Coultas family needs her. Jelka is having a crisis as well. Then there's all the scribbling in her black books. It's the writing that makes Jovan desperate to find a way to free them for a trip up north.

By the time he gets to his white panel van, his head is swimming. He reaches into his pocket to fish out the keys. Pulling them out, he fumbles the keys to the ground. He leans over and feels he might tumble onto the asphalt of the car park after them. Rust along the bottom edge of this van, that he has sanded back once already, puttied and painted over. Yet there it is again, beginning to bubble beneath the paint and eat at the edges. The metal was old. You couldn't patch it a million times. Eventually it gets to a point where there's nothing left to work with.

A young woman is talking to him before he realises someone has approached and is catching up while she's halfway through already; he opens his thick mouth and attempts a smile through lips that feel made of rubber. "Yes, hospital. I work in there."

"I thought, since I needed to get down there as well, maybe you could give me a lift? Public transport from here to there is a bitch. It'd be a tram and a train, a ten-minute walk or a bus, and it sucks when you have to go from point A to point B, just so you can get to point C, and then finally to where you need to get to. You know what I mean? Point fucking K or something."

Jovan wishes he could tell her in one facial expression that the long explanation isn't necessary, and all she needs to do is tell him they work in the same hospital, and they would already be on the road by now. His nodding doesn't stop any of it, and eventually he's able to mumble, "No problem. We go. Get in. Point K. Direct."

She gets into the cabin of the van, though first she's got to be told it's alright to shove the paper and Melways, the jumper and cap and smelly boots to the floor. To push his lunch box aside while Jovan returns to the dentist for the sunglasses he's only now realised he left up there. His own sunglasses, the ones he swapped for the dentistry sunglasses when he lay back on the seat.

So it's past the old man with his little bottle of O^2 again and the child that was now pulling on his mother's arm to go now, *can we go now please!!!* Back to the annoying Janusz who is the dental receptionist upstairs and his Polish-style ultra-camp flouncing and fluffing over every detail of his cubbyhole of an office and its eternally running, locked-on-soaps, five-inch television.

"Oh yes I have the sunglasses for you. But you left them here on purpose. You must be desperate to come back already. To see Janusz again. Don't forget, that I will see you again on the Fourth of July. Maybe we should celebrate with fireworks. I will call you, to remind you," Janusz says through his flavourful Polish accent.

Jovan blinks through all this, thickly says, in his blockish English, "What?"

"You know, American day. When the Americans celebrate themselves. You won't forget again at least." It baffles Jovan what he means by *forget again*. As it was, for this appointment Janusz had called him three times during the week to shift it around by half-hour slots, and there was certainly no possibility of forgetting when Janusz called once more this morning.

When Jovan gets back to the car, the girl is scribbling in her book. Maybe technically she's a woman and old enough to be a nurse. She's the kind of petite woman who stopped growing at about age fourteen and will continue to look like a teenager for the next ten or twenty years. Jovan will go on feeling as though he's clocking in as an octogenarian. Dentures not too far away now. Having a child certainly isn't going to be a remedy for that.

She's talking again as he starts the loud Ford which makes birds in a nearby tree leap for open skies. Has to gun the thing so that it doesn't stall. Gives her a misshaped smile by way of saying, *sorry, I have to do it, and seriously, this car isn't a hot rod in anyone's imagination.* The anaesthetic is making the right half of his head feel like the aftermath of a stroke.

He's not listening to what she's saying while he navigates the heavy crate through the busy traffic. She goes on talking and he's prompted to correctly say "yes" or "no," "why," and "I understand," which is enough to keep her going happily. Talking and drawing in her sketchbook. Jovan drives raggedly today, getting beeped at twice, almost crashing into an ice cream van because of his bad brakes, which makes the nurse laugh so hard she has to wipe tears from her eyes.

Buoyed by her goodwill, Jovan tells the nurse that the van is an old love that will continue to need to be seduced even when she's ninety. That doesn't make her laugh again. She smiles and nods at Jovan because now she's the distracted one. By the time they get to the hospital she has drawn a portrait of Jovan in pencil. The nurse asks for his name and writes it above the image. *Romance of the Crash,* she adds below his face.

"My name's Leni by the way. Thanks for the lift," she chirps. Leni gives him a playful peck on the cheek and leaves the sketch on the seat beside him. Jovan doesn't know what to do with it. He folds it and pushes it into the overfull glove box. He crushes the image to make it fit. There's a lot of stuff in there he knows he'll never need. Inside that compartment is also sunscreen Suzana used on those beaches up north. He can feel the kiss through the fading numbness of the anaesthetic.

"**DON'T KNOW WHY**, but I never think of you as a refugee. But you *are*, aren'tcha mate?"

Jovan is pulling up his overalls in the hospital's change room, his jaw still sore on both sides. Bill's a janitor that works in the hospital with Jovan. He says he is Greek because he's the son of immigrants, yet besides the stockiness, hairiness, and olive skin, there's nothing about him that Jovan sees as actually Greek. He's Australian, whatever the accent.

"When you think refugee, you think black, brown, or Asian. Skinny and small, because there's never been a lot of food. But look at you. Raised by basketballers. Smiling like a fucking wood duck. *Usually*. Not today though, hey? You've got your refugee face on this morning." Bill throws a can of Coke he's been drinking at a bin. He misses. They both watch it roll away.

"So where's the wood-duck smile today? What happened?" Bill asks.

"I go to dentist this morning," Jovan answers.

"You'll be walking around with that stupid fucken smile soon enough, hey? Maybe later on today I'll see you walking along the halls with that little smile that tells everyone everything is OK. 'No problems.' I don't know what you've got to fucken smile about. I hate this shit. Had to fucken clean up an old man's vomit in the lobby this morning. But maybe that's why you go on smiling. Being a refugee, you seen all kinds of shit, hey? What's an old man's vomit when you've seen old men gunned down? Happy to be in the land of the fucken free!"

Jovan finds it difficult to think when Bill's in this mood. Bill likes to rant every few days and all Jovan can do is let him go on for a few minutes. The fading anaesthetic and the general discomfort he feels make it that much harder for Jovan to deal with Bill today.

"You want go back to Greece?" Jovan says. "You say this sometimes. Freedom there, even if your parents run from their islands,
give everything away to make it to over here. Doesn't make sense
to me. Things get worse in Greece. Not better, since your parents leave there." Jovan sits on a bench and puts his feet into his
boots. Pulls the laces up and begins to tie them with hands that
feel clumsy.

"Fuck yeah. They know how to live over there, man. We waste
all our time working here. They know what Life is over there. You
know what I'm saying? We have to plan to fit it in. Save up for years,
and then go over for a few weeks. Call it a holiday. Fucking hell,
man, what do we call the rest of this fucking life here?"

"It is easy to make picture cards of places." He regrets even saying
this much. Smiles at Bill closed mouthed—a "wood-duck." There's
no point talking to Bill. Jovan usually walks out on him, mid-rant.
Jovan doesn't know where he gets this idea of life. A holiday that
never ends is the daydream of a spoilt child.

"You mean postcards." Bill kicks his locker shut. From the way
he's behaving, Bill might have been on this same job for thirty years.
His father, Tom, had done just that, and retired recently. Bill hasn't
been a cleaner for a year yet.

Bill says, "No Bosnia postcards, that's for sure. Fucking Muslims, fucking up their own shit, and then they come around fucking
up everyone else's. Acting as though not eating pork is gonna mean
shit to God or the devil."

Bill leaves the change room thinking he's offered Jovan a pat on
the back, as though to share a hate is to share a love. Tossing Molotov words with his eyes closed. The type of thing you lob around
a football ground during a rival match. A flare and nothing more.
Not something that could set the air alight—a kind of napalm that
would keep burning for generations.

Jovan feels the fluttering, and then he's within the feathers and claws of the black crow. He makes it to a toilet cubicle and is able to close a door. All he can do is place his head in his hands and breathe while the crow crashes his brain with adrenaline and fear. Promise himself that it will pass. Sit and wait. Close his eyes and press his palms into his face. He knows it will pass. Curl his shoulders over and bring up his thighs until he's above the balls of his feet and on the edge of the toilet cover.

Someone enters the cubicle beside Jovan's for a long piss. Music erupting from his ears in long stuttering beats and jack-hammering trills. Jovan can hear it clearly though the speakers are plugged directly into the man's head. Drilling his brain with this ceaseless roar of sound. Words are barely made out in the noiseless grappling of thoughts in Jovan's brain. The graffiti on the walls of the cubicle around him is as black as disease and threatens him with the noxious penetration of the shit-stained fingers that wrote it, reaching through his skull, even with eyes closed and hands over ears.

Graffiti that talks about sucking someone's dick, or fucking some woman in the arse that works in the hospital, or drawing out images of sloppy cunts and dripping cocks. Everywhere this same kind of toilet graffiti and its puerile assault on decency, as though it's written with one omnipresent hand everywhere in the world, scribbling these insults to thought for the last two thousand years.

Maybe it is only fifteen minutes. In the cubicle, his elbows pressed hard into his knees, he allows himself a moan that is soft—brings it back within himself as soon as he can. He's afraid of it, and what it might become. He knows it's a spark, and if it's given fuel, it will rage and burn everything he has, from memories to bones . . . and then it begins to release him. He breathes and raises his head to breathe again.

Must have been the dentist, his drills and needles. Must have been Bill and his Molotov muttering. Must have been everything finding a moment to burn again. Silently and imperceptibly.

He washes his face and wishes there was a way he could wash any of it clean. The crow has settled, sitting on its perch in the cage of his chest. There's no way for it to ever get out again now that it's in. Jovan's last breath will be to cough up one final black feather. He looks at himself and sees none of this. He looks calm. In the mirror, he looks fine.

He dries his face with a powder-blue hand towel he keeps in his locker. Bill's boots aren't placed on top of his locker, they're abandoned on the floor. Someone else's problem. Jovan picks them up and does it for him. He'd rather throw the boots into the trash yet he places them together, heel to heel, on top of Bill's locker.

Old men gunned down, as Bill said. And women and children as well. Regular clean-shaven men, fathers and sons of those other victims, destroyed by Jovan and his kind. Is this what Bill thinks? Jovan wasn't only a refugee, he was responsible for the war. Because he is a Serb he is responsible for a decade of mutilation and death. There's no conversation. Nothing can change a mind made in ignorance, but Jovan wishes he could speak anyway. To explain that there had been lots of ordinary people with ordinary religion, who started killing each other, for reasons less and less clear as more and more people died. He doesn't want to think of what the Serbs did to the Muslims, and can't think about what the Muslims did to Serbs. To his friends and family. To him. To Suzana.

Bill doesn't know a lot about hate, and not a lot more about love. He thinks he hates a boss or a politician or someone at his local pub but he hasn't seen hate turn into fire, free-floating and exploding throughout a city, and then materialising again into a blistered red monster more real than any creature children imagine in night-time terrors. Moving from city to city, and village to village, blazing across a whole country, uncontrollable and annihilating. Breathing fire around Jovan, and murdering before his eyes, raping and maiming all with a dying grin never quite dead.

Calling that explosion of murder "War" makes it seem familiar.

Elementary as much as elemental. When it rises from the ground, reeking of sulphur, war is hard to disguise as anything other than the devil himself. Turning mailmen, barbers, greengrocers, electricians, and taxi drivers into dismembering demons. Burning up entire generations of men as if their souls were made of hay. The devil was never a comic book character, with a red face and small horns protruding from his skull—he is a force as real as gravity, raging through the minds of men with the fires of hell.

It does not restore faith in God for Jovan. If he puts his hands together, and he does that most nights, it is to bring the cool and quiet closer to his face. To enfold himself in silence, and find some kind of peace in it. He prays because prayer itself is as close as he can come to containing the devil. Pressing him, if only for the space of a few breaths, between the palms of his hands.

Jovan takes his face out of the clean hand towel, which still smells fresh from the lavender detergent Suzana uses, and puts it back into his locker. A lavender smell she used in Bosnia as well.

He feels it all recede again, back into the postcard images of places he's been to. Places people pass through. Everything he's felt, reduced to the few lines dashed off for disinterested people never likely to go to those places themselves. Enough for them to contemplate a few images and a few words and dream themselves visions that had nothing to do with those actual places. Because a postcard from hell is a joke. Hell isn't real. The devil is as frightening as the graffiti, or cartoon, of a man with a pitchfork, painted on toilet doors, or on children's television. No, this thing we've been talking about for thousands of years, this farcical fire imp, doesn't really exist. There's nothing to fear from him, because the choices men make are all their own, even when they decide as a nation to burn everything down to the ground.

It's better to think of places like Maroochydore and Mooloolaba,

Noosa and Coolum. To hang on to postcards from those places. Let the words entice the mind back to the azure waters and sun-gold beaches of Maroochydore and Mooloolaba, Noosa and Coolum.

He clicks each metal button of his overalls closed. He opens his locker again. Takes the hand towel and breathes in its lavender one more time before returning it and locking the narrow metal door.

JOVAN IGNORES THE messages on his pager that direct him to the hospital's dentistry suite. In less than an hour, Tammie has found him in the kitchen, mopping the floors. She plays at wandering through casually, looking for something to nibble on. A slice of fruit from a tray on a bench brought back in after lunch and covered by Glad wrap. She peels back the plastic and lifts a long piece of pineapple and places it in her mouth. Pretends she doesn't see or feel Jovan looking at her. When she does look over, she turns on her one-hundred-watt smile. For everything Jovan can say about Tammie, he'll give her the sincerity of that grin. He can't help but return the smile.

She does love this, even if *this* is a sideshow to her life. This is dessert after the meat and potatoes. It only requires a bit of moral flossing after each meal, and that gets easier every time she allows herself to indulge. This sneaking around with a janitor, a brutish foreigner who can barely speak the language yet who fucks as if fucking is vital, as though it comes up from the bones, as much about marrow as semen, and not the distracted *lovemaking* of a lawyer husband who is never off the clock. Never really present. Simply turns over his body to necessary duties. The half-swallowed moan at the end of it as much a sigh of resignation as of satisfaction. Not that she actually sees Jovan. He's more a part of the *now* of her imagination than he is a man with his own history and his own future.

Jovan kills the smile on his face with his palm across his mouth as though he was crushing a cockroach that had snuck out from behind his ear. He doesn't know if he can help himself. Tammie's smile is an offering, a reminder of a sweet place; a deep, rich, black oblivion. Already a taste in his mouth as she begins to move towards him again, pausing at the edge of the wet floor he's mopping. Then proceeds as though daintily stepping, naked, into a cool, wooded lake.

Suzana's whisper across his pillow, "I saw you smile at her Jovan." Pretending to be asleep.

Tammie doesn't speak. She takes ahold of the handle in his hands with a firm grip. As though she's taking ahold of him. Waits for Jovan to respond, a slight swaying through her body. Ready to sink below the water with him again and to feel the weight of his body and the pool of trivial bliss that he will always be surrounded by for her. Holding on to the long wooden handle of the mop. The smooth grain of it, which in this moment, seems to possess the solidity of a tall ironbark reaching up for a blistered-red dreamtime sky swimming with crocodiles. With eyes already closing to slits as she lets herself move into the corner of her brain that generates these fluid, running daydreams. Made by memories and stories she heard when she was a child, swagging out under the hurricane of stars, spinning and opening up to gather the infinite black into a storm of light, with her father, their backs to the ground, listening to his stories at night. Never mentioning God, but God at the centre of everything he told her out there, as though he felt the beginnings of cancer even then, a different kind of storm brewing in a soul only he could believe in. The smooth feel of his axe in the crisp crystalline mornings. The handle almost too heavy to lift. For her father, it was as light as a switch. The axe head red, and shiny sharp blue steel at its cutting edge. Later watching him swing it up high, hanging in the air, using all its heavy momentum to cut down through a fallen boab. Feeling as small and helpless within the space of Jovan's breath, swaying above her and massively broad, and wanting him now to lift her up with the same kind of vast power and safe strength planted into the stream of her blood so long ago out in the Kimberley. Wanting Jovan to cut through her until she can spill out with all these rushing incantations and all this vaporising desire.

Jovan pulls the mop out of her hand with an angry jerk. The force of it shudders through her whole body, almost dislocating her shoulder. He dunks the mop head into the water and brings it out and down again at their feet. The dirty, foamy water splashes across her lovely, professional shoes, her stockings, and flecks her charcoal skirt with black and foam. Satin-top French stockings complete with garter belt visible in hints below the tight, hip-hugging skirt. No underwear below the garter belt. He's seen the outfit once before. Jovan's never known a woman to wear a garter belt or these kinds of elaborately elegant costumes before. He can't help feeling the appeal of its ornate seduction, vicious in its gathering power. He might want her in this instant more than he's ever wanted Suzana. Maybe that's true. The blood has a way of rushing through the brain, surging with those kinds of lies. He can't do anything else right now, shove her away when the only other option is to demolish her with desire.

Kitchen staff are beginning to trickle back from their lunch breaks, and she must know how apparent all this would be to them. So she steps closer to Jovan and raises a finger slowly to his mouth, pulls back his cheek, and examines his teeth.

"Looks as though they were rough," she says, her face pretty with all its perfectly applied makeup.

Jovan is already mopping again as she begins walking away across the now dry, clean kitchen floor. He's thinking about what she said long after she's left, and can't understand what sounds so seductive about those words, *Looks as though they were rough*. He lets the black water from the mop bucket run down the drain of the kitchen sink.

THE CHANGE ROOM is busy with people leaving or coming in for their shifts. Voices fill the room with the traffic of conversation. Everyone passes through this room—an intersection with busted lights.

Robert Sewell sits down to put on a fresh shirt as he asks Jovan whether he remembered the cleanup in room 302. Jovan nods. Says, "No problem." Nods again as Mr. X-Ray sings a bar of *Hey Joe* for the first time in weeks. There are two Indian men chatting in their language by a locker, their words interlaced as they seemed to talk almost at the same time, shoulder to shoulder. Offering him no smile today, Jovan walks by bare-chested Bill.

The "Greek," who struts at a standstill, turns on his heel. Picks up a can of deodorant, waving it under his arm as he goes on talking, now into his cream-coloured metal locker, plastered with images of over-exposed pneumatic women screaming in pink, vanilla, and blond. With bodybuilders glowing cherry red with high-tension tendons and well-oiled muscles.

A newspaper has fallen on the floor and the hospital handyman walks across its pages as he says goodbye. Nobody notices, and from the way he says it, he himself isn't expecting acknowledgment. Steps over images of a city being bombed from the air, at nighttime—the explosions are like the flashes of fireworks illuminating the buildings from below.

Bill has been explaining that Australia is full. Bill says that he went to the supermarket last night, and he was surrounded by Indians. A brown invasion. Customers and check-out people. "What the fuck is going on, letting so many of these people in?" Talking out to the two Indians who go on with their interlaced conversation across the room, though speaking ostensibly to Robert Sewell, who is trying to clarify with Bill whether the toilets on the second floor were cleaned as requested, and whether a problematic toilet, prone to blockage, was operational again. Sewell has been asking him all day. Bill's also directing his thoughts at X-Ray, who is leaning up against a locker not even pretending to listen as he flips through the pages of one of Bill's pornographic magazines. "Look at these wobble heads," Jovan hears Bill saying as he passes through. "Why do we need these clowns?"

Jovan is in his own head. He's taken his boots off. His feet and legs are tired and heavy, so he's very slow about it. Removing his overalls and then sitting back down on the bench as though to catch his breath. Suzana is spending more of her time scribbling into her notebooks. The only place safe for her in the time since Bosnia, was somewhere buried underground. Coming to the surface isn't going to be easy. What he can do to assist, or impede, isn't clear. Perhaps what he should do is look at what she's been writing. So far he's operated on an idea of honouring her personal space. If he can make a decision today, it's that he can't afford to do that—let this thing run its course when the destination is likely to be underground again. And this time he will be left with a mouth full of dirt and worms.

"Let's not have any racism here, please," Sewell says by rote.

"Racism? I'm Greek mate," Bill says in reply.

"If by that you mean that you've been a victim of racism and so . . ."

"Are you fucking listening to me?" Bill takes a step towards his manager. "I'm trying to say something. Everyone is pretending it's like *this*, when it's like *that*. Even here, between a group of fucken guys who get shat on by pretty much everyone. We supposed to pretend to enjoy the taste of it as well? That's what those clowns do. They come over when it's already fucking hard enough as it is and make enjoying the taste of shit part of cleaning up after the giant arsehole over our heads."

Jovan goes on thinking about Suzana and the notebooks and the hours of scribbling that was going into them, and wonders what should be done, knowing that there's nothing he *can* do. Not about the tossing and turning he feels from her side of the bed, the sweat-drenched nightgowns she leaves hanging in the bathroom most mornings now, or the babble that is beginning to emerge from her mouth as she sleeps, or the unconscious scalp scratching and hair tugging as she writes in those black-skinned books. Nothing he could do about it last time in Belgrade and nothing he can do about it this time either.

Truth is, Jovan always fails Suzana. When she asked whether it's a good idea to leave Sarajevo, in 1990, and live in Belgrade with Ana and Dejan, and maybe look into the possibility of teaching in London, he laughed. Teaching what? he asked her. Who cares about Yugoslav literature, and what else can he offer anyone? And why would he want to live in London, packed in a concrete box with over six million strangers who will never be anything other than strangers as long as he lives, ants streaming from hundreds of thousands of other concrete boxes. So, no to an exit from Bosnia, in 1990, when an exit was still possible.

A few years later, there's a bathtub with a ring of red. There are towels soaked in blood left lying around. Open doors and windows. A tap in the kitchen still half on. The water running in a quiet, empty apartment, as loud as any alarm he'd ever heard in his life.

In the bathroom. In the bathtub. And there's nothing he can do in Belgrade to stop it or to get her going again afterwards. She'd done a lot of writing then as well. She stopped after getting out of the hospital, and when she says maybe she and Jovan can go and live in Australia, because she has an uncle living in Melbourne, this time

Jovan says yes. Let's go to the other side of the world. He doesn't want to fail Suzana again.

Jovan walks into a toilet and swings the door shut behind him as he takes a piss. Thinks these thoughts. All of them thought through, beginning to end, the same way as he had a hundred times before. Millions of times, back in Belgrade, after Suzana opened up her veins as easy as bathtub taps. Saved by her sister, visiting on the off chance Suzana was home. Jovan would have come home a few hours too late, to the corpse of his wife in the bathroom.

When he turns he notices new graffiti on the door. Sprayed red over the other graffiti going on about cocks and cunts. Graffito's work. Jovan puts his finger to the paint. It's almost dry. There's a slight stickiness.

A river of Waste
Just below Your skin
your Bones rot in
history's flowing Shit

The sharp smell of paint, so this went up a few minutes ago. This is the same door that he saw at the start of his shift. He might have passed Dr. Graffito in the change room or hall.

Rushing out into a red steam that has risen from the concrete floor, Jovan shouts, "Who put words on the door of toilet?"

"What the fuck?" Bill turns around from his locker. Shirtless with his singlet in his hand. "Made us jump mate. Slamming that fucking toilet door." Bill talks in a customary bellow. Bill spends a lot of time in the gym. The muscles are packed onto his squat Greek frame—seeming to cluster and crowd beneath the skin. "Calm, the fuck, down, Wood Duck." Starting to grin, Bill shakes his head. "And maybe you should wash your hands after going to the toilet."

He's looking for laughs from the other two men as Jovan moves towards him in three quick strides across the room, and has one massive tarantula hand wrapped so far around Bill's dwarfish throat that his fingers press around the sides towards the spine.

Bill can do no more than half grunt the word "fuck" in response. Stunned. Unable to reach out his short arms along the long out-stretched limb of this sudden Goliath. Bill gurgles.

"This red words on door?" Jovan asks again. All three of the men in the change room are quiet. "You talking about shit. The graffiti words talking about shit. Did you read? Or did you write?"

Robert Sewell lays one hand on Jovan's shoulder and the other in the small of his back. "Hey," he says, "Mr. Brakochevich, please." There's no strength in Sewell's arms to pull him off. One of the Indian men has come over and he is hauling at Jovan's shirt so hard it's beginning to tear, yelling, "Hey! Hey!" as though he doesn't know any other words.

"This isn't good," Sewell says, attempting to do his duty and respond to what is happening in the change room between two of his employees. "Please, Mr. Brakochevich."

None of these men have paint on their hands and all of their faces show surprise or fear. Jovan moving into the room so rapidly. Attacking Bill. Such a drilled movement.

"Hey, stop this. Hey, stop. Stop." Jovan does not feel or hear the Indian.

Bill's eyes are swelling. His lips move uselessly and it won't be long. It's easy to turn someone off. Jovan can feel the switch just below his fingertips. Is that true? Is it that simple? One way to find out. Do it. Squeeze that fucken dwarf throat. He never need hear another poisonous word from this toxic mind. There would be some silence when the body slumped to the ground and for that moment everything would be perfect.

Jovan releases Bill. Turns to the two other men as if he might attack either one of them next. "He must learn to keep his mouth closed. Or do we learn to walk in his shit?" Jovan says.

Bill has stumbled away towards the toilets, taking air through a throat that must feel half crushed. His shoulder bounces off a wall as he attempts to get away from his assailant. He is disorientated for a second—gets a grip of a basin and gathers his wits. Splashes water onto his face.

X-Ray shakes his head with a smile at the locker room scene and makes a quiet exit. Robert Sewell walks to the toilet to have a look at the new graffiti. When he returns Jovan is putting on a denim jacket and is about to leave for home.

Bill begins swearing at Sewell for employing madmen. Bill punches and throws his shoulder into the lockers as he watches Jovan walk to the sink and wash his hands. Bill swears at Sewell again as he watches Jovan use his special, soft, powder-blue hand towel from his locker. Sewell says he doesn't hire hospital employees and asks Bill to calm down, explaining that no one wants any more violence today. He gets shoved away brutally for his troubles as Bill begins to yell abuse at Jovan and to all Serbs. Jovan leaves the room as he entered it. As though everything around him has nothing to do with him, yet the words in the toilet are for Jovan. Of course they are. It's simple. No surprise in it at all. Dr. Graffito knows Jovan in the same way as he knew the optometrist.

He walks to the break room a door down the hall to get something to eat. Suddenly ravenous. Slices of soft white bread in a plastic bag. The television has been left on. There's no one else in the room. A host is offering up some news about two men attempting to circumnavigate the world in a hot air balloon. They have set an endurance record. In the air for 233 hours and 55 minutes. Their names are Colin Prescot and Andy Elson. Jovan assumes they're English with those names, but they could be Americans or Australians. He stuffs a second slice of bread into his mouth and looks up at the screen to see the balloon, thinking it can't be one of those jaunty balloons with vivid stripes of colour seen on advertisements for Kodak film or some such brand. It'd have to be a more impressive balloon, denoting adventure. An expedition, not a joyride. Emphasis on endurance rather than pleasure. Jovan gets a brief glimpse of something silvery and NASA-like, then it's back to the host signing off for the day. A commercial comes on, advertising a television set that will give its prospective owners a new world of experience, entertainment, joy. Jovan walks out of the break room before the ad has finished extolling the virtues of the new technology involved in the product. Jovan calculates it was almost ten days in the air for Prescot and Elson, and wonders whether they got bored with their Everest views and turned on their portable television to a new world of chatter and trivia.

Jovan's new world began with two suitcases, and Christmas in summer, living in a bungalow at the back of Suzana's uncle Mirko's house in St. Albans, Melbourne, with the novelty of "footy" and cricket on the television, and English in Australian accents. A little over forty hours of flight for Jovan and Suzana. That's how a world begins, and because it comes with different newspapers and street names and currency, the old world can be packed into a box, and left to gather dust, and be rarely seen. More and more rarely as the years pass. The two worlds drift further and further apart.

Of course, the box doesn't disappear. It will always be exactly where it always was—in the centre of their lives. It is made of the thinnest sheets of porous material, the most fragile membrane, leaking without warning at any point. The two worlds appear far apart. Sarajevo is across the seas, and as time goes by, the separating waters seem ever broader to Jovan and Suzana, yet the box, which they cannot open, and cannot close, contains their Sarajevo lives. Nothing within it is dead, though they both often think otherwise. They will sit in their Frankston home watching television and not notice the Australian accents anymore. They allow themselves to think fondly of Christmas snow rather than the December heat of Melbourne. Weeks and months pass and the seasons here have a way of offering easier transitions from year to year.

Yet an odour remains, the sickening smell of melting flesh from the heat of a radiator. There are sounds, Suzana's voice as it murmurs pain in solid thumps. Vanishing a moment later.

The war didn't start everywhere at the same time in Bosnia. It was part of the civil wars of Yugoslavia, yet where it petered out quickly in other parts of that federation of states, in Bosnia, it grew into something far worse and protracted. It was fought from village to village, town to town, and in cities, street to street and building to building. It was resisted for long periods in some quarters of the state, as it raged full gore in others. It was fought by peasants who had known each other for generations and had often celebrated weddings together, or Yugoslavia's victories in sport, or mourned the deaths of locals, Muslim and Christian alike. Which should not suggest a paradise of brotherhood. The war, however, was fought by policemen turned generals. By sports stadium hooligans turned sergeants. It was fought by high-school children, trained up to then by PE teachers. In short, it was fought by loose groupings of people organised by no grand plan, leader, or movement.

Muslims vowed to Serbian neighbours that atrocities committed in another town wouldn't be perpetrated here. Yet they were. Of course, that was also true the other way around. Serbs made promises of decency that they didn't keep. Promises are part of a currency, and as long as there is an idea of social economy, then these notes can be traded on. A society can become bankrupt through various causes, and all parts of the world have witnessed these collapses of a moral economy.

Jovan and Suzana were part of a group of teachers at a university that insisted that their institution should provide a beacon of under-standing in the rapidly rising, murderous idiocy all around them. They hadn't yet seen more than images on television broadcasts, which as horrifying as they can be, are only ever images as one might see in a film. They don't penetrate and become one's own. They excite passion, and then fade away. If they had known the difference, they would have packed those same two suitcases, and walked out of Bosnia, into Serbia, or through to somewhere else. They would have taken a bus or train anywhere—wherever it was going.

At their university there had been students who continued attending classes even as their courses became absurdities. Jovan still had a handful of pupils coming to read and discuss the merits of Mesha Selimovich's masterpiece *Death and the Dervish*, drawing contrasts with Ivo Andrich's monumental *Bridge on the Drina*, with Milosh Tsernianski's *Migrations*, or Danilo Kish's *Garden, Ashes*, irrespective of which author was a Jew or Muslim, Orthodox or Catholic. He still gave these desperate, delusional students assign-ments, which they completed. He graded them and made his com-ments, and returned them to his students. Until none of them came at all, and his books became truly useless. He couldn't read them himself anymore. And still he didn't leave. Their flat in Sarajevo was taken and they began living in the university. Jovan walked around the university in a daze that wouldn't lift for a second. A head full of bees is how he described it to Suzana. He couldn't understand what bees were at times. The world was full of insects erupting from peo-ple's mouths. She didn't say anything, but even with Suzana's mouth closed, he could hear humming.

They had already sent Ana and Dejan to Jovan's parents, who lived in a village outside Banja Luka, where the war was not an immediate threat. Jovan and Suzana understood the danger well enough to protect their children—not well enough to protect them-selves. Losing their home had not convinced them that they had lost their city and were soon to lose their country as well. They flat-tered themselves, thinking they were fighting for what remained of their culture, before it went up in flames in the general conflagra-tion of their society. They were unable to let go of their lives; had not accepted a more basic existence, beyond what they had lived for, in their devotion and belief; beyond even children and a future. Pure existence. Bodies in the world, breathing and blinking because bodies kept breathing and blinking beyond reason.

There's the smell of sweat burning on a radiator, that sickening smell similar to arm hair burned above a gas flame on the stove top during a rushed dinner preparation. The radiators in the university were industrial strength, screwed onto the walls. When they were fired up they stayed on most of the harsh Bosnian winters. During brutal blizzards students didn't leave their university. They crawled under tables into sleeping bags. In the morning woke to whatever classes were scheduled by teachers who were also sleeping there. The radiators kept running, for weeks and months, the oil within them staying molten the whole time.

When they were turned on for Jovan it was late autumn, and still warm during the days, and cool in the evenings, not quite requiring gloves or scarves. They asked Jovan to remove all his clothes before they turned them on. Used bicycle chains to bind him to the cool surface of a radiator. Turned it on to full, and sat at a desk to play a card game called Tablichi. A game children play. These men weren't far removed from such playful years.

It was pain Jovan could smell. Is that the smell of pork frying? one of the young men asked. Is it Saint George's day? another asked. The Serbs must be celebrating a *slava* somewhere near, because another one is sure he can smell pig on a spit. The jokes about pork went on. Funny because it was practically the only thing that differentiated them from the man they had bound to the radiator, though they'd eaten pork themselves often enough. They went on playing Tablichi.

Jovan was not an extraordinary man. The pain was terrible. He tried to be quiet. His wife was hiding in the ceiling and if he cried out he knew it would be worse for her. Oddly, the words that kept running through Jovan's mind were ones that would never make sense again. *This is necessary. This is necessary. This is necessary.* Jovan didn't know what sense it made even then. He went on saying those senseless words.

Bored with the game, one of the young men stood up, and walked to Jovan with an American gun he held sideways as he's seen gangster rappers do in video clips. "I think I'm going to give you an F, Mister Teacher. That's fair isn't it? You remember giving me an F don't you. I got punished for that F, Mister Teacher, you know that? I got a caning with a branch from a birch tree. And I wasn't a child anymore either. But there's respect and my father's a peasant and they don't understand F. I don't know what it meant to him. It must have been like something coming down from on high. An F, he kept telling me. Crying as he was beating me with that birch branch. Like I'd told him I was a faggot, and brought eternal shame to the family name. I let him beat me. I was too big to be beaten like that, but I let him anyway. My peasant dad. I felt ashamed of him, as much as he felt ashamed of me, so I let him beat me one last time. For old times' sake. An F, he kept telling me. An F. An F. How could you! And do you see how little it matters now, Mister Teacher. But my F is going to matter. You will remember it. Tell Porky Pig down there in hell that I gave you an F. Tell his brother, Jesus Christ, as well." And who knows if young Zlatan would have pulled the trigger on his gangster gun? It was enough to make Jovan close his eyes. Enough to whimper in the last moment before feeling the bullet.

Suzana didn't let that happen. She pushed the white square of a ceiling segment aside. Announced herself to the four young men below. Who asked her to come down. Who did not need to discuss what would happen next. Who did not need to think about what would happen next.

Do not visualise the details. Do not try to imagine what husband and wife may, or may not, have thought or felt. As those images on television broadcasts could not fully penetrate the minds of Suzana and Jovan, or anyone watching anywhere else at the time, so no one will ever know anything of this experience. Which wasn't unique to this husband and wife in anything other than the particulars. It can only excite brief feelings, in the way something might from a film, one of Jovan's books, or the poetry that he used to put to paper and publish in various literary journals around Yugoslavia.

Outside, on the university grounds, Jovan would find the four bodies of these young men a few hours afterwards while Suzana slept under sedation. Shot down by Serb militia. Not because they were rapists. Because they were armed Muslims. And Jovan did not feel relief. Did not feel the hatred for them consummated in this violence. Maybe it was because they looked young. Young enough to still be his students. Young enough to be anything they wanted to be. No longer young. They had no age now. Hate would have been easier. Jovan searched for hate, and wanted to find it. Easier than the obliteration he actually felt.

The demolishment he still feels, even here in Melbourne, Australia. A different world altogether in which what happened in Bosnia was some kind of horror show where monsters killed other monsters. A place with no heroes, and therefore of little interest to anyone he talked to, except as far as they looked at him and wondered whether he was possibly another one of those Balkan monsters. Jovan smiles at people in the hospital, blokes like Bill, and assures them all he's not to be feared. He's just a cleaner in this world. No problems. There are no problems here that can't be cleaned away.

He walks down the hallway, away from the change room and the noise of Bill kicking in metal lockers. Jovan moves down the busy hospital halls, patients making their way along to rooms for examinations or rest, with doctors and their purposeful faces and others, similar to himself, heads full of directions, moving here and there, looking to keep it all running. Everything going on as it should in this fully functioning moral economy. The hum of a healthy hive, audible through every wall, at least to Jovan's ears.

That hum had been harder to hear ever since Doctor Graffito had emerged, his mind breaking out across the walls, a rare, exotic disease that was yet deeply familiar as well. As common as a cold. The cough and the frustration. As basic as hate. The venom from a wound, sucked up, spat out. Had Jovan been fooling himself about his own hatred? Enough of that poison and a man becomes toxic, the walking wounded, more dead than alive.

Outside radiology, he stops for a drink from the new watercooler. The white plastic cups are small, child-sized, so Jovan refills his cup and drinks again. The water is slow and he thinks of Graffito's Origin of the Species oil. Leni walks along the hallway and pats his elbow lightly as she passes, absentmindedly says, "Hey, Jovan," pronouncing it correctly. Returns after a few steps because a thought has occurred to her—for a brief chat with him at the watercooler. It's one of those social phenomena, *people talking at the watercooler*, but he hasn't seen it often and he's never been part of that kind of conversation. It's a small thing, yet it lets the toilet graffiti slip away from his mind as nothing more than the spat-out madness of Dr. Graffito.

Jovan walks through the hospital feeling as though these people belong to him. As if the halls and rooms were in a home he owns. A feeling he used to have in the university. He knows them all in brief moments. He wants them to find their way with as little confusion and pain as possible. The grid pattern of the plastic floors along the way pleases him; the three tones of a comforting grey. So clean you can't see a scuff mark or bit of rubbish all the way out to the car park.

When he puts his key into the lock of the panel van, he thinks, Maroochydore and Mooloolaba, Noosa and Coolum, and wishes he could find a way to free them both for another drive up to the Sunshine Coast. They bought a pile of postcards while they were up there and sent them to no one. Jovan collected them at different service stations along the way.

There was a place called Cotton Tree. They spent a month there. Every day so bright it dazzled the brain all the way into evening. A gold-flecked heat, that blasted without blistering—the water freshening the air whenever it began to feel heavy. A place where he felt for the first time that they might actually survive Sarajevo.

Cotton Tree doesn't rhyme with the rest of his Sunshine Coast names but it's the centre of a useless compass he carries around with him in Melbourne. Jovan drops into his car seat and feels the shock travel up his spine and jangle up into his teeth.

He drives out into the homeward-bound evening traffic and doesn't mind the push and pull of the metal river around him, the long stops, crawling along for sections of the road home. It gives him time to think about Leni. The conversation about her art. Asking him to be her subject.

He laughs out loud now, because back at the watercooler, he had thought she meant she wanted him to stand in a room for her— naked. Just him and the pretty girl. Had she noticed him blush? Had he actually blushed? His face wouldn't have flushed, yet she was watching closely. There were almost invisible signs. The pupils dilating. A blush response in his eyes? Jovan brakes for a cyclist pushing out into the lane because of a parked car up ahead. She must expect that reaction when she asks someone to pose for her. Wouldn't most people stumble on the idea of their own nudity? Not a brief nakedness, as it was most of the time, or part way. Fully nude, an hour or two, for the careful scrutiny of canvas. All of the people she's asked, laughing with the same kind of embarrassed shift of warmer blood in their faces. He passes the cyclist and admires the fixed attention he gives the road ahead. The way the cyclist leans forward, poised and very still but for the perfect rhythm of his legs pumping up and down. "Almost killed you," Jovan murmurs. Shakes his head in the rear-view.

X-Ray walked past the watercooler, stopped to see what the laughter was about. Impossible to explain and Leni laughed harder when Jovan attempted to describe the misunderstanding—what she asked him and what he had assumed. X-Ray walked away as if he was angry at both of them. Especially Jovan. He couldn't help laughing at X-Ray's confusion as well.

Jovan had looked back at Leni, enjoying her laughter. Might he have been persuaded to pose nude? He knew that, had he wanted to reveal himself, he wouldn't be able to. Nothing showed in the mirror. Suzana said there were a few marks across his back. The sharp radiator fins had put a vague pattern into his skin—even those industrial-strength Bosnian radiators couldn't melt flesh. They weren't quite as hot as an electric iron. Was that why a demented mind needed to explode across hospital walls in graffiti? Spell out every vague wound pattern inflicted on a man's mind.

He could wear his overalls, she said. In fact, the overalls were good. Wear the overalls, she told him, though he hadn't agreed to be her subject. The clothes were a part of the world they both lived in yet she would be looking to draw him out of it. There would eventually be a kind of nakedness anyway, she said.

When he parks the van in his driveway the lights are on in every room of the house. The curtains are pulled aside. He doesn't see Suzana walking from one room to another as he has in the past. Or he might see her sitting at the dining room table over her books, her spine as rigid and straight as her writing arm is relaxed and serpentine. Not at the table either tonight, though her books are there.

Isn't this a kind of nudity as well? They were never this careless before. Maybe there were children to protect and privacy was part of that function. Now their furniture is always second- or third-hand anyway and there's nothing to steal or protect. The open blinds and lights would confirm it for anyone walking past the house.

It reminded Jovan of an ant farm they built in a science class when he was young. *Prayers for Cracks in the Glass*—the title of a poem he wrote back in those school days, where he used those ants and their compressed, exposed world, as an elaborate metaphor for his own petty high-school frustrations.

He pulls the latch and kicks open his car door. Walks towards home. There's a small slab of concrete in front of the house that serves as a step to his front door. He looks up and there are no clouds tonight. There are few stars—random dots of light which have managed to struggle through the city's light pollution. He finds a scrap of poetry as he walks towards his illuminated house.

No stars in the sky
Frankston forgets
every evening
every dream
My genesis graffiti
scrubbed clean
every dream
every evening

Jovan doesn't open the front door. Charlemagne, on a chain, barks from Silvers's yard. Rosellas squabble on the power lines along the street. Cicadas roar from the eucalyptus tree in his yard. A neighbour's truck coasts home along Reservoir Road—a few houses down the street. Silence beyond the door. Jovan's keys are in his pocket but he can't move his arms. He turns away and faces the street. He stands there, breathing and blinking. Pure existence. That phrase drifts through his mind, connected to nothing.

Jovan remembers the sketch Leni made of him when he drove her to work in the morning. The Romance of the Crash. Suzana might find the drawing. The portrait would hurt her. Wouldn't it be clear a woman had drawn it? Might he seem a philanderer? Jovan walks back to his van and opens the passenger-side door. He leans in for the glove box. Pops it open. The compartment is empty other than for a small parcel. On the front of it are the printed words

This is a Bomb

Jovan picks it up and knows he's meant to open the package. Graffito wants him to feel a jolt of fear that his car has been broken into. Anger that there has been a theft. The doctor is directing the janitor to read another message within the small box, carefully prepared for him.

Jovan walks the parcel to the green wheelie bin. Changes his mind. He doesn't want to be tempted later on by a curiosity that will be sure to grow. Given enough time it will be irresistible to know what Graffito had to say in a personal message to Jovan.

This is not a game Jovan can win since it can only be played on a madman's terms. No doubt what's in it. Harm. Pain for Jovan. An invitation to torment. He shakes the package as he walks towards the street and feels a weight within. So it wasn't words today. The toilet door was enough, thinks Jovan, as he bends down. He drops "the bomb" into a storm-water drain that will sweep it away to Port Phillip Bay.

He walks back up to the front door of the brightly lit house and notices the dim, flashing lights of his television. The set is turned away from him. He can't see what's being televised. It's illuminating his wife. She's sitting on the carpet before it, as he'd seen his children do when watching a show. They were captivated in the same way at times. Tears running from an immobile expression of fascination on her face. Mesmerised—a woman who almost never watches television. Suzana doesn't look like she's crying. Jovan can see her wet face as television light plays across it. She's childlike, arms wrapped around her legs, watching. Doesn't notice Jovan through the front window, three metres away, until he knocks on their front door. And then she flinches as though slapped.

SIX

SUZANA HEARS THE DISTINCT ROAR OF the panel van before it comes into the drive. Listens for the sound of his car door thumping shut before she stands up. Runs her fingers through her hair. Stops halfway as if halted by knots. Suzana sits down again on the three concrete steps of the backyard door, watches the rosellas line up on the unpainted back fence. Nails in the wood have leaked rust in streaks. The rosellas remind her of the colourful metal outlines in a shooting gallery at a fair. She has often wished she had a rifle to test her skill because while the rosellas are colourful they are also noisy in a way that makes her feel as though she might go mad again. He's walking through the house, turning off all the lights as he goes.

Their television sits on the grass in the middle of the yard. It might have fallen over, forwards or backwards, when it was thrown down. Facing her, ready to be switched on by a remote control. Jovan mustn't have felt a need to demolish the damned thing. Removing it from the lounge was enough. Yet the fall would surely have destroyed at least one or two essential mechanisms within the box. Had it rained overnight? The day since had been overcast but Suzana hadn't noticed rain. Even a minor sprinkle would have got into the television. Maybe that fucking idiot Silvers watered the grass and the television combined. From where she was sitting the box wasn't cracked and the screen pristine, its grey static heart ready to pulse back into life.

Jovan knocks on the mesh of the security door because he can't open it while Suzana is sitting there, blocking the door. She stands up and lets him take the three steps down into their backyard. She drinks the final sip from a cup of chamomile that went cold hours ago—so she has something to do with her hands. She took a sleeping pill. It's wearing off and Jovan simply standing there is too solid and big, and altogether too awake. Suzana sits down again.

"All the lights were on in the house again. It makes me think there's been some kind of emergency. And then you're just out here, sitting."

"You worried about the bills?"

"I don't give a fuck about the bills."

No pleasantries today. Unusually aggressive. She looks up at him.

"I haven't made dinner," she says.

"I'm starving," he says.

"Why don't you call me before you come home? Maybe you should start doing that. I can't guarantee a three-course dinner every evening."

"Fuck off with the three-course bullshit, Suzana. Let's work out how to feed ourselves regularly."

"You should go out. Sit down at a table in a restaurant like a civilised man. Enjoy a glass of fine wine. Why not?" she suggests.

Jovan's teeth come together. Grind once and then he lets it go. The quick conversion in his eyes, fury into pity. Suzana is happy to go to bed without dinner. It's something Jovan can't imagine doing. He might sneer at a three-course meal yet three meals a day form a structure that he can't do without. He wouldn't know it was morning unless he'd had breakfast, afternoon unless he'd eaten lunch, and evening if he wasn't sitting down to dinner.

Jovan says, "There's a new place I passed along Wells Street the other day. Thai food. It reminded me of Cotton Tree." The first time he'd had Thai food.

She turns her face from Jovan, back to the fence. The rosellas have taken to the air. Maybe he thinks she's been sitting here for hours, no birds to look at, staring at that unpainted wooden fence or the television on the grass in the middle of the yard.

Those birds: they're vivid drops and splashes of colour, applied directly from God's paintbrush. The red so vivid, not blood or rose or lipstick or any of the cliché reds. A purer, more startling red. She'd wanted to share that thought with him because God was a word that didn't feel bankrupt from his mouth—that quiet way he folded his hands on his chest when they both settled in bed and the pathetic silence as he said his prayers.

"How's that sound?" he asks.

"Why not?" she says. "Order me whatever you think. I might peck a bit, like one of those rosellas. 'Sing a delighted song from the palm of your heart,' afterwards."

"What the fuck is that?"

"What the fuck is *what*?"

"Sing from my *palm*?"

"Don't read into it, Joe." She uses the name they gave him in the hospital, speaking to him in English.

"The next thing, I'm putting you in a cage. Is that the metaphor you're using?" Resolutely in Serbian.

"I was quoting one of your own poems, you idiot."

A slight movement of his face backwards and a double blink. "I don't recall. Must be one of the early ones."

Suzana looks up at him, not blinking. "I thought you were starving."

"So, Thai?"

"Alright."

"Okay." He nods at her and then nods again. "Okay."

The two okays make her think of Glen Coultas. She was at Prospect Grove this morning and she was supposed to go back there for her afternoon shift. There are messages on the machine. Jovan never notices it no matter the red light blinking or number of calls recorded. Suzana hears him snatch up his keys from the kitchen table. She sits down again. So many keys, most of them needed for the hospital, clattering from a variety of circular links. A system he's developed to navigate hospital and home. Jangling through the house and out the front door—ignoring the two messages on the answering machine. The phone rang twice while Suzana sat on the back steps. Coultas, she assumes.

The panel van roars into life again. She closes her eyes. Hates that sound more every day. The Ford drove them all the way up north and back south to Frankston without leaving them stranded anywhere. Unbelievable. She shakes her head. The damned thing will not die. They'd slept in the back of the van a few times. She hated the vehicle even then and on the way back down the coast told Jovan that would never be an option again. The vague smells of turpentine, paint, motor oil, could never be washed out, no matter how well he had cleaned the entire vehicle, inside and out. Not that it bothered Jovan. It was as though he'd been a fucking tradesman his whole life.

Jovan has said he'd paint the fence, across those rusting nails, and Suzana told him not to be a fool. It wasn't their house. Slavko is paying off his own home now; before he did, he lived in a rental as well and spent time painting things, replacing and improving, putting in a skylight in the dreary lounge to open it up to a brilliant waterfall of sunshine. The landlord was happy to see all the improvements but never offered concessions in rent. In the end, the landlord kicked out Slavko and his family and sold a much improved property.

Suzana stands up again. Walks into the house—dark except for the light in the hallway. Such a lightless bunker of a building. Even during the day, at the height of summer, it has a cavernous quality. She's already dreading winter. The windows are too small, badly arranged, and the place is surrounded by sunlight-swallowing trees. East facing, so they get light in the morning for about fifteen minutes. Suzana has been outside for hours, watching the afternoon dissolve into evening over the back fence.

The rosellas are quiet. They don't have a song. It's a scrambled Morse code when they congregate. A chaos of squeaking that can't mean anything even in their stupid heads. When she's hanging clothes they will often mill about her feet, as if they've never been kicked or scattered, and have nothing to fear from people. When they're quiet, they're beautiful and she moves across the grass carefully. Today she took a sleeping pill so she could go out amongst them to hang the clothes. The huge, water-heavy overalls belonging to her husband, her worn-out dresses weighing nothing in comparison, the other odds and ends of their lives. She watched them drying and waving with every movement of the air.

Suzana leaves her handbag and takes nothing with her as she walks towards the front door, pausing only to put her shoes on and to take an envelope of money she got from Coultas in the morning. She has a vague intention—of seeing the water. They lived near the ocean yet almost never saw it except through car windows. Every night they talked about how to free themselves, how they might drive up there again, how to find the time and energy. A holiday all the way up north, pushing out around the continental belly of Australia to get to a stretch of coast, when there's sand and water nearby. An easy half-hour walk away from where they live right now. Suzana leaves the front door open. The security door bangs shut behind her as she walks out onto the street.

SUZANA GIVES THE man at the counter a false name, Rhonda Johnson, so she won't need to spell it out for him three times. So she won't have to answer questions about her origins and then be forced to be an ambassador for Serbia for some motel flunky, who, five minutes later, would be thinking about the footy scores, interested in the statistics of bombs but couldn't care less where they fell—as though they were sports stats in a game that no one cared about in Australia. Just *chit-chat*. Rhonda Johnson. Suzana is forced to repeat it. She can see the motel concierge doesn't believe her. She can't be Rhonda Johnson. Suzana signs it carefully, remembering the silent h in both words.

"That's an interesting accent," he says.

"Thank you, if 'interesting' is a compliment. If not, keep quiet. You might avoid insulting your guests."

"Yes. A compliment. I'm sorry. I like your voice. That's the main thing. I wasn't trying to offend you."

"Trying to offend? When would anyone *try* to offend someone?"

"I wouldn't. I don't know. I . . ."

Suzana stops, leans forward a few millimetres. His earnest eyes in his fat face. The tight motel uniform, pushing at the buttons traversing the mountain of his belly. It's a pathetic thing to do—pin someone working behind a counter in a shitty job. Despite that, desperate to keep it. And it isn't as if he wants this conversation either. Maybe that's why the English expression "chit-chat" reminds her of shrapnel. Of the countermeasure explosive and the word "chaff."

"My apologies." No more chit-chaff.

"It's fine. I'll take it as a compliment." She gives him a curt nod. "Can you confirm that my room has a view of the ocean?" Suzana isn't interested in the sea. Not really. The bed is all she cares about. She walks away from the counter feeling conspicuous by her lack of luggage. She's wearing a summery yellow blouse she bought a few days ago in Brighton, so at least she doesn't look as though she's desperate and homeless. Maybe she strikes the concierge as a forlorn wife escaping the clutches of a violent husband.

She walks the hallway, thinking about the bed, fatigue deep in her bones. She knows she'll be able to sleep tonight. That's all she needs. To fall asleep quickly and stay that way for eight hours. Even a solid stretch of four hours will do. A door ajar, she pushes it open. Wants to get inside to collapse on the motel bed—sagging in spots that thousands of bodies have worn into the mattress over the years. To find rest in that kind of patina seems perfect and poetic to her sleepy mind. A nest to curl up into.

A woman and a man. Noises first. Muffled grunts. The surprised oh, again and again. Suzana takes another two steps into the room before she can stop. It takes her a second to understand that there's been a mistake. That's how sleepy she is. This wasn't a show on the television. Motel porn. They're fucking on the bed. The man is behind the woman, his eyes closed, the final few thrusts. The woman is looking up at Suzana. Muted. Unresponsive. Waiting for her lover to finish. Not wanting his last blissful moment to abruptly cease. Unable to indicate her surprise even by blinking.

Suzana backs away, thinking, perhaps the other woman was the kind that will tell her lover afterwards, and they will laugh. Suzana closes the door on her way out. Before she does, she makes sure it's locked. Pulls it shut loudly. Angry at the swelling embarrassment. She doesn't have room for anything else in her mind. Yet another emotion to deal with. Maybe sleep isn't a certainty here, after all. And no sleeping pills to help now.

Her room is the one next door and she unlocks it with the key and steps inside. The television in the room, silent, up on the wall. A red light indicating it is on standby. A push of the button. She gazes out at the ocean instead. The grey steel of Port Phillip Bay, the way its leaden stillness kills the idea of an ocean. A large body of water is not the same thing. That was why they went all the way north, to see the pulse of the planet throbbing back towards the land. The clear blue immensity of it unrolling their souls for them so they could see the reflected reaches of stars and cosmos in themselves. More of Jovan's poetry. No escaping him, it seems. The red light in the television—a hook in the corner of her eye. She picks up the remote, doesn't press the button. Chucks it back onto the coffee table. It clatters and the batteries spill out.

Up north was the last time they were able to function as a couple. Both of them had thought it was a new beginning. It turned out to be a new end. What do they have now? It isn't "making love" as they say in English, and it isn't fucking, it's that kind of anomalous thing they call "having sex." So delicately referred to when it is phrased that way. She doesn't use Serbian words because she doesn't think about the act without everything else flooding through, along with more familiarity. So it's the sedate English way of doing things when they "have sex." She couldn't hear the couple next door. Maybe they were already gone.

Suzana winces. The last two times might qualify as having sex but Jovan had not been able to ejaculate the time before those. That had surprised her. It would have been more understandable if he hadn't been able to get an erection. The useless back and forth was worse. A tearing impotency. Pulling away and slumping down onto the bed. An apology. A week later they tried again. His body above, locked elbows, a suspension bridge, both of them silent. His eyes needed to be closed. His mind had to forget everything. That was the trick. And yet, neither of them found much more satisfaction in the two times since, even if technically "successful." Pleasure was beside the point. It was a decision to have another child. Another new beginning now ending.

When she lies on the bed she realises she's ravenous. Sleep will be impossible. That hunger growing within her. A void sucking her away. She calls the front desk. It's the same man she talked to when she checked in. He tells her everything is closed. There's a pause, silence. Suzana wonders if he will hang up if she doesn't speak again. Maybe they've got a bag of nuts somewhere. Some bread. She doesn't ask.

"There's an all-night pizza place. I could call them for you."

"Thank you," Suzana says.

"What kind of pizza do you like?"

"Any kind. Except the marine pizza."

"Do you mean marinara?"

"Yes," says Suzana. "I mean marinara."

"OK," the concierge says. "No marinara."

Suzana decides to take a shower while she waits for the food. The water blasts out of the shower head. On Reservoir Road their water pressure, ironically, is weak. The water in the Best Western hurts it has so much force. She turns up the heat until she's being scoured. Washes her hair with the motel's shampoo and conditioner. Running the knots out of her long hair with her fingers. The two tiny bottles are empty after her shower. She dries herself with the white towels, the flat kind motels use and not the fluffy, luxurious ones they have in hotels. The motley array of towels on her line at home would be dry. She hung those before going to the Coultas home this morning. Jovan would have brought them in by now.

Her bare feet on the cool tiles. The wet footprints. One towel for her head and another for her body. Dries herself as she glances in the mirror. Feels as little for the naked image of herself in the mirror as she did for the woman being fucked in the room next door. A hotel would have a robe. That's another difference. One of those fluffy robes would be wonderful. She moves back to the main room and its bed. Places two pillows behind her as she waits. No view of the ocean out her window because the lights are switched on inside now and there's no illumination out there—no stars and no moon and no ships. The pitch-black glass. Her reflection again. An anonymous woman propped up against a bed head and an exposed brick wall.

A nurse, hand on Suzana's shoulder. That careful shake to awake the sick. Jovan is outside. Suzana tells the nurse she doesn't want to see him. The nurse comes back a little while later and gives her a glass of water. Helps her drink. Sits on the side of the bed and helps Suzana hold the glass. Holding the glass of water is almost impossible. She never thought she'd be this weak. Amazed that she can be so feeble. The nurse tells Suzana her husband is still waiting outside. Suzana recalls other times the nurse has given her this information.

Suzana is so enervated she is afraid to go back to sleep. It's as though sleep is heavy and it will fall onto her with the weight of a collapsing building. Had that been one of her dreams when she was asleep? A collapsing building. Dying in the crumbs of concrete. Her arms bandaged. Despite the painful changes of bandages the nurse has put her through, the white fabric soaking up dots of strawberry colour, reminding her of a handkerchief used to wipe red jam from a child's lips.

Too exhausted to say no again, she nods at the nurse this time and when Jovan walks into the hospital room, the room becomes a

room, the man in the doorway a man, and the suicide in the bed is a
suicide. It is Belgrade, this is Zemun Hospital, the same hospital she
was born in thirty-one years ago, everything real and concrete, yet
incomplete because she is still alive and there is this room, and this
man, Jovan Brakochevich, is waiting for her.

That Goliath doesn't move from the doorway and she has never
seen him cry before. She has never seen his face fall into such open
grief, arms useless by his sides, unable to lift and hide his face from
the nurses or doctors and other patients in the room. Helpless in the
doorway until she manages to raise a hand to him and when he takes
it she knows he has pulled her back into the world. For an instant she
feels nothing but fury. As if she's been tricked. His stupid fucking
tears, crying like a child.

Had there been a knock at the door? It registered somewhere
in her brain. A few minutes for the information to reach awareness.
Suzana gets out of bed and opens the door. The pizza is sitting on
the carpeted floor. The proud face of a chef kissing his fingers sten-
cilled into the top of the box. The hallway long and empty. She picks
up the warm box and takes it inside. The red standby light is not
on because she pulled the plug on the television before having her
shower.

The small motel room is quiet and perfectly bland. Not one
thing in it to draw her attention. She can barely eat a slice of pizza
before her eyes are closed. She manages to get beneath the sheets of
the bed. The flat pillow. That rough anonymous feel to the sheets.
Lovely. The vague whiff of hospital bleach. Ammonia. The word
drifts through her mind. A place like Patagonia. More asleep than
awake, she thinks, What a wonderful place that would be to go for
a holiday.

Ammonia.

JELKA SITS DOWN in an old wooden swivel seat beside Suzana. Jelka tells her she's never been to the State Library as she leans upwards from the chair to admire a green reading lamp.

"Why are we here?" Jelka asks, already bored with the vast reading room, vaulting above them, four stories high. Slumping into the backrest. Swivelling left and right. Head dropping back, lolling. The imperial dome above exciting little interest.

"That might be the dumbest question I've heard you ask," Suzana tells Jelka, feeling rigid and upright in comparison.

Jelka's eyes pop open. "You can't read anywhere else?" "Frankston library?" Suzana runs a palm across the page she was just reading, twice, as if to clean away dust. "A community centre for every degenerate in town. I can deal with the wafting aromas of sweat and piss. Don't get me wrong. It's the unconsidered, unconsulted books on those bleak metal shelves that make me choke."

"A Belgrade snob. That's what you are." Jelka says it approvingly. Leans over and gives Suzana a kiss on the cheek. She reaches over to the book Suzana was reading when Jelka arrived—closes it on Suzana's finger to see the cover. "Of course. You couldn't be entertained by anyone less than Tolstoy." Suzana doesn't remove her finger. She flips the book open again as though she intends to keep reading.

"I'm not a bimbo. I've read Tolstoy," says Jelka. "I can see you think that there's a personal connection there—between you and the Count—but Tolstoy is like the newspaper. Even if you haven't read him, you know the news."

"Have you read a book since high school?"

"Don't be a bitch." Jelka tilts the book in Suzana's hands to get a better look at it. "You're not supposed to mark the fucken books, Suzana! Talk about *high school*."

"It's only pencil . . ."

"And there's a librarian who has an official rubber and the duty to go through each page in the library. Is that what you think?"

Suzana shrugs and winces at the same time. "Alright. It's wrong. I did a bad thing."

Jelka snatches the book away from Suzana, reading from the marked page with the exasperated expression of a high-school teacher: "'My life stopped. I could breathe, eat, drink, sleep, and could not help breathing, eating, drinking, sleeping; but there was no life, because there were no desires whose satisfactions seemed reasonable to me. I could not even desire to know the truth, because I guessed of what it consisted. The truth was that life was an absurdity.' Even when you haven't read it you feel as if you *have* read it. That's what I mean about newspaper Tolstoy."

"You look *gorgeous* today, by the way." Suzana leans back in her chair. A smile on her face. Jelka glances at her friend and sees Suzana is both sarcastic and sincere.

"Makeup gives me time for meditation. It's the space I give myself to reflect." Jelka winks and casts a Marilyn Monroe smile.

"The Count was wrong." Suzana takes the book back and closes it. "Life is not absurd. I'm not sure what it is, but 'absurd' is the easy way out. And what a terrible cliché."

Jelka nods. Motes of dust drift around them and Jelka waves her hand before their faces, as if she were shooing away flies.

"Every now and again I have an hour where I look around and seem to understand," Jelka says. "I notice something beautiful without dismissing it as instantly irrelevant. It's worse afterwards because it makes me realise I live the rest of the time in some diminished state—barely thinking, barely feeling—as the Count says. Everything around me in shadow. And I blame Ante, who's a normal guy, working hard every day of his life. You've got to respect that kind of man. And you can't expect that he's going to light up your life like in the television matinee romance of the week."

Jelka has a few shopping bags arrayed around her, from expen-

sive boutiques in the city. She complains about living so far south
of the city all the time. It's because she isn't close enough to these
stores she so cherishes, also because she can't comfortably wear the
clothes where she lives without feeling foolish. Fashion, and the art
she means when using that word, doesn't belong in the part of Melbourne they live in. Jelka's wardrobes are full of clothes she wears on
the weekend or when she can get dressed to go shopping. There's a
half-hidden world she finds on the streets of Melbourne city; discreet
and delightful places where the air is perfumed by the many women
coming and going, and special lights make everything appear not
simply new but eternally reborn as in a fairytale where no one gets old
and nothing gets worn-out. There are wizard-made mirrors in which
you can find the spells that work for the lost princess in the mirror.

"This has been going on for a while—the way you're feeling.
And I'm not sure what I can say but I'm sure there's got to be a way
to move forward," Suzana says. A powder of concrete drifts through
the air. Jelka plucks a flake of paint from Suzana's hair.

"What's going on?" Jelka asks, glancing upwards with a palm
out, as though searching the skies and gauging the chance of rain.

"Renovations," Suzana says.

Jelka dusts off her arms. "Sometimes I feel incapable of one fresh
thought. And I realise that's gone on for days on end. Maybe longer.
That seems alright. Is it alright? I ask myself. I should want more
than this. This is what I was born for? Cleaning people's houses.
Gathering bits and pieces for my nest. Have my little birds so that
they can get big enough to fly away and do the same. And I'm alright
with that, yet every now and again I have a moment that feels like
an inspiration. I see a woman look up at the sky. I don't know why.
Nothing up there. No clouds. Not a bird. An empty sky. And then I
notice how white her eyes are. The lustre of the white, and how beautiful that is. That clear, perfect white she has in her eyes. And then
I'm looking out for it in other people's eyes. It takes days, I finally

catch it in another person. A particular luminous white with a hint of blue beneath it. I know it doesn't mean anything. And I wonder, has anyone noticed that particular bit of beauty."

Suzana says, "Maybe you should be a photographer. Or learn to paint. They have those classes."

"How fucking pathetic would that be? Imagine me doing that? *Fucken hell*." The last, Jelka says in English, with what she imagines to be an Aussie accent.

Raised heads around her make her lean closer to Suzana and ask again why they're meeting in the Victoria State Library reading room. Jelka had been whispering. She'd gradually forgotten the need for quiet and by the end of what she'd been saying had offended five or six studious readers and note-takers with her first English words. Two of them have already left for parts more tranquil.

"We should have met in a cute little city café," Suzana says. "Just another way I've been going wrong."

"Back home, you can talk in a café for hours," Jelka says. "Over here, a café lets you sit in one of their chairs as long as you're drinking coffee or nibbling biscotti. Even if they're not busy. I'd like to *talk* with you. And we can't really speak with all these stickybeaks around us." Another reader leaves their vicinity.

Jelka is a pretty woman. Naturally so when she was younger. Now it's an earned beauty. Her hair is attended to by South Yarra hairdressers. She drives over forty-five minutes each way to see them every few weeks for touch-ups that cost a fortune. Her face is managed by expensive makeup. Nails and jewellery and shoes and handbags skilfully coordinated. Her breasts are her pièce de résistance, almost always on display, especially when she comes to the city, Melbourne weather permitting. She got them a year ago and she's still paying them off.

"If it's important, we can go somewhere else. I've got some work I'm doing. I came here because this is the only library that has the particular book I needed to look at again. And I don't have the whole afternoon to spare. Why don't you tell me what you want to say? I'm listening."

Suzana leans forward. Attentive. There is no confidante for Jelka other than Suzana. Back in what was once Yugoslavia both of them would have had extended circles of friends. For all occasions and all modes of companionship. Here in Australia, where everyone is locked into their suburban backyards and the biannual BBQ, Suzana and Jelka have to assume all of the kinds of friendship they still need.

"So . . ." Jelka leans forward and touches Suzana's hand. Pulls back quickly. "So, okay. I know you said not to talk about it with anyone, but I told Ante about your plans to have a child, and he kind of went berserk. Why are they going to have children at their age when we should be having a child, and why haven't we already had one?"

Suzana asks, "This is what you wanted to talk about?" She turns back to her books but closes them and returns to her friend. "This is the conversation, is it? It boggles the mind that people can eviscerate as easily as communicate. And then we'll call it a pleasant *chat*." The last word in English.

"What? Why be so dramatic?"

"It's something we're thinking about. Me and my husband. It's not as if we can order a pizza. A baby doesn't just show up. It's not easy. None of it is that simple."

"I know it's not pizza. I'm talking about you and Jovan being together such a long time and then this sudden desire for a child. Is it that good old biological clock ticking away?" Jelka leans forward in her chair as well and they're close enough now to talk in whispers. "I never know what you're thinking. You always act as though no one could possibly understand your reasons, thoughts, and feelings. And God, you do make me feel like I'm a bimbo some days."

Suzana is sitting at the edge of her chair, looking at Jelka intently. "What can I say to you? This is what you want to talk about?"

Jelka says, "Yes. Because I'll tell you the truth. I got angry after we talked on the phone the other day and you told me what you and Jovan had decided. That's why I didn't call you a whole week. Then when I spoke to Ante and he got angry at me for exactly the same thing, I realised that I wasn't angry with you for wanting a child. Honestly, I wish you the best with that. It's because when I see Ante now, I think about how having a child guarantees another ten, fifteen, twenty years with this guy. Twenty, plus. Life. You have to plan for that long. *Life.* What would I be in twenty years after children? And there's no way. No way. That's what I'm thinking over and again in my head. *No way.* So it's kind of obvious, but it's the first time I've thought about it clearly. I've got to leave Ante. Don't I?" Then she halts, still leaning forward with her feet firmly on the ground, on the edge of the library seat, searching Suzana's eyes for an answer.

"You can't be serious? Asking me that question."

"I'm asking for your opinion. I know you've got one."

"No. I don't. I don't know Ante. I've never even met him. All I have is *your* opinion."

"I can see it in your eyes. You don't think I see it in there? What are you, some kind of genius? Walking around with a head full of thoughts no one is entitled to ever see because they'd never understand? Tell me what you think for God's sake!" Gradually their area in the library has emptied.

Suzana closes her teeth with a snapping sound and then opens them again. "I think you're a drama queen. I think you don't know how to be satisfied, let alone happy. I think in six months from now, you will have changed your mind, and will have decided that *of course* you'll have Ante's children. Because the resistance you feel isn't about him. It's about you and this perfect package you've got going on"—waving a hand at the Las Vegas show that was Jelka

Tomich—"beginning to bulge in the middle and those sculpted breasts beginning to leak. Pregnancy is simply too graphic for you. You prefer to contemplate the white of someone's eyes. And all these beautiful fabrics you surround yourself with, this mask you apply every pitiful morning just to walk around your house, the whole song and dance of this life you want to live, will end soon enough. Then it's down to the Frankston Target for Jelka. Then you'll be buying durable, stretchable, boring old cotton for those babies to throw up on. That is when you come down and rejoin the rest of us, my darling little princess." Suzana gives Jelka a stinging kiss on the cheek. Jelka is motionless. She's never been slapped with a kiss before.

Jelka leans back into her chair, blinking. She collects herself. Stands up and gathers her many bags of treasure. Leans over and kisses the air near Suzana's cheek. "Don't worry about us. Friends have to give each other a bit of honesty every so often. Sometimes it's sweet. Occasionally bitter." And then in her Aussie accent, "It's all good, mate."

Suzana knows she's offended her only friend, yet Suzana suspects that Jelka loves being talked about in this manner. Being the subject of serious contemplation thrills her. To be cast as someone worthy of consideration, even harshly, makes her feel real. What Jelka yearns for more than anything is some kind of proof of existence no one wants to give her. Instead, she's surrounded by a reality that tells her she's simply another woman, not remarkable in any way. No one sees she is the woman with the clear eyes gazing up into the empty blue sky, filled with her opening soul. The wondrous expansion of her unknown potential.

Suzana doesn't think she is all that different to Jelka in her own pretensions. Isn't the Victoria State Library her own special place, as the clothing, jewellery, perfume, makeup, shoe stores of Melbourne are for her best friend? All the ways she is deficient, remedied by the wizard-mirrors of books, making her feel she isn't utterly alone, getting older, diminishing, more and more useless every day of her life. And these words she is trying to put down to paper, one last effort to prove to a world that is happy to go its way, with or without her. With or without Serbia and her history, with or without anything and everything that is dear to her. Trying to prove that her life is valuable, her soul worth its weight in paper, if not gold; and that the people she comes from deserve to be known—because she isn't the one voice, the one woman. When ink is put to the page she is history and her children will speak again. If anything, Suzana thinks her own delusions are more foolish than Jelka's Las Vegas daydreams.

A few more flakes of paint on the table. There's also a mist of concrete so fine she'd think dust except for the taste in the back of her throat. Distant sounds of construction. The thump, thump of hammers. Bolts into walls. The metal clang of scaffolding going up. Thump, thump, thump. As sporadic as mortars. The real work was set to begin in the next week when the dome reading room will be closed, maybe for years. Suzana has seen signs giving notice that this room will not be open the next time she needs to use the State Library. There will be another place to read. She makes a pile of the books she was looking at before Jelka. One by Tolstoy. The rest are history books relating to the Ottoman Empire. She places her notebooks into her bag. Returns her special pens, black and blue, red and green, her array of pencils, into a leather case she has kept since her university days in Belgrade.

SHE WAKES UP coughing. Not sure when she wakes what the nightmare was about. Her ears are ringing. There had been a roar above her which had hurt it was so loud. Lungs full of concrete dust. Fighting for air. Surprised she can breathe easily now. Relieved it was a trick of sleep. *Just a dream.* What a wonderful thing—to be able to say that. Silence in the Best Western motel room. When she focuses on the sound of her breathing, the ringing in her ears doesn't seem so loud. She looks at the digital display on the bedside clock. 3:35. About four hours sleep. She counts each hour every morning. Time crawls along as she tries to find a little more unconsciousness. The ocean outside her window shoosh-shooshes along in the black water of her thoughts. She's too hot with the sheet and blanket and too cold with the sheet alone. Her arms and legs trickle with adrenaline. Suzana opens her eyes again. One of those clock radios with a phone. She picks up the receiver and dials. She counts the times it rings. How many before it cuts out? She loses track and puts the phone back in its cradle when the line goes dead. Jovan is a sound sleeper. He's not liable to wake even when there's a car alarm going off on the street outside their bedroom window let alone the polite trills of the phone in the kitchen. She considers calling him again. It's 3:45 in the morning. Suzana closes her eyes and a little while later finds an outgoing tide of sleep.

SUZANA CLOSES HER eyes below the water when she is far from the surface. Her back almost touches the bottom. Exhaling a few more bubbles, she feels her shoulder blades make contact—balances on those two points. There's a lovely interval here. A space between everything. Before and after. A dark smudge of now. As long as she can hold her breath. A minute. A minute and a half. Submerged, she is at ease and buoyant. Whole and complete. She becomes a perfect living balloon, with nothing to push or pierce her. It's hard to stay under until all her air has been released. It leaves her with a few more seconds.

She bought a swimming outfit for the occasion. The teenager at the counter said Suzana would look good in pink with all her black hair. Black and pink is classic, the girl assured her. Suzana tried on the navy-blue bikini and an olive one-piece and went for the bikini despite how pale grey her skin appeared in the mirror. The point was the feel of the water and a one-piece was too much fabric.

The girl told Suzana she looked good. A compliment she threw to anyone buying bathers. The teen saw the sceptical expression and said, "No, honestly, you have nice breasts. And a woman your age usually gets saggier and heavier by the year and you don't have a bit of fat on you." Suzana grimaced as she thanked the blunt girl. Yes, a woman my age. That particular qualifier.

Clinging to the teen's words as she walked from the counter to the change room and put on the navy-blue outfit so she could swim in the public pool. Even when she felt she was beyond puerile vanity, a stupid girl's comments could obliterate every other thought for minutes, then laughing at the idea of wearing the suggested pink bikini.

Suzana holds her breath down at the bottom of the Frankston pool. She turns and begins to swim. A breaststroke across the tiles. Passing random bits and pieces. A Band-Aid. A hair clip. Some yellow sand swirling beneath her strokes. No bathtub-white surfaces here. And then the arched spine and kicking for the surface. The graceful arc back. Almost impossible not to be *graceful* below water. Lungs screaming for oxygen and yet water burbles, a lazy stream across her ears, shoulders, and face, swallowing every possible noise she might make. Above water, she splutters, heaving in air, and thinking too much again.

She hasn't been in a public pool since her university days. Was that true? Not since Belgrade? It wasn't as if there were many pools in Sarajevo. Yes, there were trips to the ocean with Jovan and the children, but a pool takes her back to when she was a student desperately needing to depressurise. And Jovan can barely swim. If dropped into the middle of the ocean he might paddle around for about ten seconds before sinking to the bottom. No, it's not surprising that it has been such a long time.

Suzana swims a lazy freestyle to the end of the pool and places her elbows on the edge and rests her chin on her forearms and closes her eyes and thinks about the dream last night. That terrible feeling of lungs being filled with dust was worse than the thought of lungs flooded with water. Water took the edge away. Softened flesh and the mind, especially when hot. Suzana's legs dangle at the deep end.

Eyes closed, she becomes aware of the roar of the water through the grates in the side of the pool, of voices echoing in the huge room, calling to each other across water and from opposite ends of the twenty-five-metre pool. Mothers shout at their children. Boys laugh and yell and drop into the water, clenching their whole bodies into huge fists, to punch out big splashes. There's a sign on the wall prohibiting running, jumping, and these bombs.

Suzana opens her eyes. Seconds ago there had been a silent bubble around her head, where she hadn't noticed a sound. Thinking about Jovan and the children, Belgrade and Sarajevo. Then it pops and the world comes flooding in again.

A girl of about five has been playing and swimming with an orange swim-ring since Suzana got into the pool fifteen minutes ago. The girl pushes the inflated plastic circle down, over her thin hips, and steps out, back into the water, and sinks straight down.

A simple failure of logic in a child. Exhaling the air in her small lungs in a single line of bubbles. The only buoyancy left in her little body, gone. Suzana pushes away from the edge of the pool without urgency. She gets ahold of an arm. Not even waving in panic. As though the area on a five-year-old, between shoulder and elbow, is a handle. A perfect fit for Suzana's hand. She pulls the girl back to the surface and places her on the edge of the pool.

The girl walks away from her, crying and coughing. Suzana watches her until the girl's mother isn't distracted by older sons making trouble at the other end of the pool. The mother doesn't listen to the girl's blubbering. She folds the girl in a towel and takes her away to the change room.

The mother doesn't thank Suzana. Maybe she didn't notice. Also possible is that it's because of the marks on Suzana's wrists. The way Suzana has them folded on the edge of the pool hides most of the damage. Only the briefest glimpse was necessary.

The stuck glances, the double blinks, second takes, were common on the beaches of Noosa and Maroochydore. That thought flaring quickly in every set of eyes. Suicide. As if she was death. Failure and loss incarnate. The same primal response to extreme suffering buried in their own minds explaining the moment of horror, however brief.

Easier, of course, to always wear long-sleeve shirts, no matter the heat of Australian summers. Or the desire to swim free and loose-limbed in a pool of water. Rare for someone like the teenager to register the suicide scars and lean forward into the realisation and suggest pink to match black hair. Compliment breasts and figure.

The mother comes out of the change room with her girl, dragged along by the wrist, crying again. The mother yells at her two boys, tells them that it's time they went home. Suzana pushes away from the edge and slides down through the water again.

SUZANA HAS A mug full of pens and pencils set out on the small round table in her room at the Best Western—a bouquet of cut flowers with all their heads lopped off. Ink in green and red, blue and black. Prettier than a selection of roses, whether in the clichés of red, pink, yellow, white, or lavender.

Suzana hasn't used pen and paper for her compositions since she was a child. Now she enjoys the tactility of words applied to the page by hand. The way the ink rises on the paper, welts you can feel if you run your fingertips lightly across them. She isn't in a rush to meet deadlines as she has always been in the past. She orders herself one coffee too many and watches it cool in the cup. Feels it go cold looking at it.

Back in Belgrade she used a typewriter though other writers she knew had already made the move to computers. She persisted with this habit until Sarajevo. When she started working at the university her typewriter became a memento and she did all her work on a computer, the same as everyone else. She got the most up-to-date computer she could find and there was no going back. Forgot entirely what she'd found so charming about her typewriter. Writing more than ever. All of it was academic and meant nothing at all to her. No, that wasn't true. Everything she wrote meant a great deal to her mind, sometimes her heart. Never her soul. That was what the fiction was for and she'd written none since that typewriter.

She smokes cigarettes. It's been a while. Her taste for tobacco isn't what it used to be yet the weight of smoke in her lungs is pleasant. She watches her exhalations shift with the morning light until it changes into afternoon light. Blows out her cigarette smoke like she's evaporating and only her bones remain. She tamps the bottom of another cigarette on a hardcover book from the local library. A history of the Ottoman Empire that told her nothing she didn't already know. Poorly written to boot. Research is easy. This is what she does so well and it gives her the feeling she's working. Meanwhile the actual work has not actually moved. There's no getting away from the feeling that her novel is dying. A death which does not feel as abstract as her "soul."

Suzana sits at her small round table, paper before her, a pen in her hand. Not writing a word as she looks at the blank void of the paper the whole day. Eventually she finds her retired Janissary again, riding from Istanbul to Belgrade, and follows him into his story as he rides into a deep forest and becomes sick. So ill that he has to find a place to stop and camp while he waits for his fever to pass. Except that the fever doesn't pass. He gets worse.

She intends to have him suffering, on the threshold of death for days. There is something about being sick to the point of helplessness in a deep forest that interests her. Somehow she has to work out a way for him to stay alive. Coming back from the brink isn't easy. So he'll have to meet someone. Perhaps a witch.

Suzana has an idea of what real witches may have been in those days. Operating in remote areas as doctors and herbalists some of the time, and as priestesses and visionaries beyond the scope of the prevailing religions. And, yes, they were also needed to summon rivers full of venomous snakes, a black storm of destruction, malformed children, etc. People would pay for spells yet there was never a date on them, and life was long enough for some evil to eventually befall the victim of a curse.

Right now, Suzana is only interested in who her Janissary is. She wants to explore his life through the febrile disordering of his warrior mind and veteran body as he struggles to keep breathing despite lobar pneumonia. The histories of the wars he's fought for the Ottomans. Was he perhaps involved in the battle for Vienna, in 1683? She might describe the greatest cavalry charge in the history of warfare if she chose that date as her marker. There are other dates with different narrative possibilities.

For now, she allows her imagination to open to his dreams and visions, as he lies dying amongst moss-covered stones. In the half-formed mouth of a cave in the side of a hill by a stream, his rifle ready to shoot the forest animals that will come to drink. He has noted the various marks their feet have made by the water. She stops and wonders if she can throw in a little information about how the Janissaries were the first soldiers in history to use rifles as standard weaponry. Also the first to use grenades. She lets that go and writes what the story needs.

The Janissary has a memory of a well from his childhood in a village he doesn't know the name of anymore. He is at the bottom of the well. Face tilted all the way back, searching upwards, until his neck hurts so much he is forced to drop his head. He recalls watching the clouds move above in the circle of blue. The time it takes for one cloud, shaped like a bear, to slide from one edge of the circle above to the other. Another cloud in the shape of a turtle, reminding him of the race his mother told him about. In this one, not only a turtle and hare, there's a bear to devour them both.

This last part, from a dream the Janissary is having, remembering and dreaming in fluid transitions of fever. The black bear, no longer the soft white cloud shape, catching the slow turtle and ripping apart his shell, as easily as peeling an orange, and afterwards, catching the hare, sleeping by the side of the road—thinking he has all the time in the world because he's racing a turtle, and a bear, who's not much quicker. The bear tears off the hare's limbs and finds that the white fur comes off too easily, that it's a costume, within which, a little boy has been hiding.

The Janissary wakes. Horrified by the dream, yet settling himself quickly. A man used to waking from nightmares of one kind or another. He has opened his eyes. When he focuses, he sees a red deer is drinking from the stream below his stone alcove. His rifle is set on a prop of boulders and a thick branch. He lifts the shoulder stock and takes aim, stops his breath so there's no movement in his body, doesn't blink for a few seconds, fires and drops the deer with a bullet to the centre of his chest. Not the head, protected as it is by a nimbus of bone.

The Janissary is too weak to get up. He closes his eyes again and remembers more details about being forced to stay down at the bottom of a dry well for days. At first, it's a kind of brutal punishment and it seems as though it might be another of Aesop's fables. He remembers more. His parents lowering food down on a rope in the well bucket. Their desperate mouths whispering of patience and love. Their voices rain on him, drops of honey as he stands amongst the frogs slapping around his feet. His father's hoarse voice and his mother's cold tears.

The Ottomans discover the boy. Of course they do. It's impossible to keep a secret like little Mileta Alimpich. The brightest and fittest of that village he was born in, somewhere near the two rivers that cross through the heart of Belgrade. That's a clearer memory for the Janissary. Fishing with friends, boys bigger than him, one of them is an older brother, at that concourse and wondering where the two great rivers came from and where they are going. The Ottomans take Mileta for their elite corps, the Janissary, as everyone in the village was sure they would. This had been going on for hundreds of years—the blood tax of the *devshirme* system.

After six hours of work Suzana has over thirty pages of her handwriting. The second chapter. A working title for the manuscript: *Kalimegdan*. The four colours of ink interweave across the pages. Black for the story itself. Blue for fragments of narrative in the future of the book. Green for notes. Red for corrections. All of these new pages in Serbian. She will translate them into English for her second draft. The important thing is to be absolutely free first time through the novel. She's happy to leave it for today, with the Janissary remembering Mileta Alimpich. The name he was given by parents that hid him at the bottom of a well.

Suzana knows what she will write tomorrow: The Witch finds Murad Selim, shivering and insensible in his stone alcove. The sound of his rifle has caught her attention. She is grateful for the red deer and returns with a cart to haul away the animal carcass. She has little concern for the Janissary and will leave him to die. The deer is not quite dead however, and in a final pulse of life, lifts its head and scratches the Witch across her face with its antlers. Drawing lines of blood. Almost taking out her eye. She hears laughter from the alcove. She walks over to examine the recumbent figure, removing a knife from her robes. Takes the top of his head in a hand, a savage grip of hair, and exposes his neck. She is ready to slaughter him as though he were a sheep. He says, *Hvala*. Eyes open. Eyes close.

The Witch is still bleeding. She sits back to wipe her face. Glances back at the red deer and then the half-dead man. She will drag the Janissary back to her cottage on her cart and coax him back to life. When she asks him for his name, the Janissary will say he doesn't know. Suzana is not sure which name she will use for her Janissary. Perhaps Murad to begin with, and later she will call him Mileta, as he takes part in the First Serbian Uprising in 1804. Suzana is set on the new date as she puts her notebooks into a leather folder and zips it shut. She gathers her many pens and places them back into the mug in the middle of the round table.

She picks up the phone and orders food from a local café that delivers. Not another coffee because her hands are already shaking. Her eyes go out of focus and everything she sees is a blur. It might have been as long as a day since she ate a proper meal. She's not sure. It's morning now. The night has passed. Suzana loses herself in the haze of her starved body and her exhausted brain. All she can do is wait by her motel room door for someone to bring her something to eat.

THERE'S MUSIC BEHIND the door. She notices it when she steps inside the house. She doesn't move. For an instant she thinks perhaps he's tricked her, deliberately not parking the panel van in the front, so she'd walk inside thinking he was not home. If Jovan walks down the hall she will turn and leave. For good this time. She stands by the open front door, waiting for him. Listening to classical piano with a bewildered expression on her face. She calls out his name. Jovan doesn't answer.

A radio announcer tells her the song was by Debussy, and that a previous piece was by Ravel. He begins to talk about Impressionism.

She follows his voice to the lounge, perplexed because they don't own a radio and music has never played in their Reservoir Road home.

In the lounge there's a new stereo system where the television had been before Jovan picked it up and threw it into the backyard. Her notebooks and folders are stacked on the coffee table in a neat pile. She wonders if Jovan has been reading her novel.

The announcer signs off for the morning and a brief piece of music signals a transition to the midday news. Various details are rattled off about world events, Y2K preparations dominant. Four hundred billion U.S. dollars will be spent globally by governments and companies before the end of the year for something as simple as clocks ticking over from 1999 to 2000. Following with the state of the stock markets of Europe, America, and Australia, the sports and the weather. Twenty-six degrees today. Fine and clear. A perfect Melbourne day in autumn.

Suzana sits on the couch. She's wondering if Jovan has made any notes while reading her manuscript. Giving each other feedback on their writing was as common as a conversation about how the children behaved with a new babysitter or a bit of annoying university gossip. Jovan's comments on her work were often brilliant. A difficult essay, that wasn't going anywhere, might come alive with a particular insight, and she would race it all the way to the finish line.

Suzana pages through her notebooks. She's disappointed to see no hint of marginalia, no phrases underlined, no scratch of ink to indicate that he had indeed read what she'd written. The first chapter was in English, so perhaps it wasn't as easy for Jovan. Or more likely, it was this separation. How could he possibly comment on her novel when she'd walked out of the house one evening? Without leaving as much as a note. And then an unbroken silence for a week.

That time of words and sentences, of ideas and philosophies, inspiration and passion, driving each other forward and upwards, to be better and clearer, more eloquent, more alive, more beautiful—

had felt for a moment connected to her. Slumping back into the sag of the couch, there's the cold, divorced reality between her and that past. No, of course, he had not read these drafts and notes. That'd be as difficult to imagine as coming home to find new pages of Jovan's poetry.

A news segment follows the general update on the radio. "'The noise starts around half an hour before the bombs fall as the animals in Belgrade zoo pick up the sound of approaching planes and missiles,' director Vuk Bojovich said." The reporter shifts from the intro directly to a pre-recorded interview, a segue to a heavy Balkan accent, "It's one of the strangest and most disturbing concerts you can hear anywhere. It builds up in intensity as the planes approach—only they can hear them, we can't—and when the bombs start falling it's like a choir of the insane. Peacocks screaming, wolves howling, chimpanzees rattling their cages."

The radio reporter says that the zoo has been particularly hard hit by NATO's air strikes campaign aimed at forcing Belgrade to accept an autonomy deal for Kosovo, particularly when the alliance attacked Belgrade's power system and water supply.

"'I had one thousand eggs of rare and endangered species incubating, some of them ready to hatch in a couple of days. They were all ruined. That's one thousand lives lost.' Meat in the zoo's freezer defrosted and has gone off, making it suitable only to scavengers like hyenas and vultures. Belgrade people donated meat out of their home freezers when the power went down, but most of that wasn't even fit for animals. The lack of water has meant that some animals, particularly the hippos, are literally swimming in their own excrement.

"'We had to give dirty drinking water to a lot of delicate animals. We won't know the effects of that for two or three months,' Bojovich said.

"'While the zoo overlooks the confluence of two major rivers, the Danube and the Sava, both are heavily polluted by chemical and industrial waste. The nightly air strikes, with their accompaniment of anti-aircraft fire lighting up the sky, has had other, possibly longer-lasting effects on many of the animals,' the director said. 'Many of them have aborted their young in the latter stages of pregnancy. Birds have abandoned their nests, leaving eggs to grow cold. Even a snake aborted some forty foetuses, apparently reacting to the heavy vibration shaking the ground as missiles hit targets nearby. The worst night the zoo can remember was when NATO hit an army headquarters six hundred metres away with a huge detonation.

"'The next day we found that some animals had killed their young,' the director said. 'A female tiger killed two of her three-day-old cubs, and the other two were so badly injured we couldn't save them. She had been a terrific mother until then, raising several litters without any problems. I can't say whether it was the detonation or the awful smell that accompanied the bombing. I personally think it was the detonation,' he added.

"On the same night, an eagle owl killed all of its five young, and ate the smallest of them. 'It wasn't because she was hungry. I can only think it was fear.' The most disturbing case is the huge Bengal tiger, who chews his own legs. The zoo has tried to stop him but every time they put a bandage on, the tiger rips it off. The ends of his legs are a hideous red, the flesh exposed.

"The grimmest spinoff of the bombing is the sight of armed guards patrolling the zoo. 'They're not here to keep people from harming or stealing the animals,' Bojovich said. 'Their job is to shoot the animals if the zoo gets bombed and some of them try to break out.' The zoo's animals remain trapped in an increasingly desperate world of sonic booms, air raid sirens, and dwindling hope."

Suzana turns off the radio. Walks to the kitchen and looks out the window into the backyard. Her uncle Mirko gave them the television out there on the grass when they found their first place in Australia five years ago. Their washing is on the Hills Hoist. Some of it on the dry, patchy grass and dirt below. The same washing she hung a week ago. The rosellas are gone. Jovan probably isn't feeding them anymore and they've moved off to Jubilee Park again.

She read about the zoo in the newspaper yesterday. Hearing the voices on the radio struck harder. Suzana had televised images of Belgrade being bombed in her mind any time she closed her eyes. Always from a distance. So far away, even Suzana couldn't recognise the city. A nondescript collection of lights on the darkened horizon. Enough though to have seen the missiles blazing across the black skies. That was what the telecasts were really about—the display of godlike power of Zeus lightning bolts. At a press conference, a uniformed man with the countenance of a war god, after talking at length about his surgical precision and the supreme efforts made to limit civilian casualties, states that he has at his disposal "enough bombs to turn Belgrade into crumbs."

Suzana takes the three steps down into the backyard. She places the hanging clothes into the laundry basket. She picks up two towels, a shirt, singlet, socks, and Jovan's overalls, that were on the ground. Shakes them off. Drapes them over her shoulder. Walks into the house again and puts the towels and clothes in to wash. She spoons detergent in and turns on the machine. She goes outside to collect the washing basket with the clean washing that had remained on the line. Her tea mug is sitting by the steps. It's filled with rainwater now. Must have rained in the last week. She didn't remember a downpour. Always hard to remember rain on a day as blue and wide open as today. Fine and clear. A perfect Melbourne day in autumn. Lightning flashes in an evening sky every time she closes her eyes.

The security door slams behind her. The sound of the washing machine stops as it pauses to soak. The quiet of the house. What a lovely thing it had been when ice covered the windows and snow piled on the window sills outside, a white curtain rose up the glass, muffling everything within, making the silence soft. It wouldn't last long, so when it was found, she would fold herself within it for as long as she could. Until the inevitable noise of children waking or returning, laughing or falling. She walks to the lounge and turns the radio back on. No doubt in her mind why Jovan bought the stereo system. She sits on the couch and hears the big dog from next door half bark, half cough—barking to himself as some people talk to themselves.

The washing machine begins again. The cycle will take fifty minutes. And then she can hang the wet clothes and even if it will already be almost two o'clock in the afternoon by then, there's a chance everything will be dry before late evening. She never leaves the washing out overnight. She could feel the groove of habit just thinking about taking out the washing and hanging each bit of their clothing. The deep trench through her time of that mundane practicality where it was easier to keep thinking only about the very next peg. The very next shirt. The handkerchiefs—there were six of them in this wash. Each one hung by two pegs and each peg had no future and each peg had no past. The simplest mechanism. Pure function. The trench of habit she had made going out there over the years, every day, sometimes many times, to feel if the clothes were still damp, fabric between forefinger and thumb, a trench so deep sometimes she couldn't see anything else at all. Shaking her head, thinking, trench warfare in the nuclear age. Nowhere to hide. Never again. That was clear. As bright and obvious as an explosion.

When the washing machine finishes its cycle she barely notices the click. She is absorbed by a book that Jovan has been reading. *Der Zauberberg* by Thomas Mann. Jovan's German is much better than hers so she can't comfortably read the text. She's more interested in Jovan's marginalia. Some of it in German, mostly in Serbian. His best foreign language is Russian, and a book by Dostoyevsky or Chekhov would have comments in the language of the book. It could almost make her laugh to think how useless all his languages were to him here in Australia.

Reading his marginalia was initially of little interest. She'd been reminded of it because of the absence from her own manuscript. Perhaps he'd read her pages, searching for clues to her disappearance. She was doing the same, each of the comments revealing that the man she knew from Sarajevo University hasn't simply vanished.

Something Jovan doesn't know is that she knew him before they ever met. He published something in a Belgrade newspaper. No title for the poem and only the name below, *Brakočević*, as though they'd forgotten his first name, didn't think he or they needed to worry about it. When she met him years later she thought he was nice enough. Not bad looking either. Too tall, and he moved around oafishly when he wasn't playing basketball. He acquired grace only on a basketball court. He was intelligent enough. Not brilliant as a lecturer. Not a Vladimir Mitrovich. Adequate in most other ways as well. Passable.

For years, she used that word in her mind—passable. It took her such a long time to realise she loved him. It was when he was dying from that UN poison that she discovered he was no longer "passable." Ana and Dejan had already been carried away in canvas. Suzana knew there was one response to the death of both her children. There were weapons everywhere and so many people had already used them on themselves. Suicides in Bosnia were a dime a dozen. So it was an easy decision and it calmed her as she took the last few steps towards it. All her grief subsided into a deep ocean of death. She was already below the waterline, holding her breath for another few seconds. Watched each bubble escape her with a strange kind of pleasure. Suffering and sorrow can be sweet in those final moments before death burbles down into the stomach and then the lungs. She looked at everyone as if they were already dead as well. She saw trails of bubbles leaving their noses. She imagined flesh getting bloated and separating from bones. She saw their faces dissolve. Every one of their words nothing but underwater murmurs. Her own death was a cherished event. As though it was a birthday for a child. Every morning, getting closer, and she held off because there was pleasure in the expectation, of the special day, coming soon, of unwrapping a wonderful present, when she finally decided on a way to peel off her skin.

Then a nurse called Dragana Mihailovich came and told her Gospodin *Brakochevich* was dying. Using his surname like he might be unfamiliar to Suzana. Gospodin Brakochevich will be dead before dinnertime. *Dinnertime,* a word used when speaking to children.

"Jovan *Brakochevich* has been dying for a few days already. He seems to be taking his time," said Suzana.

Dragana Mihailovich had no judgment in her eyes. She sat beside Suzana on the metal cot, so close to the ground, they were practically sitting on their heels.

"Death is a small part of life." The nurse said it as though it was a common bit of lore she'd learned from whichever village she was raised in. Even so, it made Suzana turn her head. Dragana had two gold teeth in her mouth. A peasant fashion. Suzana looked at those gold teeth and felt revulsion for the old crone.

Dragana said, "Gospodja Brakochevich. Please come and help your husband die. He should already have passed days ago. Maybe he needs to say goodbye."

Suzana walked to the tent with that word in her mind again. Passable. An adequate husband. He was simply not Vladimir Mitrovich, who was filled with such genius and glory, malevolence and destruction. Mixtures of life and death that would infuse Suzana's soul for the rest of her life. Jovan was steadfast and a moderately talented poet, who would never stir a revolution in the blood of anyone.

Suzana sat beside his cot and held his hand, deciding she could be dutiful for at least a few hours. Jovan Brakochevich didn't die by *dinnertime.* He suffered through wracking fevers that wrung agonised moans from his chest. Made him whimper when unconscious. His grip on Suzana's hand went from a crush to something that reminded her of Dejan's distracted handholding when they walked through the supermarket.

They moved through the night in this way and by morning she saw Ana's face in Jovan. She heard both her children in those whimpering noises of suffering and she found that the closer they got to his end, the looser that grip was, and then there was nothing but her hold on him. She found that both her hands were wrapped around that massive bundle of bones and fingernails, and that she was praying into that fist, to a God she had never believed in, for Jovan Brakochevich not to die.

She remembered that first poem and she began chanting it into her husband's ear. Whispering it again and again. Praying to whatever remained of the soul within the poisoned body to keep listening and to stay. To not be *passable*.

She never kept the newspaper that poem was published in before she met Jovan, and he'd published so many by then, and there were so many to come afterwards as well. Many better poems. More significant or ambitious. She doesn't remember that first poem, as such. She *sees* it. Poorly printed, with ink that had bled, blurred slightly, with uneven type, on cheap newspaper stock.

White   Cloud
Over
Blue   Water

———

Red   Sky
Weeping
Black   Ocean

Brakočević

SEVEN

THE PHONE IS RINGING. HE STUMBLES through his home with extended palms brushing the walls to guide him along the hallway and to the kitchen telephone. When it stops ringing he's standing in the kitchen rubbing his eyes and blinking. No idea what the time is, yet a middle of the night call is an emergency and it can only mean something has happened to Suzana. Is there another possibility? Is there anyone else in his world but Suzana? Jovan takes the two steps to the telephone. He picks it up and puts it to his ear. Hears the dial tone. Places it back on its cradle and sits down at the kitchen table. Perhaps he should go back to bed now.

How long had it been ringing before it woke him up? Had it been a long emergency call that finally gave up after minutes of ringing? Will they call back again? Outside the kitchen windows is nothing—not a glimmer from a streetlight. Turning on the kitchen fluorescent is an intolerable idea. The double tubes in the ceiling are so bright they remind him of the hospital. An examination room. Jovan sits on a chair at the table, in the darkness, and waits for the phone to ring again. The dim red glow of the oven display tells him it's 3:45 a.m.

SURROUNDED BY THE smell of paint, turpentine, and methylated spirits, a mixture of other chemicals, old and new. Breathing hard. Both of them. Tammie's forehead is against the carpeted cabin floor in the back of Jovan's panel van. She's chuckling as she shudders. Each impact of bodies jolts through the sound of deep laughter, burbling up from her lungs. That noise registers every thump, rising and lowering, shifting from giggle to murmur and back again. As she approaches her climax the heat within her rises and it brings Jovan to orgasm as well. The laughter goes on a little longer. Tammie stretches out her arms as she pushes back against Jovan, extending every throb of pleasure for as long as it will last.

"What's this?" Jovan asks.

The lights from passing cars outside move across her body in diffused beams. A truck roared by a second ago with a larger array of lights and the van was illuminated as though it was the flash for a picture being taken. When she doesn't respond to the question, and her annoying murmuring goes on, he says more forcefully, "I *ask*, what is this."

"Oh, *sweetie*, you're distressed," she says. Mocking or playful, even she's not sure which.

"What the fuck this thing?" he asks. A slap and push into her back. She falls to her side.

"Take it easy, Joe." She reaches her arm out for her shirt. "Seriously. Calm down."

"Why put this on you back?" He drops down to his arse to pull up his jeans.

"It's a fucking tattoo, Joe. They don't have tattoos in your part of the world?"

"But why his words?"

"And don't push me. I won't be shoved aside with those bear claws. Unless I ask for your hands to push and shove. There's a fucking difference you should be very clear about in your bear head by now."

She shoots her arms through the sleeves of her shirt. There's some paper towelling on a roll Jovan would normally use to clean oil or paint solvent from his hands.

"I ask about this. The Trojan Flea?"

She makes a bundle and places it below her to catch his semen. She finds a place to sit by shoving a roller brush on a long handle out of the way, leans back against the side of the van, pushes the hair away from her sweat-sticky face—has three goes at plucking out a strand in her mouth.

"Why put Dr. Graffito's words into your body?"

"Why not? What am I supposed to get tattooed? A butterfly or a unicorn? The Chinese symbol for my star sign?" Tammie pulls the front of her shirt together and buttons up. "Maybe I'm supposed to get your name. Jovan. How'd that be? Maybe you'd like that better. J O V A N. And what about getting it done in Serbian letters? Cyrillic is what you call that jumble of Greek and Russian, isn't it?"

She chucks away the wad of paper towelling and finds her knickers and skirt. She screws her stockings into a ball and throws them at her handbag by the back doors of the van. Not wanting to move towards Jovan. He doesn't talk again. Buttons up his jeans. Opens one of the doors of the van and gets out. He closes it behind him quietly, as though she might want to sleep there for the evening.

She enjoys the smell of the paint, turpentine, and methylated spirits for now. The cars shoosh by, less and less regularly. The after-work rush of traffic is petering out. Soon she'll have to go to her home in Brighton. It would be lit up from every room, glowing white light out into the cypress trees surrounding their property. For Graham and the guests he has invited over for dinner tonight. That are already there now, eating the meal that she'd organised for his colleagues and their accessory wives. Drinking the wine that she'd selected. The music of her choice playing in the background, an appropriate backdrop to the sound of their refined conversations. The modulated light delicately falling across their cultivated faces. Their mouths working through the sections of flesh cut from animal bones for them and then arranged on their plates. Their teeth cleaned off by a swipe of a greasy tongue behind their clean lips and a fold of crisp linen from the serviettes she'd also provided for them. She'd sit and perhaps she would feel a trickle of Jovan, still leaving her at the dinner table. Tammie is sure she'll make it home for dessert.

JOVAN STOPS AT a 7-Eleven and buys two hot dogs, orange juice, and milk. He drops the bag onto his passenger side seat, remembering he needs petrol. It's all reversed. He should have already bought petrol and then the food. And yet he doesn't want petrol on his hands before he eats and he must eat soon. The toilet within the build-ing, so grimy, his hands would be more dirty coming out. He hasn't washed his hands since Tammie either. He walks around his van, looking at his watch and then looking at it again three times before he registers the time. 8:40 p.m. The cleaning products he has in the van are good for oil and paint; he needs soap and water to eat food. Ten minutes from home. He hasn't been shopping. Feeling light-headed. Disorientated. Wondering what he should be doing. Simple little choices are sometimes the hardest to make. The order things need to be done in, is important, otherwise, it all goes topsy-turvy. Food will help. Why not eat from the package? It'll help him settle. Time to get home. Actually, it doesn't matter what time he gets home. He glances at his watch again and gets back into the van. He eats one of the revolting hot dogs while a man drives into the fuelling bay next to Jovan. The man fills up. When Jovan is finished eating he starts his van and looks at the gauge rise and waver on empty. Enough to get home and back here tomorrow morning. He's on the verge. Shouldn't be driving with the black crow in his head.

He drives out onto the road abruptly, into a gap—not judging the speed of the traffic. Gets beeped by two cars. He sees the words printed into her flesh, red with the abuse of the needle that had injected the black ink beneath the surface of her skin. As though Dr. Graffito has vandalised a living human body this time. The scalpel that cut the word **INSPIRATION** into a dead woman's chest. The words in Tammie's back: **The Trojan Flea**. A black-ink skull surrounded by roses. It had looked pretty at first glance. In the small of her back. Between those delightful dimples above her buttocks. The flowers radiating out around the skull, a red-ink nimbus, the words within the head forming the eye sockets, nose hole, and teeth. Jovan didn't realise that they were words in the skull of this pretty little image until he was spent and catching his breath. A truck roared by and the light flared through the small translucent windows in his van. The skull materialised into the message. Graffito could not have managed it better. The thought hits him hard, even now, driving down the Nepean Highway to home. Another message from Graffito—cut into the body of a living woman. For Jovan. As intimate as a kiss on his face from poisonous ink-black lips.

HE KILLS THE engine. There's a light on in his house. He might have left it on. It could be Suzana. Sibelius is playing. Jovan likes the radio on, even when he's not home. He turns it off only before sleep. So, there's no doubt about the radio. Is she in the kitchen? He walks down the hallway, fingers tracing along the wall. The light is coming from the kitchen. No noise. No sound of movement. He stands in the hallway. There is the smell of food, that particularly astringent, sharply pleasant smell of *sarma*. His stomach is filled with junk. That smell still has the power to reach into him and reveal an abyss of hunger.

When he lies down in bed, he's waiting. He's lying at the water-line of an ocean, the tide about to change. The waves will start rolling in and there will be white foaming hurt. Her nightdress is hanging on the cupboard doorhandle. The hairbrush from the bed-side table, long black hair bound within the bristles, is gone. It was there this morning when he woke. Her glass of water is ready for her on the bedside table and the sleeping pills she needs every night. The bottle of sleeping pills is gone. Her slippers are on the floor. A couple of her notebooks have vanished from the lounge yet all of her reading books are where they were before she left a week ago. A body impression in the bed, head in the pillow. Jovan spreads out his arms and legs across the bed and closes his eyes as though it's a large expanse of sun-warm sand. He feels nothing but relief falling away into sleep.

THE FIRST FEW nights in the Cotton Tree Holiday Park produced little change. Both of them felt so exhausted they slept far too long in the evenings and felt drowsy during the days. They walked along the water. Saw pelicans with immense throat pouches and found no way to comment. Ate mango every breakfast and went to a restaurant that served Thai food each evening. No dinner banter. Wordless meals. Afterwards they talked about the lovely weather, as though they were strangers with little in common. They wandered around like people that didn't know the first thing about taking a holiday. It was almost out of boredom, not knowing what else to do, that they went to bed, removed their clothes and waited to see what would happen. Three years had passed since Sarajevo and the last time they'd been intimate.

Jovan showered afterwards. The feeling of euphoria hadn't lasted long. The illusion that they would be well again and they might find happiness wasn't something he could believe even at the height of the delusion—Suzana's head on his chest, feeling her drift away in sleep so deep it wheezed in the back of her throat. The trust and safety of him there in that Cotton Tree holiday shack. At home with him again. She need not worry. She could drift away.

Showering and knowing as he washed off the sweat of the day and the stickiness in his pubic hair, that nevertheless, this was the end of the line, even if it was different to how they'd imagined driving up to Queensland. They would break up after the holiday. It was clear to them both. There was no point in suffering together when the suffering was worse because they were together. One last effort to break loose and see things clearly and then they could walk away clean. They'd done everything they could. There were some things people weren't meant to recover from. There were losses you simply couldn't let yourself overcome, out of basic decency.

The water roaring around him in the shower was loud enough to obliterate the sound of weeping so he let himself go. It got away from him and he lost himself to it until he was barely able to stand and minutes or hours had passed. Suzana came in from the bedroom. She entered the shower wearing her nightdress.

Naked and crying, Jovan pressed his forehead to the shower wall, away from her, and found the blunt edge of a tile and forced it to split the thin skin above his left eye. He would have searched for more blood to hide his shame, if Suzana hadn't forced herself below his face and pushed him back, the watery blood spreading, getting into her eyes and mouth.

He thought he was a good man. He thought he was right. He didn't want the devil to win, yet the devil always gets in and takes what he wants. Where was the safety he should have given Suzana? Where was the protection? The simple foresight of a caveman would have been enough. He should have taken them away from death. It should have been easy to run. He could have taken them to safety. He didn't protect his daughter. He didn't protect his son. And now what can Ana and Dejan mean? Did he let them go so they could be dragged down to hell as well?

Utterly useless. He'd proved that. The most basic task given to him by God, the simplest function in this world, the only thing that mattered to his heart, mind, and soul, was the preservation of family. He should be washed down as well. If he wasn't a coward he would have already found a way to slide down to the devil.

The water roared around them and he thought she would never speak to him again. That they would hold each other and she would simply walk away and that'd be the end of everything. She whispered words he couldn't make out into his ear, long senseless fragments of words without pauses to separate their syllables, and continued to tell him this endless story filled with nothing he could understand until he picked her up and carried her back to that Cotton Tree bed.

JOVAN HAS AN early start the next morning. He gets the van going and then places a brick on the accelerator so the engine won't stall while it warms up.

There is a bag of seed in the garage. He takes a cupful and walks to the back fence and drops some down in the flat dry grass for the birds. One of the planks of unpainted wood is coming loose. The nail has leaked rust in a brief streak. He pushes the plank back into position and uses his callused thumb to press the nail back into the wood.

The rosellas are already dropping around Jovan's boots to get at the seed. Might not be much for them to eat around here. He's not sure how they survive. Rosellas don't seem the most resilient type of bird. Neither scavenger nor predator. They don't peck straight at the seed as seagulls or pigeons. They don't threaten each other. They take the time to pick a seed up in a foot and lift it to their beaks, eating at leisure.

He gets into his van and pumps the engine in the predawn darkness. He notices a scrunched up ball of paper on the floor. He leans over and picks it up. It's the drawing by the girl he gave a lift to the other day. A picture of himself at the wheel of this car. Graffito emptied out the glove box when he placed his Bomb message, but mustn't have noticed this bit of rubbish.

Jovan is more used to seeing the slice of time that a photograph offers, and usually all he sees in a photo is how much older he's looking these days. With a portrait or a drawing, there's a particular perspective, an aesthetic. He sees the artist's impressions rather than some scientifically objective document. There's the pain from his swollen jaw in what Leni noticed that day though that doesn't seem significant to her. She's sketched him looking out into the oncoming traffic. Cars shooting by in blurred lines past his face and shoulders. Vehicles by the borders of the paper are colliding but appear to have little more impact than that of rain on a windshield. The man in the sketch has a kind of patient resilience which he wishes he actually did possess. The man in Leni's vision rides through crashes like a surfer breaking through foam to get out beyond the waves. *Romance of the Crash*, written below his image. He can almost imagine that place beyond the waves.

Jovan reverses the van down the driveway. It dies and he lets it coast out onto the street. The gauge tells him he's out of fuel.

JOVAN GETS TO the hospital late. Even so, it's early enough in the day that he can get through a few essential duties quickly before anyone is inconvenienced. He rushes around from one thing to the other and then he pushes a cleaning cart towards the men's and women's by the main entrance. The most frequented toilets in the hospital. A very rudimentary clean today should be enough. A quick look to make sure they're all flushed and nothing atrocious in the bowls and that there's toilet paper for the day. Perhaps a quick wipe of the benches. There should be enough of the pink liquid soap in the dispensers.

The fluorescent lights flicker into life. On the floor are black-lined stencil markings of dead bodies. Police drawings marking the outlines so that the place of the murder victim is displayed for future reference. Not one body on the floor—ten, twenty, maybe thirty, were overlapping each other. Different-sized bodies, implying different ages and sexes. One of a baby, has a word scrawled into its body. **Obliteration.** In another stencil of a pregnant woman, over the bump, the word **Oblivion.** Just those two words in the massacre of bodies that is depicted on the hospital floor.

Jovan steps outside and lets the bathroom door shut. On the other side of the door, perhaps the title of this work, **Ethical Cleansing.** He fumbles with his keys. Can't make sense of the jangle. So many of them. He focuses his mind as well as he can and tries one key and then another. Manages to lock the door.

"Hello, Jovan. We should set a date for that portrait. Whad'ya reckon?" She stands there with an open smile on her face, natural blond hair around her head in a ragged corona, clear sky-blue eyes tired, an exhausted angel at the end of a long night shift.

He nods towards Leni's "hello," otherwise doesn't move. She's walking down the hall. He can't remember who she is. He nods. The nurse that drew the sketch. The one he gave a lift to after the dentist. Who kissed him on the cheek to say thanks.

She says, "You look like someone's punched you in the guts. You alright?"

"I am not sure where or how. Punching, for sure. I want to find a way down maybe. Stop with the fighting."

"What's going on? Can I help?"

"I'd crush you for help."

"What?" she says, the smile on her face faltering. "Sorry?"

"You cannot help me."

"But what's happened?" She waits for him to explain, which he does by hooking his thumb over his shoulder.

Jovan unlocks the door and Leni walks to the doorway with the door held open and peers inside. It takes her breath away. The amount of work alone that has gone into this. It must have taken hours. She takes a step inside. When she walks around the toilet it's the slow steps of a patron visiting an art gallery. Even in the cubicles, there are the outlines of the bodies. In two figures there is a message:

Obliteration. Oblivion.

"That's very cool," she says when she comes back out into the hallway. "That's fucking amazing."

"That's work. My whole morning. Cleaning for hours."

"This is that guy, right? That's doing all that shit around the hospital?" She shakes her head at Jovan, her eyes not blinking. "That dude's hard-core, man, I'm serious."

There were hospital employees, X-Ray, Tammie, and others, and now Leni, that thought of Dr. Graffito as an artist. They had become cultish about it. X-Ray had created a site on the Internet that displayed every message, and many people commented on each new "piece."

"Hard-core . . ." He says on an exhalation and locks the door.

The first thing he will clean is the message on the inside of the

door. A pun for Jovan? *Ethical Cleansing.* Jovan walks with grit-
ted teeth to retrieve the cleaning equipment he uses for Graffito's
"work." *Oblivion* was already out of his hands; Jovan would make
sure, in this instance at least, of *Obliteration.*

JOVAN BUYS A lemon, a loaf of bread, and a prime cut of beef from
the local supermarket. He also buys three pieces of grilled trevally
from a nearby fish'n'chippery. He carries the food down to Frankston
Pier. It's a long boardwalk that takes him and Charlemagne a good
distance across the ocean. The dog is used to dusty dry food from a
bag; it doesn't take long before he's savouring the cut of beef. Jovan
slices the lemon with his pocket knife and squeezes both halves
across the grilled fish. A few slices of lemon come with the food but
Jovan enjoys fish soaked in lemon juice. After they've both eaten,
they listen to the water moving below them. It's a warm autumn
evening and people are walking the pier. The dog closes his eyes for
a snooze. There's restlessness in hunger and there's a few moments
after eating a good meal where even Jovan can sit and feel at ease.

Before going to the supermarket Jovan stopped in at the
newsagency. He picked up a copy of *Novosti*, a Yugoslav newspaper
he didn't often buy. He read about Zoran Djindjich, who seemed to
Jovan the only rational politician in what remained of the country,
portrayed in the article as a traitor to his people. A trial for treason
would soon be under way. Jovan thought going to trial would be
a victory for Djindjich though it was possible he would simply be
assassinated first. Miloshevich had initiated mafia assassinations of
political opponents—Slavko Churuvija gunned down in front of his
own home in Belgrade by two masked men, the most outrageous
of these murders so far. The byline for the article read: Vladimir
Mitrovich. Jovan put the newspaper down and walked out of the
newsagency.

Jovan had been in Belgrade for a conference when he met Vladimir Mitrovich. He'd been expecting a refined, well-spoken man. That'd been the impression Suzana had given him of her great Belgrade professor. Perhaps that had been the way he was in his prime. He'd become bloated with bad food and alcohol; fingers, teeth, and eyes stained tobacco yellow. A man without friends and family in a city he'd live in his whole life, and perhaps because of this, he pursued political and professional contacts with all the more vigour.

Jovan heard Mitrovich was staying in the same hotel, but before he could seek Mitrovich out, Jovan found himself buttonholed at the bar. A finger tapping him on the chest any time Jovan looked as if he might rise from his seat. Not as a threat, as punctuation for the story Mitrovich was telling about that bitch of a woman Jovan had married.

A slap across the old professor's face made him lift both his arms as though he might fall backwards—they remained raised. When talking he hadn't appeared so drunk. After the slap, with his eyes closed, dropping his hands onto his head and then into his lap with a series of small nods, he seemed almost paralytic.

"Oh yes, I understand. Hit me if I prove rude company again." The speed with which he opened his eyes and began talking intelligently again surprised Jovan. The man lit a cigarette, despite having a half-finished cigarette in the ashtray. "I'd like to tell you a story. I'll mind my tongue but don't slap me again, comrade. Women slap and I'd prefer a punch. It'd be better for both of us."

"If I punch you, comrade, a soft bag of shit like you is going to split at the seams. It'll be messy, for both of us," Jovan told him.

"I'll be honest." The cigarette made Mitrovich cough when he inhaled; he took a long drag in any case, exhaling the smoke with another two coughs. "I'd like to be honest. You won't strike me over the truth. That's all I want to do, speak to you." He raised his hand for the barman's attention. "You need the right person to tell a particular story. After all, words only live in communication. The rest of the time words are half-dead fish in a bowl of rank water. Maybe I'll understand how I lost everything over the kind of weakness you yourself, I'm sure, have occasionally indulged. I'm not talking about a great evil. It's a simple function yet it's easy to get lost in something so simple, because you stop thinking. If it was more complicated you would give the situation proper contemplation."

"I won't listen to babble. You'd want to make sense right now," Jovan told him, mocking Mitrovich's "punctuation" by tapping him on the chest with a knock, knock, knock, as though on a heavy door. It made Mitrovich cough again.

He patted Jovan on the hand, and then left his palm on the back of Jovan's wrist, as if they were old friends. The barman arrived and Mitrovich didn't order a round of drinks, he bought a bottle of *rakia* and began pouring glasses.

Jovan sits on Frankston Pier with Charlemagne as he remembers that conversation with a shake of his head. Even drunk, Mitrovich had come up with that line about words living only in communication—half-dead fish in a bowl of rank water the rest of the time. Jovan couldn't help but agree that some subjects could only be understood when talking with a particular person. It was the moment he decided not to lay the rude bastard out on the floor, or at least to hear the story he wanted to tell before he did. There was no doubt in Jovan's mind that's how the conversation would end. A punch to the solar plexus to watch the old windbag gasp for a few minutes.

"A particular love. A particular hatred. A particular heart." Vladimir Mitrovich said that after his first drink. He then began to speak about the day he came home to find Suzana sitting in his kitchen with his wife. Suzana had explained to Vesna that she was one of his students and that she would soon be leaving Belgrade and there was a last-minute detail to attend to. She had also brought cake as a gesture of thanks for her wonderful professor. Vesna insisted she come in, at least for a coffee. It was a cold day and it had just begun to snow and the girl was so thin, pretty, and polite.

When Vladimir came home there they were, his wife and his mistress, eating a cherry torte Suzana had made herself. Drinking coffee and laughing, happily talking about all manner of things.

Suzana was "dressed for church," is how the old man put it, in that hotel barroom. He didn't know what to do when he came home to this nightmare scene. Since everything was going along so pleasantly he sat down and had some cake and coffee with the two women. Soon his son and daughter came home from high school and hit it off with Suzana as well. "She'd never been more charming," said Mitrovich, drinking another shot of *rakia* and lighting a cigarette before his lips were dry.

Vesna even asked her to stay for dinner. Suzana sweetly explained that she couldn't. She really had to run. She had an early start and the bus would take her an hour and a half to get home to her cramped student apartment, where there were four of them living in a place with room "for one person and a bad-tempered cat." That was another expression Mitrovich remembered as he poured more drinks for Jovan and himself. Jovan wasn't drinking. Vladimir Mitrovich didn't notice.

There was an envelope that had been sitting on a pile of papers Suzana brought with her. Sitting there on the kitchen table with them. Suzana explained that tomorrow morning she was going in for an abortion and wanted the Mitroviches to come to the hospital with her. After an hour or two she had proved herself intelligent and funny, lighting up the afternoon with her sparkling black eyes. They all genuinely liked her but her request left them cold. Vesna Mitrovich said they would help, of course they would. Suzana sat at their kitchen table, not talking, not blinking. The girl they liked so well had disappeared. It was as if a totally different woman had appeared in the room.

Suzana smiled again and explained that since it was the professor's baby they would be terminating, perhaps they should come and help her get through it. "Hold her hand" are the words she used, because, as she pointed out with the most believable naïve insouciance, it was certainly not for a nineteen-year-old girl to go through this kind of ordeal by herself. She admitted that she was ashamed to tell her own mother and father about her pregnancy, or rather, the need for an abortion so soon after leaving home. A close, warm family was what she needed right now.

Because while abortion wasn't a novel idea, and it wasn't a baby they were talking about, it wasn't quite the same as cutting out her appendix either. There was no question of murdering new life, yet there was a bit of life nevertheless that had been bound to a man and his words, and perhaps, even if they weren't promises, there was a great deal of hope and affection in this fragment of life, suddenly cancerous within her—that now had to be cut from her body. Which is what made her think about a close, warm family.

When the Mitroviches said nothing, Suzana asked Natasha Mitrovich, a girl only a few years younger and still dressed in her high-school uniform, how she would deal with such a circumstance. Especially if a man as respected and accomplished as her father, the august Vladimir Mitrovich, so charming and caring, abruptly lost all feeling, became unrecognisable, inseparable from a street thug, and told Suzana to go away and "deal with it." How would Natasha Mitrovich deal with it? She looked at Vesna and asked her if she'd ever had to deal with this kind of circumstance before.

Vladimir Mitrovich had since been fired from university work. It wasn't because of the few times he'd seduced students. It was his trouble with the bottle. And afterwards he had degenerated into the worst kind of demagogue and propagandist, endlessly talking about the glories of Serbia, its pride and power. Jovan was told by Suzana, and others that had known him, that in his better days Mitrovich really had been a superb speaker, a grand educator inspiring many on to worthy endeavours. If there was a tally, then certainly Professor Mitrovich became responsible for far more damage and destruction by the end of his career.

Jovan didn't punch Mitrovich as he'd intended. He gave him three hard pats on the back instead, making him cough up his last shot of alcohol. He left the old fool spluttering instead of gasping. There was no point in hurting him when Suzana had been far more effective than Jovan could ever be. When Jovan returned to Sarajevo from the conference he didn't mention that he'd met her great Belgrade professor.

Jovan gets up and walks the long pier back with the dog. He enjoys the quiet company of the animal as they stroll through their neighbourhood. When he gets home the phone is ringing. He doesn't rush to pick it up. He unlocks the front door and stops by the answering machine. There have been calls and messages from Glen and Rae Coultas. It was almost ten in the evening and they wouldn't call so late. He doesn't press the button to play the message, walks to the kitchen, and drinks a glass of water first. The red light stops blinking when he presses the button. He listens to his wife's voice.

JOVAN HAS A vacuum cleaner strapped to his back for the whole afternoon. The noise isn't loud, the hum is easy to get lost in. He could go on for hours barely thinking. A meditative drone in his mind often continued for an hour after switching the machine off.

"Good morning, Professor Brakochevich."

He doesn't stop. His work daze is so deep it's as though a memory has drifted up out of his unconsciousness. He blinks as the drone goes on and raises his head. A woman is sitting on one of the moulded plastic seats in the waiting room, very near him. The head of the vacuum cleaner is close to her feet. She lifts one up as if he might want to vacuum the area beneath her seat.

She's a patient. That's all he sees, the generic shape of a pregnant woman waiting to see a doctor. There are always so many pregnant women in this part of the hospital.

She places her foot back on the carpet. "You aren't ignoring me, I hope."

"Why would I ignore you? I'm not sure I know you."

"You don't remember me?"

"My memory isn't what it used to be. Don't know if my memory ever was great, truth be told." He turns off the vacuum cleaner. Looks at her properly. "Silvana. Was that your name?"

"It still is."

"Yes, of course." He straightens his posture from his vacuuming crouch and finds he's towering over her so he sits down in one of the seats opposite her. He holds the tube of the vacuum cleaner across his lap. "Over here it feels like a different name even when it's the same name."

"That's a good thing sometimes. The Silvana Pejich back in Sarajevo isn't someone I ever want to be again."

"Congratulations," he says, nodding at the large baby mound she's rubbing with one palm. "I'm guessing you're a month or so away. You must be excited."

"We're looking to have our second, but it's been difficult. I keep bleeding. I'm here for yet another check-up. Make sure the thing in here is alive and kicking." The light tone as she says "the thing in here" doesn't match the worry in her eyes.

"Have you been waiting long?"

"Fifteen minutes. Feels a lot longer." She glances at the clock on the wall. "Fifteen minutes in purgatory is all it takes to lose your mind." It's a quote, she can't remember which book or author. Jovan doesn't appear to recognise it from one of his lessons. Perhaps she misquoted and it should be *underworld* instead of *purgatory*. She feels embarrassed by the possible mistake.

They don't speak for a moment. Silvana says, "I heard about what happened to your children. Sorry for your loss."

Jovan nods. Not a flicker of emotion. As big as he is, it'd be easy to think he feels little about anything—a colossus. When he was her professor of literature she'd often been struck that despite his size, not only tall but very broad and solidly built, his personality was so light, his face mobile with his rapid thoughts and every electric surge of enthusiasm. He'd clap when a student was brilliant, yell out bravo.

"Very sorry for you and your wife."

No sadness. No smile. Nothing. "I never taught you how useless words are, did I?" As expressionless as a death mask. He stands up and switches the vacuum cleaner back on.

The drone continues for five minutes and then a nurse calls her name and Silvana stands up and leaves the room.

JOVAN KNOCKS ON the motel room door. He waits long enough to wonder whether it's the wrong room at the Best Western. Suzana opens the door as he's lifting his hand to knock again.

"Sorry," she says stepping back into the room. "I just got out of the shower."

"I think I'm a little early," he says, following the smell of freshly washed hair, the warm soap perfume lifting from her skin.

She's barefoot. "No, I got caught up talking with Glen and Rae." She's moving easy. Lightly. "I went out to Black Rock. I thought it was about time I explained myself to them."

"What was the explanation?" Jovan asks.

They are standing in the middle of the motel room, both surprised at how quickly they've arrived at the question.

"All I had was the truth." She is wearing a white bathrobe, tied around the waist, held together at the neck by her right hand. "I spent a week thinking of elaborate lies."

"Were they happy with your answer?"

"I'm not sure if I know how to do that—make anyone happy."

Jovan has a box in his hand. He places it on the small round table by the exposed brickwork wall. It's a wrapped present that he doesn't want to offer Suzana yet, and feels foolish holding it before himself. Her mug of pens is in the middle of the table. Her novel is progressing well—the filled notebooks are neatly stacked atop each other.

When he turns back to her, the hand that was holding the bathrobe together at her throat is by her side and the knot at her belly has been untied. Suzana's long hair is still damp and sleek black down her shoulders. When the robe falls open it reveals skin that still has the blush of water at full force and furiously hot. Her breasts are half revealed, nipples remaining hidden within the soft white. Her pubic hair a hazy shadow behind sheer cotton. She pulls the robe closed. A blink of both eyes—a wink. She opens her bathrobe and lets it drop to her feet with a smile that jolts his heart. Adrenaline flooding through his blood, ready to run a marathon, he walks towards her with steady slow steps.

"WHAT'S IN THE box?" she asks.

"It's not a box. It's a present."

"Well?"

"What do you think the point of wrapping paper is?"

"It's a surprise?"

"Not for you," Jovan says, poker-faced.

She's already swung herself out of bed, pads across the room to the round table.

"You might have bought flowers. A present is silly, isn't it?"

"It's not for you," Jovan says.

The present is wrapped with images of lions and giraffes, monkeys and zebras. He mustn't have realised it was wrapping paper for a child. He might have had a hard time explaining himself at the counter of whatever department store he bought this gift. She rips off the wrapping paper. The cardboard box within gives her no idea what's inside. She pulls it open and finds a red metal tractor. The toy doesn't look new. It explains the nondescript cardboard box. Jovan didn't buy it from a store. She stares across at him, lying on his side in bed, his expression unreadable.

"Is this a joke?" Suzana asks.

"No. It's not for you. I told you that twice. Why'd you open it?"

"Who's it for then?"

"What a foolish question."

She catches her breath. "It's for Dejan."

"Do you think he'll like it?"

She can hear them arguing in the next room, fighting over Ana's Christmas present—a complete set of 150 coloured pencils from Paris. Ana won't share so Dejan runs into the room, crying. He stops when he sees his mother, standing there with the red tractor in her hands. The tears instantly end in a brilliant smile. Is that for me? he asks. Yes. She holds it out and he comes to her. In another moment the dream will end. She knows she is dreaming but she gets down to a knee as her son approaches. She can feel Dejan in her arms as she wakes. She can see him so clearly in her mind. I've forgotten your face, my love. Those dear hazel eyes. That sweet small voice. Less than murmurs as she blinks in bed and listens to the sound of Jovan breathing beside her. She lets him sleep. Knows she can keep herself quiet, sobbing almost noiselessly.

IN THE MORNING Jovan is brushing his teeth. Suzana walks in and sits on the toilet, eyes closed. Half asleep. He finishes and rinses his mouth with water. She puts her hands under the running faucet to wash. She blinks her eyes open.

"You used my toothbrush?" she asks.

Jovan nods and Suzana leaves the bathroom with a shrug or shiver, he's not sure which.

Jovan gets dressed as Suzana orders breakfast for both of them over the phone. She steps into her knickers and puts on her bra and then opens the curtains and a window.

The bay is rolling with waves today. Seagulls hover on currents of air above the white foam, wheel and coast to the sand, settle and peer out across the water as though waiting for something to come in on the tide. Perhaps fifty of them, all looking away from the motel and its occupants. An audience only interested in survival—the sea's washed-up waste, or crumbs in the sand.

Suzana puts on a lilac blouse and jeans. She must have gone shopping. There were tags in the vanity unit's bin in the bathroom and he flatters himself with the thought that she wanted to dress up for him. Jovan watches her make the bed and reconsiders. Her wardrobe was at Reservoir Road, of course, so she bought a few things.

"There's some news from home," he says.

"What?" Suzana asks, turning her head towards him, the sheet in her hands settling on the bed. He looks at her and realises that when he said *home* she had thought he meant somewhere other than Reservoir Road. He turns away from her, to an immense container ship in the distance inching towards the horizon, then returns his gaze to see her blink away the notion.

There's a knock on the door. A young man with a tray comes in, says "good morning Miss Johnson," and sets it down on the small round table. Jovan picks up the present and loops it through the air to Suzana. She catches it and holds it as though she might choose not to open it. She tears off the wrapping and finds a Mason Pearson hair brush—the same one she used to own, that she used to love. She'd had it for two decades, using cheap supermarket brushes ever since.

"Where'd you find it?" she asks.

"There's a place in the city." He sits at the table, ready to eat.

Suzana sits down at the end of the bed. There's a mirror on the wall opposite and it resembles a window into the next room and she's peering in on a woman brushing her hair. She sees the surprise in her own face and smiles at the foolishness of that expression.

He pours milk over muesli. There's a very small cup of fresh fruit he tips into the bowl as well.

"Thank you Jovan," she says, brushing. He nods and continues to eat, blinking rapidly and unable to speak. He opens one of her notebooks and begins to read her novel.

She lets him read a page before interrupting. "What's the news from home?" she asks.

"What?" He lifts his head, distracted. "You mentioned news before the boy came with breakfast."

"Oh, it's sad news."

"When is it happy?"

"Our neighbour died a few days ago," Jovan tells her.

There's a brushing rhythm to her hand movements, and she doesn't pause. "Who?"

"Silvers. He wandered out across Cranbourne Road. A truck couldn't stop in time."

"That's funny." She's not laughing. As far as Jovan can tell she's still counting strokes. A habit she picked up when she was a child. It's the counting—that's the reason she never cut her hair. Sitting on the side of her bed and counting strokes of a hundred, in the morning and in the evening, without fail. Her eyes half closed, meditative. "And I assume Charlemagne is OK." Five strokes. "And yet, Silvers gets run down." Five strokes. "That monster dog gets to keep romping around the neighbourhood while his master ends up as road kill." Ten strokes. "And what about Jane? How's she?"

"She's selling the house. And she's already asked me to take Charlemagne."

Suzana stops brushing. "No *fucking* way."

Jovan can't help himself. He's laughing.

THE REST OF the day at the hospital passes quickly. Jovan drives the van out into the street and is about to head home when he notices the nurse who drew his portrait. Leni is standing in the bus shelter on Bluff Road. The bus is leaving her behind. Jovan stops and waits for the opportunity to U-turn, thinks perhaps he should keep driving when he sees the nurse waving the bus driver away. She's not signalling the driver to leave or stay. She's swearing at the bus and throwing a Zippo lighter at it.

She's still in uniform and the hospital she's employed by is twenty metres away. She's wearing a cardigan but Jovan knows she'd get fired for this kind of behaviour. Leni drops onto the metal bench and the back of her head bumps up against the glass of the bus shelter, large handbag clutched to her chest. Her mouth opens in an expression of surprised pain and she clicks forward again.

Jovan turns his blinker off, turns it on. When the next break in traffic comes along he swings the panel van through it and stops before the bus shelter. He doesn't get out and Leni barely notices the white vehicle stopped there for her, let alone the man within, waving a greeting. Her mouth is chewing frenetically and her eyes are blinking as if she's trying to wake up and losing the battle with sleep. Her head bumps up against the glass of the shelter again, and this time her eyes don't open, her mouth does.

Jovan takes a long minute before he puts his car into gear and drives back out into traffic. He thinks it would be best not to get involved, to leave her in the bus shelter, and a moment later decides he can't do that. He forces his car through unyielding drivers to do another U-turn. So a chorus of horns alerts the nurse. Even now it's not clear whether Leni recognises the vehicle or its driver.

Jovan comes back around and parks in the bus shelter and honks in what he hopes is a happy sound. He smiles at her and waves her in. Then he has to get out of the vehicle and call to her. The drugged nurse with the blond hair searches his face and after staring for long seconds, identifies it as the face of a friend.

"Hey, Racket. You're a riot, but no one's laughing."

She pushes off the bench and manages to make it to the van. Jovan helps her with the handle. Leni slumps into the seat and closes her eyes. Jovan winds down her window, thinking the fresh air might revive her.

"I take you to point K," Jovan says with a smile. The girl is too far gone, or simply doesn't remember the point A to point K of their first conversation.

"Can't stay and can't go. Don't want to drive but there's nothing but traffic. They had a bed for me in there but I need to get home. Or anywhere else. Just not in there. Not in there. We need to go. Can we go? Took too much, I'm sorry. Thanks for stopping. I appreciate it. I just wish there was a way to get out of my own skin."

"Where is home for you?" he asks.

"Go to Elwood," she tells him. "Please. Thank you." She closes her eyes, her right leg rapidly jumping on the spot. Her hands twisting around each other in compulsive hand washing. Her head lolls on the top of the car seat. The breeze through the window calms her yet she starts with eyes wide open in five-minute intervals, muttering "Okay, okay, okay, okay," to herself.

He drives along the beach thinking the ocean air will be best for the nurse. He notices his brakes are getting worse, and now there's the grind of the brake pads. Jovan thinks to hell with the weekend, when he gets home tonight, he'll change his brakes by torchlight after dinner. Until then he gears down to every stop.

He had an uncle in Banja Luka who drove his car for years with no foot brake, using his handbrake every time he came to a stop. Funny that's about all he remembers about the man who died of stomach cancer all the way over in Zagreb, where only a few members of his immediate family would see him die. At the time Jovan had thought it would have been better to die closer to home, where everyone, down to second cousins and neighbours, could be around him in his last moments.

Of course he was fighting for his life and hoping that the doctors in Zagreb would save him. Instead he found a quiet place to die, where he wouldn't hear weeping, have tears splashing down on his face, or have his hands desperately squeezed, as if dying were some catastrophe the world had never seen before. Jovan has changed his mind and thinks that it's as good a way to go as any. Quietly, alone, with as little fuss as possible considering how much a fuss the rest of it is beforehand.

Jovan gears down to stops at red lights like his uncle would have done, and only remembers one more thing about him. Jovan was a child, listening in on adults talking, and this uncle was saying that when he looked at his two daughters he felt such an excess of love he felt like strangling them. A strange thing to say, but the child Jovan was, he thought he understood it. It's not something he understands anymore.

When they're passing through Brighton, Jovan asks the drugged girl for further instructions, gets them after he's passed Elwood Park and is driving up Marine Parade, almost overshooting into St. Kilda.

"Turn here." Only a right is possible onto Dickens Street. To the left it's a flotilla of moored yachts and boats in St. Kilda Marina. A half-second along Dickens, she says, "Turn," again with one option. A right into Hood Street. She says, "Stop," without opening her eyes.

There are small apartment blocks and houses around them and Jovan wonders where she lives. He sits in his seat not knowing what to do. It isn't clear how conscious she is until she asks him if this is "point K," a precarious smile struggling to emerge around her dry teeth. Her eyes open again. Clearer for the drive along the beach from Sandringham to Elwood.

"Yes. Point K."

"Can I trust you?"

He leans away a few centimetres.

"I think I can. How can I know for sure?" she asks him.

"You don't need trust me." Jovan moves his hands to the steering wheel and keys and starts the van again. "I say goodbye now. And you safe."

"Hang on . . . I want you to come inside with me. I need you to come inside. Make sure about the flat."

"Make sure of flat?"

"Will you just help me inside please? I'm scared and I'm not sure of what. Please come and make sure I'm alright. I'll be alright inside my apartment. I should be alright then."

"I help." He turns off the car again. "And I am safe I think." He smiles at her and she nods at him.

Gazing into the jumble of Jovan's possessions around her feet, Leni says, "You know when people say this is one of the best days of my life? Like when they've just had a baby. Or they've just revealed a million dollar scratchy. Or they'll say this is one of the worst days of my life because they found their pet goldfish belly-up that morning." She turns her head towards him and says, "On the actual day . . . there's no doubt in your head. You know it. There's never been another like this one."

He follows her along the short path of concrete discs set into a small uncared-for garden of a four-unit building, into an art deco foyer that had seen better days some twenty or thirty years ago, smelling of the passage of all those decades and its vanished inhabitants. Climbing up stairs on which a red carpet had begun to wear through to white cross-hatch threads along the centre.

Leni walks carefully, balance an issue. Jovan watches her weave from wooden railing to wallpapered wall and back again, stumbling to her hands on the stairs and getting up again. He puts his arm around her to help her with the bend in the stairs, onto a landing, and up to the next floor. The light woollen cardigan Leni is wearing falls from her left shoulder. Hangs halfway down her back. Her dress is ripped and dirty. Her left elbow grazed. She's already fallen once or twice today.

Leni is pretty, even in the bland nurse's uniform, even this battered and wasted. She spends a long time before her door fumbling around in her handbag, tries various keys before she manages to fit the right one into the lock and turn it. Jovan stands back, three steps down, watching her.

She turns on the light, walks into her passageway with eyes closed. Stumbles into the wall and finds her way to the left and through a doorway into her lounge. It's a train-cabin style apartment with one long passageway leading from the front door most of the way along to what would end in the kitchen area.

Leni walks to an armchair, vomiting into her cupped hands. There's a vase of flowers on the coffee table. He pulls out the flowers and throws them to the floor and brings her the vase if she needs to vomit again. The cardigan has fallen off one of her arms anyway so he pulls it down the other arm and wraps it around her hands. She has sense enough to be able to use it as the intended towel, lifting a dry spot of her cardigan to her lips. Jovan returns to the front hall and closes the door and walks down the corridor towards the kitchen. He will get her a glass of water. She needs a wet towel and a proper bucket.

It's a three-room flat—one long corridor along the side. The kitchen is small, barely usable. He passes her bedroom and the neatly made bed, and notices there isn't a lot of furniture in there. A chest of drawers and standing wardrobe, open, everything contained within it in tidy lines. The long lounge is about half the apartment in itself, extending out onto a sunroom. Not a lot of furniture in here either, a three-seater couch and two armchairs. Leni is sitting in one of the armchairs, head tilted back, blinking and taking in deep lungfuls of air. As far as these things go it is all fairly ordered, yet the flat is a vast, spewing, collapsing, impression of chaos otherwise.

Stacked along every wall are canvases. Some are hung above, mostly they are arranged in readiness for some kind of exhibition a few years overdue. On the parts of the walls he can see, there are drawings and paint applied directly onto the plaster. Hand-painted vine leaves crawl along the wooden door frames. There's more paper on the floor. Sketches and drawings, of things seen at the hospital, along the roads, at the library, on a bus, on trains; everywhere that she goes. There are also many attempts at depicting the massacre scene in the toilet they saw together last week. A canvas up on the wall depicts a man, kneeling down, face hidden from view, drawing out the words: Oblivion. Obliteration. He is painted in such a way that he resembles one of the murder outlines he is drawing.

Kneeling beside her as she retches again, listening to her moaning into the bucket, Jovan knows it is going to be a while before he can get out of this woman's apartment. She calms down, slumps back into her armchair. He sits on her couch to decide how long he has to stay here before leaving. He might check her handbag for more of the drug she's using yet she could have a stash anywhere in her apartment. She hadn't previously struck Jovan as a drug user. Perhaps this was indeed something out of the ordinary, "the worst day of her life"—it didn't mean she wouldn't harm herself in other ways. All he could think of doing was driving her back to the hospital and that's exactly what she didn't want. He takes a few deep breaths, closes his eyes, and because it's the first time since six o'clock in the morning that he has rested, he falls asleep.

HER HEART IS beating in quick thuds. She can hear it thumping in her ears. Someone has been whispering *Waste of Life* over and again. Black lips in the cup of her ear. *Waste of Life.* Leni opens her eyes, afraid and disorientated. She's home. Vase and flowers scattered around her. Her cardigan and a towel at her feet. Sees a big man on her couch and she can't remember who he is. She's shivering as wave after wave of anxiety breaks over her. Leni is drowning within herself. She has no idea how to come up for air. She's got to do something. She's not sure what. There's got to be some way to get out of her own head.

She hasn't been working long at the hospital. Hasn't been a nurse all that long for that matter. But she had loved the *idea* of a hospital. Being around people during their greatest need had made her feel as if she wasn't stuck at the periphery of people's lives. Floating out on the outskirts of life in general. She told her friends she was interested in finding a way to look at the human experience from a more ragged and raw perspective. It had given her ideas for her art and that feeling of being at the centre of life, where it was really happening.

Leni thought she was prepared for the ragged and the raw, the ugly and brutal, yet there was no way to be ready for what happened this morning—for the body in the bathtub, face down in the water, letters written in thick black marker across a woman's back and along her arms and legs and across the back of her neck: **Waste of Life.**

Leni stood there. Took a step forward because maybe the woman was alive. The smell in the air, as well as the vicious pale colour of her skin, killed the idea dead. She had seen so many images on television and cinema screens, on canvases and in books, that the image refracted through all those mediums first, then got lost in these reflections, in the images she had seen, until she didn't know what she was seeing, and where she was, or who she was, whether she was the murdered woman with those words printed onto her skin coming back to see what had been done, a spectre taking steps backwards until she was stopped at a wall behind her. Solid after all. Nothing but a woman ready to die in the next moment in a bleach bath.

A woman with long blond hair going white, floating around her head. Tiny bubbles in the liquid burst and dissolved slowly in the air coming through the door Leni had opened. The smell of chemicals in the room burned in her nose and throat. Bleach. Bottles of industrial bleach were scattered around the room. The naked woman, face down in a bathtub of bleach, her ankles and wrists tied together behind her back. Hog-tied is what it was called. The brutal rope forming livid marks in her flesh. And that message on her back, along her arms and along her legs and across her neck—fading below the line of bleach, clear and black above the waterline.

She closed the door and walked back into the bedroom outside that bathroom. There was a nurse's uniform laid out without a wrinkle on the bed with the name tag still on it. The name belonged to someone Leni worked with, a girl called Melissa Martin. They have talked often about men and the world, about music especially. They went out dancing once. They had called themselves friends though it was hard to find the time to go out a second time. The woman with her face in bleach was Mel Martin.

Leni walked out into the hospital hallway, where people were strolling by, saw them pass, and had a thought of slipping out amongst them, and into the same oblivion. She stood by the door with an idea that no one else should see it. No one should be allowed to wander in and discover a woman in a bathtub with its bleach and that message and the contorted position Melissa Martin was in—that most of all. It wasn't over and done, like when she saw a dead body for the first time in the hospital. This was a different kind of death and it was just beginning.

As Leni stood there, back against the hallway wall, she saw every detail whenever she shut her eyes. She'd never had such a clear image in her mind before. It was as if the same photograph was being taken over and again, opening her eyes, flash—closing her eyes—there it was, every minute detail. The braided white rope. Blue nail polish. The cluster of fingers bound at the wrist. Another flash when Leni opened her eyes. A mole on the left hip, match-head black below the waterline of bleach, and she thought, What if I can never see another thing ever again. Blinking. The hog-tied woman. What if every time I blink, I see Mel Martin, with those words on her body? That cruel, taut, white curtain rope. It was that thought more than anything else that made her start blabbering words in a chain, my-god-my-god-jesus-christ-jesus-my-god-my-god-god-oh-god, a meaningless prayer for a demolished god. Babbling louder and more desperately, until enough people had moved into her orbit for her to speak the one sentence that would open the door again to Melissa Martin, drowned in a bleach bath—a hog-tied woman with the words:

Waste of Life

Life of Waste

Life or Waste

She blinks and wants the morphine pills in her handbag. To crush them between her teeth again so they are quicker, dissolving into her bloodstream without the long wait of stomach acid to break down the hard pills. Enough of the morphine to eradicate what she saw. She's blinking at the huge man on her couch and wondering if it might be him, and knows that of course it could. Who can say that it isn't? He might be the author of Obliteration and Oblivion. Wasn't that a horrific joke now? It was his industrial bleach. The halting English simply a great cover. It's easy enough to prepare words and sentences. They are found in books, on the Internet, everywhere, anywhere. The cause of all the trouble and the author of all the graffiti in the hospital.

A janitor going postal is not a stretch in anyone's imagination. All of the mayhem culminating in this murder. And Mel Martin has told Leni she's been seeing a janitor at the hospital and it had to be this man, pretending to help Leni so he could win her trust and do to her in her own house what he did to Mel in the hospital. Exhausted for now by his struggle with the other nurse, he's resting before beginning again.

Leni looks at the phone in the corner of the room and thinks it might be better to walk away quietly, while he's sleeping. Perhaps he is pretending to be asleep. She is quick—out of her chair and across the room without making a racket. Leni calls the police on her neighbour's phone downstairs.

When the police storm into her apartment the janitor is still asleep. His first response is violent objection, speaking in a different language or in English that no one can understand. She can hear the noise through the ceiling above her as they begin a long struggle to subdue the colossal brute. Thumping into walls. She's babbling with her eyes squeezed shut, into the chest of another police officer, as they haul him down the stairs and drag him away.

EIGHT

TAMMIE HAS A NEW PATIENT AT the end of her work day. A check-up/ clean. The woman in the chair isn't a talker and she doesn't need to be, yet she doesn't say good afternoon to Tammie, not even a head-nod by way of greeting. Sits in the chair, waits, and watches her prepare. Tammie does pleasant chatter better than anyone. She can do it for the both of them. Talking about the up-coming referendum, the weather, or about a film she saw the other night, it doesn't matter, it's the same as talking to dogs—the tone of voice is key.

It's important to Tammie that her patients feel at ease and confident that they are in good hands. The best hands around. Not true, of course, but she knows she isn't the worst either. A great dentist is a natural. It's a feel for pain, economy, and precision of movement. Still, that sense for another person's pain is crucial.

Tammie gives herself that escape clause, about how some are "naturals." She doesn't believe it. That's everyone's favourite cop-out. If she's honest with herself, then what it comes down to, is how much you care. After all these years, gazing into the straining maw of a stranger continues to be the slightest bit revolting. On bad days she feels as if she's a vet who despises animals, from their pathetic moans to their awful smells, from the hair in their noses to their fearful flinching.

She moves around her dental surgery efficiently, directs her newbie assistant courteously, to the point, and it will all be under way in a few minutes, over in about thirty. She natters on pleasantly, thinking about other things entirely. Daydreaming about those big hands, those steady yellow eyes, the crude, heavy voice from a deep chest, and that wonderful cock of his—Jovan and the clean smell of his body, even after a day's work.

When Tammie puts on her white coat she begins her performance. She knows it's not necessary. She might go about her job efficiently yet she's eager to cultivate her business. Wants her patients to speak well of her to their friends. She feels the same way when she puts on a dress for Graham and they go out to a fund-raiser, an auction, or dinner party. She knows it's not *her*, but what is? Role-playing is what it's all about. Graham has that ugly horsehair wig with curls down the sides that he puts on top of his head, his black gown that makes him look like a religious nut or Halloween diehard. She's never gotten used to it. He walks a different way and speaks as though his every word has weight when he enters barrister mode. So Tammie is mostly happy to play her role as well.

"I was watching this interview the other day, with John Howard," says Tammie, to fill the dead air as her dental assistant suddenly discovers she desperately needs to go to the toilet. Using the word "toilet" in front of the patient. Tammie feels hard-pressed to erase that word for a woman with her mouth half-open and waiting. "And this was on British television. The host asks the Prime Minister of Australia, what he said to people that suggested England would become a republic before Australia did, and that perhaps it was, after all, inevitable. The host says it with a wink. Little Johnny gets this sour expression on his face, and says, 'The only thing inevitable, is death.' Glares at the Pom. 'And taxes,' he adds. Here we are gearing up for a referendum on whether Australia is ready to be an independent nation, finally ready to cut the Queen's apron strings, and our Prime Minister can't conceive of ever doing away with that silly Union Jack in the corner of the flag."

Her patient is a foreigner so there isn't much chance of upsetting her. Tammie mentioned the same interview at the dinner at her home the other evening, the one she came late to, yet because she was speaking to right-leaning bigwigs, she'd used it to highlight the dogged resilience so many admired in John Howard. Whether Australia becomes a republic or not is about as interesting to Tammie as the results of her neighbourhood dog show.

Her dental assistant returns and apologises for a stomach bug when Tammie wishes she would keep her stupid mouth closed and not say another word about bowels and toilets. The assistant fumbles around now, searching for a new surgery mask. Has to be reminded to fish out a fresh pair of gloves.

Tammie waits, and feels the slightest remaining irritation from another tattoo she got two days ago, on her shoulder blade. A Norse compass this time. Björk, one of her favourite musicians, has one on her arm. Tammie often turns around in a mirror at home or her change room here at the hospital admiring the new ink. Graham hasn't seen it. Who knows when he will? He hasn't seen the last one either, the skull with a halo of roses. She's interested in how long it might take for him to notice. A few days, and it would tell her that maybe things aren't all that bad between them after all. It might take weeks, and then what will it tell her? What if it's months? What if he sees the two tattoos on her back a year from now and doesn't think they're worth mentioning? Maybe he'd be as outraged as Jovan. Her husband would understand she hadn't bought into her role, mind, body, and soul.

The message in the skull doesn't mean much to Tammie. It was a joke, wasn't it? Fleas on the Trojan Horse. Who knows what he actually meant? Clearly fucking crazy. And who cares? Dr. Graffito had become such an interesting presence in the hospital. Where previously a person could die of boredom listening to people bitch and moan about every mundane detail in their trivial lives, now there were these biting messages to make everyone jump, scratching at their Trojan Fleas.

More than anything she loves the way her first tattoo seems to have hit Jovan. It surprised her. All along, since the Christmas piss-up, and this little *thing* started, he's had a nonchalant attitude, as though he can walk away from Tammie, as easy as that. Like she was worthless. She'd finally gotten through to him the other night in his van. Not a bit of graffiti he can clean away. And when they said good-bye he seemed afraid. He'd been altered at least. So yes, an impact.

Concentrate, Tammie, she tells herself. Two cancellations today. Also space on the schedule for an extended lunch break, and who wants a three-course meal for lunch every day? There were times in the past when Tammie could not fit in a bite to eat the whole day long, her schedule was so filled with waiting patients. An assistant who understood basic dental surgery etiquette would help, yet Tammie knows that when she talks about "growing her business" really the desperation she feels comes from wondering how she can stop it from dying.

Since she's thinking of Jovan, and also because this patient has a surname that might be Serbian as well, one of those names ending in *ich*, she remembers a movie she recently saw.

"I saw this great film the other day, which might not be everyone's cup of tea, but anyway, it was called *Being John Malkovich*. And I don't know, maybe you could tell me. Is he Serbian? John Malkovich?" Tammie is about ready to begin now, and it doesn't matter what the woman's answer is.

The patient has murmured something around the white pellets that have been replaced in her mouth by the assistant.

Tammie is obliged to lean in and ask what she said. Her patient hasn't spoken since she walked into the surgery.

The woman says, "He is American."

Tammie blinks at the woman on her chair and feels the hair on the back of her neck rise. She looked familiar earlier. There's no way Tammie could have expected this woman to come and lay herself out in her dental surgery, for *a clean and a check-up*.

The woman's mouth opens again, gazing up at Tammie with unblinking eyes. There's no doubt in her mind that this is Jovan's wife.

"Of course," murmurs Tammie, hardly able to remember what they've just said, "with a name like Malkovich, he must be from your region." Those hard black eyes don't blink. "I mean, originally."

"My region is now Australia. You and I are in the same region." Suzana closes her eyes and leans back into the chair. "You can continue to talk as you work," she tells Tammie.

Tammie has nothing else to say. All her small talk has dried up. She asks Jovan's wife to open her mouth, and Suzana does that. She also opens those cutting eyes again. Suzana does not flinch as Tammie brings down her sickle probe and applies it to her back molars. Barely blinks as Tammie slips into the soft gum of her mouth, to bring out a bead of blood.

Tammie's own silence feels suffocating. She keeps thinking, I've got to find something to say to this woman. Finds her mind blank. There's a trembling in her hands and her arms are beginning to feel weak. She should continue talking about the referendum, the cold weather of late autumn in Melbourne, or anything at all. Nothing will come to her because this woman refuses to blink. Mouth wide open to snap off all her fumbling fingers.

JOVAN WALKS INTO the silent house late in the evening. All the lights are turned off. He closes the door and hears the echo bounce off the walls. He switches on the lamp on the dresser in the hallway. There are pictures of his children on the walls. No pictures of Suzana or himself. He's never noticed that before. Drops his wallet and keys on the dresser. He makes his way to the kitchen first. She's not there. He doesn't turn on any lights because he can't tolerate the glare. He walks past the closed door of their bedroom to the bathroom and opens the door. He sits on the edge of the bath. His eyes close and after a few minutes he sways and jerks awake.

Jovan manages to get up and turn on the lights. Squints. Not asleep, not awake. A vibration through his legs and arms. He walks to the medicine cabinet and swallows some pills and then leans against the bathroom wall to take off his pants. When he gets into the shower he uses almost no hot water. A cool shower, not to wake himself up so much as to keep himself conscious. He is slow, using the soap with gentle hands and when he gets out he gingerly dries himself with the towel. Bruises on his arms and shins, torso, head, so many he's confused by the map of them over his body—a new landscape of pain. There's a bulging lump on the crown of his head from when he hit the door frame of the squad car.

He throws his towel into the bathtub. Suzana's long blue skirt is on the towel rail, still a little damp to the touch. There's the smell of her body within the material. He breathes her in again and turns off the light.

Jovan walks to the bedroom, opens the door, and finds her body laid out on the bed. Motionless and unbreathing. He takes a stumbled step inside. So exhausted that he cannot think. He is naked and knows he needs at least a shirt and pants but can't find the energy. He lifts the sheet and blanket and takes his place beside his wife on the bed. Dead to the world a few moments later.

NURSES RUN THROUGH the hallways and a doctor nearly barrels into Suzana as she is walking through the foyer. The hospital phones ring without answer. Police park their cars outside in Emergency as Suzana gets into a car she borrowed from Jelka. Commotion brought on, no doubt, by another act of petulance from Dr. Graffito. Something for her husband and his friend David Dickens to talk about for hours on the weekend. Suzana heard one nurse say to another, *A Bleach Bath*. Perhaps that's the title of his latest piece.

Jelka's car is an automatic and it should mean it is easier to drive. Suzana has always driven manuals and her foot is restless for a clutch—she feels she's not quite in control of the car. Suzana puts the Corolla into drive and stops at Bluff Road, ready to head home when the sound of horns draws her attention to a white van pulling a ragged U-turn through traffic. She'd wondered whether she would bump into her husband at the hospital yet hadn't expected for that to happen on the street.

She watches him pull up to a bus shelter. Jovan gets out, walks around his vehicle so he can usher a young woman over, even opening the door for her. The van roars out into the heavy evening traffic. Suzana contemplates following them, her indicator ticking. A silver BMW behind Suzana beeps—two long blasts. Suzana reaches for the gearstick and realises that the automatic is already in drive. Of course. She rolls out onto Bluff Road. Heads in the opposite direction to Jovan and the blonde.

A minute down the road and the streetlights are on. They were off and then they are on—she never notices the precise instant of change. The sunlight is fading quickly and by the time she reaches the Best Western the sun is nothing but a vaporous haze on the water horizon. She flicks on her blinker and waits to make the turn into her motel, where she will be greeted as Miss Johnson if she bumps into any of the staff on the way to her room. She's already told Scott on the desk that she'll be leaving in the morning.

The thought of talking to Scott again, to explain that she'll be staying on for a little while longer, makes her grip the steering wheel tight—two weeks in that room was enough to find a little space and for that same space to collapse into less than what she had before finding it. She flicks off her blinker yet she doesn't turn towards Reservoir Road either. She can taste blood in her mouth. Clumsy nicks in her gums from the stainless steel probes.

She keeps driving down the Nepean Highway and when she passes Mornington, detours onto the Esplanade, so she can continue along the darkened bay. Her window is down and Jelka's Corolla is quiet. Suzana can hear the ocean and see the flashing white seagulls tumbling around beneath the streetlights—spaced out in regular intervals—illuminating the shore sweeping along the peninsula.

Suzana keeps the car humming, on through Rosebud, and thinks how before she'd seen Rosebud, she'd imagined the tulip fields of Holland in some diminished form, and was surprised by how drab, dismal, and utterly charmless the rudiments of a town were here. The place takes its name from the shipwreck of a cargo vessel called *Rosebud* and not from flower growing. Further along the road is Rye, another speck of a seaside town. Rye is the Serbian word for heaven. The town has as little to do with paradise as it does grain.

She drives on to Sorrento, where she turns into a car park near the waterline. When they first started looking for places to rent, this had been where Suzana wanted to live. Frankston is affordable and practical, Sorrento is neither. The white limestone buildings of the town, the way they pick up the evening lights, still appeal to her.

The real-estate agent told them, imparting a history lesson to foreigners, that the first attempt to create Melbourne had failed here. Those original colonists buried their dead and moved down to Tasmania. It was a generation later before Melbourne was given another shot at life. Had things gone differently Suzana wouldn't be sitting in an empty gravel car park by the beach. She'd be stopped at a busy intersection roaring with the power of generations—glass towers rising to radiate into the night skies from a white city teeming with spectral ambition. A failed nucleus, she thinks, and turns the car off.

Suzana gets out of the car. There's enough moonlight so that she need not watch her step too carefully as she makes her way down and over a hillock. She sits and removes her shoes, stands again and walks across the wet sand. Seawater rushes over her feet in white foam and then leaves a flawless stretch of sand as it draws back. Walking by the shoreline, tasting blood again. Pain in her gums. The shaking hands of that empty woman Jovan fell into. Suzana had thought she could pull her husband out, as if he had been drowning. They'd had an agreement about Tammie. Suzana was obviously mistaken, if not about the dentist, then about Jovan.

She can feel her sleeve sticking to her inside elbow. The swab and medical tape have come loose. She rolls up her sleeve and peels the bandage off. A blood test at the doctor's before she went in to see the dentist—killing two birds with one stone. That phrase had run through her mind. It doesn't signify the difficulty of resolving two issues at the same time. It means simply crossing both items off in one deft stroke. She is still so much more literal when she uses

English than a native speaker would be, imagining tiny bird heads, a stone, and the impossibility of that one throw.

Suzana rubs the soft part of her elbow. Her blood filled the small glass cylinder and she will be told tomorrow what she already knows. She rolls down her sleeve. The nurse blinked when she saw the scars on Suzana's wrist. A quiet one; efficient. A friendly hello as she brought out the needle, tied a rubber tube around Suzana's bicep, and found the vein with a firm, sure touch. Suzana is carrying her shoes, sandy up to her ankles, specks of mud on her calves. She'll have to wash her skirt when she gets home. Shakes her head. When she gets to the motel. Shaking her head again.

The nurse told her it was easy to miss a vein. Little of the useless chit-chat that she had to endure with Tammie, as bad as the slips of her dental hooks. Are you hoping for a little boy or a little girl? The young nurse with a lovely smile, asking as if it was the most natural thing in the world. Suzana hadn't seen the blond nurse's face as she walked from the bus shelter to her husband's vehicle. Pretty, no doubt. Did men ever pick up ugly women?

The breeze off the water is getting colder with the evening. Suzana turns, trying to work out the direction of the wind, wet feet beginning to feel icy. She takes a few steps back into drier sand. The wind gives her no choice, it's a face full of whipping hair whichever way she turns. She sits down and puts her shoes beside her and uses both hands to gather her hair, pulling it across one shoulder and tucking it beneath her cheek.

There's enough moonlight to see out across the bay a good distance, to watch it heave out into small rolling waves and settle back into its chaotic, restless skin. Suzana hadn't been able to answer the question easily; as naturally as she should. It had been neither a boy nor a girl before the pleasant nurse asked, the possibility had been enough. It was enough even after the home test gave her a positive in the motel yesterday. And Suzana's answer, after staring at the smiling nurse for a stunned second, was the easier cliché—boy or girl, it doesn't matter, ten fingers, ten toes, and healthy. The truth is she wants both a boy and a girl, both Dejan and Ana.

AFTERNOON LIGHT PUSHES through the edges of the curtain. The smell of pan-fried sausages from the kitchen, coming up under the bedroom door, has woken him. He gets up slowly and goes to the bathroom. He takes two pills and hobbles to the kitchen, his body so sore he can barely walk. He sits at the kitchen table with his head in his hands, waiting for his eyes to be ready for the blaze coming through the kitchen windows.

"I thought that might get you out of bed," says Suzana.

"Well, yeah . . . I can't remember when I ate last. What time is it?"

She looks at the clock for him as he rubs at his face. "Almost two o'clock."

Suzana lets him eat before she asks any questions. He is wearing the new bathrobe she bought him for the colder weather. It fits him well and that's a relief. Buying for Jovan isn't easy.

"Are you OK?" she asks him, when he's finished his meal, and has begun to sip the fresh cup of tea she's put before him. "I've talked to David Dickens. Or at least, he talked at me. After half an hour of his monkey chatter I wasn't sure of anything. A woman was murdered at the hospital. That can't be true, can it?"

"I swear to God . . ." Jovan shakes his head and wipes his hands across his face as though it might be possible to pull unwanted images from his eyes. "That hospital has done my head in."

"There are other jobs," she says.

Jovan looks at her. "You're right. One thing's for sure, I'm done with this job." He sips his tea, and notices the way her hand is resting on her belly. He doesn't say anything. Her hand moves away from it as if it never strayed for that particular touch.

"I spent most of the night on a wooden bench at the police station because this drug-fucked nurse got it in her fucking head that I was Dr. Graffito. Me. Like I could be insane enough, not only to write all that graffiti, but insane enough to clean up my own graffiti after making it—for months on end. That's extra insane, isn't it? As hysterical as that was, I could have been in some real trouble because of that poor woman they found in a bathtub. The police were just as hysterical, grabbing me up as though I had my hands around a second woman's throat."

"Drowned in bleach?"

"Seriously." Jovan holds up a hand. "I'm too tired. I feel broken. It's so fucking terrible I don't know what to say. She's a woman I've seen around in the hospital. A nurse called Melissa Martin. I never knew her name before getting hauled in by the police. They held me for questioning, and then forgot me in the holding cell as they got a confession from Bill Dimitriadis. I don't know if I mentioned that Greek kid—a janitor like me."

"You mentioned almost beating his head in."

Jovan nods. "Bill's old man, who was also a janitor in the same hospital for twenty years, turned Bill over as soon as he found out about it. Fucking drove him to the police station. I can imagine the old man taking him by the ear through the front door." Jovan leans back in his chair and breathes out, carefully rubbing at the swelling on the crown of his head. "Bill and the girl were together a few times and she'd blown him off for some hotshot surgeon."

"What? So Bill killed her."

"It's more complicated than that."

"And he did all that graffiti?"

"That idiot didn't even come up with the words he wrote on the poor girl's body. He's been getting letters from Graffito. Dropped off in the bottom of his locker in the change room. Saying different things, yet in each letter there's the constant refrain 'Waste of

Life.' Or it's 'Life of Waste.' One moment Bill's the confidant of the famous Dr. Graffito, and he feels special, and the next, Bill is getting his life deconstructed. About twenty letters in all, each one urging the guy a little further along a path that, step by step, gets him to kill some poor nurse who did nothing worse than kiss him once or twice."

"Graffito did something similar to that optometrist, didn't he?"

"Miss Richards was already very isolated and unhappy. If a person's on the edge it doesn't take much of a push. It's not as if the guy is a criminal mastermind."

"No, but it sounds as though he's fully invested—in people, rather than the place. The hospital is his world and everyone within it belongs to him. Twenty letters isn't a casual interest. That's real commitment."

"To what?" Jovan asks.

"To putting his pain into someone else," Suzana says, as though it should be obvious.

"How's that a relief for Graffito?"

"Seeing your madness in someone else might make it feel more bearable. Even if it's only a moment. And then you go back to the unbearable and wait for it to break you again."

Jovan thinks about Vladimir Mitrovich drinking that bottle of Belgrade *rakia*. "We all want to see ourselves reflected in the world. Is that it? He's thinking—"

"It doesn't matter what he's thinking," Suzana cuts him off. "My point is that he's not invested in only Miss Richards and Bill Dimitriadis. You get what I'm saying, right?"

Jovan nods. *"Ethical cleansing."*

"Finish your tea," Suzana says. Jovan finishes the rest of the cup in two swallows. She walks over to him, lifts his face, and looks at him for a few seconds, puts her lips to his forehead, and then pushes his head away playfully.

"So you're done with that place?" she asks.

"Done as the dog's dinner," he says in English, sounding Aussie for the first time ever, and makes Suzana laugh. She gets up and gets ice cream from the freezer and fills two bowls.

She says, "Carlo has been barking all morning. You should take him for a walk."

"I will." They move the spoons to their mouths slowly. Jovan says, "I just noticed that we don't have any pictures of us on the wall. You and me."

Suzana shrugs and turns her spoon in the cream at the edge of the bowl, where it's already beginning to melt. She says, "We should put some up."

"It's been a while since we took any photos. Let's not put up anything old."

"We should buy a camera. I don't know if we should be spending a few hundred dollars on a camera if you're quitting your hospital job. We can wait for some photos."

"David Dickens is an amateur photographer. That's part of the reason he's putting together that book about graffiti."

"Alright, but give me some warning. In fact, give me a warning any time that guy's coming over, with or without his camera." She gets up and goes to the dining room table to continue her novel. "I might get Jelka to come over and give me a touch up. She'll bring a whole wardrobe." Suzana sits down at the table and opens her notebooks.

"Maybe we should get you a computer," Jovan suggests.

"I sometimes get nostalgic for my typewriter." She's distracted.

"Slavko has been asking me to go paint houses with him for a while now. There's good money in it." He leans back in his chair and he raises an eyebrow. "And if people ask me what I do, I'll make sure I'm wearing a beret and tell them, I'm a *painter*."

Suzana glances out the window to where Charlemagne lopes along to an old fellow about to slot some advertising into their letter box, and then thinking better of it when he sees the monster dog moving towards him.

She nods. Says, "Maybe you should rest today. Carlo can wait until tomorrow." She's bent over her pages. She makes a selection from her mug full of pens. She smoothes the paper and waits for the words to emerge.

He sits awhile and watches Suzana write. He's been reading her novel and he is looking forward to finding out what happens next, now the Janissary is nearing the concourse of the Sava and Danube rivers, about to enter old Belgrade. It's strange to think that the rest of the book doesn't exist, yet here it is with the movements of her fingers. He sees her left hand unconsciously move to her belly again.

Jovan sits in the kitchen and yawns. He stretches his arms out wide. Walks his plate and cup to the sink and washes them, gazing out the kitchen window into the backyard. No rosellas today. They're frightened of the giant dog prowling around but soon should get used to the harmless monster. He pushes open the back security door and sits on the steps. It doesn't take Charlemagne long to come trotting over to Jovan. He nuzzles at Jovan's shoulder and then detects movement and off he goes again—across the lawn.

A sparrow picking at the roots of grass, head half in these emerald blades, head half in a cutting paradise, this world of crumbs from God's broken soul, head half out, amongst the emerald blades, small sharpened eyes looking for the seeds of paradise.

SUZANA LOWERS HERSELF into the water. The blue water ripples across the surface until those long, languorous moments when that luminescent skin is perfectly calm. The whole twenty-five-metre pool—perfectly placid. Pacific. Suzana takes that word down into the water with her, breaking that lovely blue surface, and paddles into the middle of the near empty public pool. Drifts out into a pacific blue.

The name a conquistador gave to the ocean after he'd crossed through Central America. The first Spaniard to do so. He called it the Pacific. Such a lovely word in English. When Suzana first heard this story she thought the ocean must have been very calm that day. She reaches the opposite wall of the Frankston pool and knows it had far more to do with the turbulence of that man's life easing away as he reached the final limits of his world.

A few remaining children by the side of the pool are plucked out of the water by their parents. A fat man trundles along to the change rooms with his sandals slapping his yellow callused heels, his arm picking out the material of his bathers from his blubberous crotch. The lifeguard has announced that they're closing in fifteen minutes and he now goes to attend to a problem at the front counter. He's already rolled up the long blue non-slip mats around the pool and hosed down some of the concrete.

It leaves the entire area the way Suzana likes it. No infant screams, no loud bellows from males exchanging lewd insights, no women and their cackled commentary. Even when they were silent, people created ripples or waves simply breathing. There was nothing like being alone in a large body of water. Suzana let herself drift— half submerged on her back, her ears subdued by the gentle lapping of the water, not worrying about getting in someone's way, a man's penetrating eyes, or women comparing themselves and evaluating.

The lifeguard hasn't returned and it occurs to Suzana that it's a bit early to do away with all the safety measures. Rolling up the long blue mats and watering the concrete before all the children had even been led away. The lifeguard gone, despite a woman well along in her pregnancy, drifting around. Suzana is happy to be alone yet she's aware of her own perversity as she feels annoyed by the way this solitude has come about. She drifts across the water, her growing belly above the waterline, a corkscrew smile works its way across her lips— how difficult it is for her to really allow herself pleasure and freedom.

Her eyes are closed. She doesn't notice a thin man slipping into the pool without a splash. Suzana tries to relax before she's called out of the water by the lifeguard. The pressure on her bladder had come much sooner than in her previous pregnancies. What's the difference this time around? Perhaps it's because she's older. Her aging bladder had forced her to the toilet every ten minutes today. She should let herself urinate in the pool as she suspects most of the children do. How many times had she waddled over the rough concrete? How many times struggling out of the wet bathing suit? She wants a long rest now in the water. Feeling the float of her new body. She feels the water moving around her as the thin man comes close.

Suzana tilts her head a little farther back so that her ears go underwater and she can hear her own breathing, and lets all of her tumbled-over thinking stop spinning for a moment, folding into the calm space of air moving cool down through her lips and out again. Listens to that hypnotic rhythm of breathing, her belly, nose, and mouth breaking the surface. Letting go of all her thoughts.

Suzana is pushed underwater. She is annoyed, not much more than that. This is some kind of accident. Her eyes are open below the water and she sees a torso black with tattoos. The arms and legs are strangely free of the ink—pale white limbs. She's that clear in her mind. She notices this disparity. Across his chest, amongst the many, many words are three fractured skulls, and within them: **The Trojan Flea.**

Suzana had been struck by that expression the first time Jovan told her months ago about Dr. Graffito. His other hand is now over the top of her head as he pushes her deeper under the water, the rough heels of his feet are brutal as they push down her thighs. She begins to struggle frantically, the nails of his toes claw down her chest, just as frantic to keep her below. Perhaps only a minute. The air has escaped her so it doesn't take long before she's taking in the chlorinated water, filling her stomach and lungs. And then there is nothing but rest at the bottom of the pool. Silence and stillness, and then not even the darkness.

JOVAN CRASHES HIS panel van. It's not a major accident. Ironic, because he finally got around to changing his brake pads a few weeks ago. Overcompensating and locking up the wheels on a damp road, making the van swerve off the side into a telephone pole. A kid on a bike darted out from a driveway. Jovan is not hurt. The van will need some panel beating, new shocks, and who knows what else? Not enough light to see what kind of damage in the undercarriage.

Suzana will be waiting so he sets off on foot. The Ford practically looks parked by the side of the road and Slavko can help him tow it home tomorrow morning. The Frankston Aquatic Centre isn't too far away from his crash. He will still be late. They can catch a taxi home. Suzana will tell him that there's no way he should get the van fixed and he'll have to buy a new car. It's amazing how much she hates the Ford. It's senseless. Well, maybe not. How had he become such a total blue-collar "bloke," as Australians said, that he doesn't have a regular car? He'd left no room for himself to be anything else other than the guy in that rust-bucket of a vehicle, his white Ford panel van. That was her point, even if she's never come out and said it. He's not wearing a watch so he's not sure how late he'll be. He begins to walk quickly. He waits for her outside in the van normally and it's often a quick ride home so she can use the toilet. He doesn't remember her bladder being this weak with the previous pregnancies.

The lifeguard is a teenager and he's on the phone having the kind of argument it's only possible to have with another teenager that he's in love with. Accusations and profanities and it doesn't matter who's around to hear. Jovan walks through the internal doors that lead to the pool area. No point waiting outside when he doesn't have the van. He decides that the first thing he'll tell Suzana is not that he had an accident, rather, that he's decided he's going to buy a new car since he's now got the new job and tonight they'll go out to Frankston Pier with some fish and chips. The last time he went out there he was feeling lonesome and the idea of taking Suzana to the pier feels good. She's got her own ideas and he wonders whether he'll be able to persuade her as he walks into the empty pool area.

No one's around other than a thin man in the water near the edge. Jovan blinks and realises he recognises him from the hospital. One of the surgeons he never had a reason to talk with. As soon as the doctor lifts his head there's a different kind of recognition. The man has tattoos across his torso, and every word is familiar to Jovan—he has obliterated most of them from the hospital's walls. **INSPIRATION** down the centre of his chest. Words pushing in, crossing over each other. Obliteration. Oblivion. Self-made tattoos, letters cut into the flesh as deep as they would go. A God of Small Knives. A Devil of Deep Cuts. And in red letters, set within three skulls lined up across the man's heart, The Trojan Flea.

SUZANA WAKES TRYING to breathe out water. She's coughing up chlorine for a long time. Coughing so much she doesn't think she'll ever stop. Taking in air is all she can think about for minutes. And then she's aware that she's lying on her side and the first thing she does is reach down for the bump. Pulled out of the water by the wrist as if she weighed nothing. She remembers the ferocious grip on her wrist, the severance beforehand, the void she'd fallen into so total she only felt it when she was rejoined, ready to go on clinging to the immense arm that had pulled her from the water.

She closes her eyes, still coughing, listening, and waiting for a movement. Nothing else can happen now. Wait for a kick or a punch. Wait. Wait. Wait. There it is. That faint tingle as an elbow nudges her spine.

When she opens her eyes there's a man bleeding from his face, his nose, his ears, and a mouth missing most of its teeth. Teeth being washed down the grates by the side of the pool. The blood dripping down his face and cleaned away by the filters. The water would still be deep blue. She can't see it. All she can see is the blood. Pacific. What a lovely word that is. Dead. The man can't be alive.

Her colossus is bringing down one rock-crushing fist after another into the man's body and then into his face again. Another tooth comes loose. Kicking within her. Alive and as deep as the Pacific. Safe and sound in those words. Her husband. How good. The only thing she can think is how powerful and great, how strong and noble. Jovan's Pacific eyes. His mouth set—a storm swallowed. As expressionless as a god's face as he does his work. Obliterating every other word. And how good she thinks, how good. Her Jovan. Her husband. Her good man. How very good. As expressionless as a god remaking the world.